D0105051

Alec

Alec

~

William
di Canzio

Farrar, Straus and Giroux

New York

Farrar, Straus and Giroux
120 Broadway, New York 10271

Printed in the United States of America
First edition, 2021

Quotations from *Maurice* appear by permission of the Provost and
Scholars of King's College, Cambridge, and the E. M. Forster Estate.

Library of Congress Cataloging-in-Publication Data
Names: Di Canzio, William, 1949– author.
Title: Alec / William di Canzio.
Description: First edition. | New York : Farrar, Straus and Giroux, 2021. |
    Summary: "A reimagining and continuation of E. M. Forster's classic
    novel Maurice, told from the gamekeeper Alec Scudder's perspective"—
    Provided by publisher.
Identifiers: LCCN 2021002648 | ISBN 9780374102609 (hardcover)
Subjects: LCSH: Gay men—Fiction. | GSAFD: Love stories.
Classification: LCC PS3554.I17354 A78 2021 | DDC 813/.54—dc23
LC record available at https://lccn.loc.gov/2021002648

Our books may be purchased in bulk for promotional, educational,
or business use. Please contact your local bookseller or the
Macmillan Corporate and Premium Sales Department at
1-800-221-7945, extension 5442, or by email at
MacmillanSpecialMarkets@macmillan.com.

www.fsgbooks.com
www.twitter.com/fsgbooks • www.facebook.com/fsgbooks

1 3 5 7 9 10 8 6 4 2

For Jim

Inspired by E. M. *Forster's* Maurice

CONTENTS

I

ST. JOHN'S BONFIRE

1

Early in the spring of 1893, in the village of Osmington in Dorset, the Scudders, Aderyn (née Prothero, from Cardiff) and her husband, Elwood (the butcher), were surprised and not entirely pleased to discover that she was with child. They had believed themselves long since finished with nappies and crying spells. Fred, their "baby," was nearly ten; Aderyn herself, forty-three. Moreover, the pregnancy conjured ghosts of heartbreak she believed she'd put to rest years ago: Susan, who would have been eighteen now, dead in her cradle with scarlet fever; and the twin boys, stillborn, unnamed, taken from her and buried before she had seen them (as was the practice then). But, come November, she had cause for joy: after a straightforward labor, she gave birth to a winsome infant. They christened him David Alexander: the first name for his grandfather and for the patron saint of Wales; the second for the grand sound. Thriving at the plentiful table provided by his father's line of work and his mother's skill, Alec grew to be a cheerful, sturdy boy and then a good-looking teenager, with bright brown eyes, thick wavy hair, and a reputation in school for brains and diligence.

He benefited from England's progress in free education. From age seven to thirteen, he learned to read (well), write (poorly), and do arithmetic (accurately). Because his father prospered and Alec behaved himself, his teachers encouraged him to stay on for three more years. He studied basic mathematics, history, a little Latin and French, and read the English poets. He liked geometry: spheres, planes, lines, angles, volumes. They gave the schoolboy pause—maybe what seemed the random stuff of everyday life partook of a complex, cosmic order, like that of the planets and stars. As for English history, he enjoyed the Wars of the Roses and the ensuing mayhem of Tudors and Stuarts; but after Cromwell things got dull in his opinion and stayed that way. Latin and French were no fun at all: the smattering they offered at the village school got barely further than grammar. As for poetry, it baffled but intrigued him; when he spent enough time, letting sound and sense come together, it could stir unnameable feelings.

His parents were delighted with Alec's schooling. Little enough had been offered to them. Even their older son had not been required to attend school so strictly as the younger; laws and customs were changing that fast. Still, they knew Alec's school days would end at age sixteen. They had no money to send him further; nor, if they had, would the gates of higher learning unlock for a village butcher's son.

Meantime, blessed with excellent health, Alec kept up with his schoolmates in sports. He played football because everybody did, though he liked cricket better because the persnickety rules prevented getting trampled by an oaf. (Also he thought the white clothes were smart.) With his good looks and quiet ways, he attracted the notice of girls. He enjoyed flirting with them, especially when they were sassy—like Rowena Blunt, who had a long braid, mocked the gentry, and made fun of everyone's name, not sparing her own or that of her brother, Ivanhoe. ("I'm-a-whore Cunt," she called him.) But Alec felt none of that lust to get under their skirts that his schoolmates hooted about. On the other hand, he did find some of those mates appealing in a way that excited him. Whenever he caught himself staring, he'd look away, because he knew that staring meant he was one of those, which was true.

His schooling, however (and contrary to its intention), taught him not to despise his queerness. The insight came about this way: His teachers encouraged him, an advanced and trustworthy student, to visit the public library in Dorchester, with holdings far richer than those in the village reading room. They let him spend whole afternoons there on his own, browsing assigned subjects, among them classical history, which he liked as much as the modern stuff bored him. The myths of Greece and Rome were best, where the gods mucked things up for the human race, and then the heroes (whose ranks he never doubted he was fated to join) fought back. He found a whole room of such books, some illustrated with plates of sculpture: Apollo and Hercules, or massive Laocoön with his two teenage sons, all three writhing in agony as the serpents strangled them. Their nudity thrilled him.

The thrill led him to explore the shelves of volumes devoted to ancient art—not just sculpture, but pottery too. The clay vessels of Greece, red-figured or black, showed stories of athletes in action: runners racing naked—bearded, thick-muscled for distance (said the captions), or smooth-faced and lean for the sprints. Some pots showed wrestlers and boxers; others, boys playing and dancing together—naked and fine. His heart would pound while he gazed; his face would flush; his cock would strain between his legs. He wanted to live in that world, to be one of those athletes, to run naked and grapple—admire, be admired—to love.

Some vessels showed scenes more dramatic: a young man with a handsome profile and dark curly beard offering a gift to a younger athlete, reaching to fondle him, seeking his love. Sometimes the athlete accepted; sometimes he refused by stopping the hand that reached. Alec thought he would welcome the gift and the touch of a man so fit and gentle; he would give love as he received it. With these noble images pleasing him, he decided there must be more to being one of those than the world's contempt, mockery, and determination to make him hate himself.

Back in the village, he'd report to his teachers that he'd read about Athens and Rome in the library—i.e., about democracy and empire. He said he thought modern-day Britain was in some ways like both. They would praise his patriotic insight and send him back for more.

Among those teachers was St. Osmund's curate, a short, scrawny man with thick glasses and a scruff of hair growing up from under the back of his collar, and whose eyebrows pumped up and down when he spoke. He came to school sometimes to give moral instruction. He took the older boys off by themselves. "Men," he'd say, "you all hail from God-fearing families and I know you're above disgracing them with any untoward behavior. But let me warn you, man-to-man: the tempter was the brightest angel in heaven before he defied the Lord God with his pride. He's cleverer than you know. He'll mask sin with beauty and innocence, like a beguiling girl's face. So guard your thoughts; thoughts too can lead you astray. Thoughts lead to words, words to action. Degenerate thoughts sap your manhood."

But thoughts were all that Alec owned, and he believed his glorious athletes had more to teach him about manhood than this repulsive clerical scarecrow, who smelled like someone who never washed below his chin. Fortunately for Alec, religious orthodoxy at home was tamed by the influence of Welsh

Unitarianism on his mother's girlhood. Not that the Scudders were openly skeptical; they attended Church of England services regularly. For his parents, though, worship was more a matter of good citizenship than faith. If a Sunday sermon got around to such rarefied doctrine as the Virgin Birth or the Trinity, Alec might hear Ma mutter, "Hogwash," and he'd snicker. This down-to-earth attitude spared him the torture of scrupulosity. But the Church was not his only enemy. There was the very family who cherished him. He knew for sure that even his mild-mannered father would rage if he could read his son's degenerate thoughts; as for his doting mother, she'd turn against him with tears and spite and insults. A dunce they could love; a swaggering thug or a thief they'd defend as their own. But a nancy-boy, a poofter? Never.

And then there was the law, merciless as granite. Certain phrases terrified him, young as he was: "gross indecency" or "unspeakable crimes." So he told no one about his longings, and he was lonely.

Sports helped, since they wore him out. Alec would race full speed down the football field, fearless if often inept, undaunted by getting slammed or scraped. But his friends' torn shirts and slipping-down shorts tantalized him, as did the melees, a dozen boys sliding all over and grabbing one another as they fought for the ball. Once, he scrambled up from a fracas so distracted he kicked the ball the wrong way and scored for the opposite team. He was pelted with scorn for weeks. He needed a release more reliable than football.

One day at the library he noticed a pamphlet left on the table: *Five Pound Dumb-Bell Exercise; Illustrated With 30 Halftone Plates*, by a Professor Attila. His heart started to pound at the sight. The cover showed the photo of a handsome bare-chested athlete, more appealing even than the figures on the Greek urns, with a smooth symmetrical torso and his calves ideally rounded. Inside was a picture of the author, mustachioed, in tights and a leopard skin. He claimed that a young man who followed his course in physical culture could achieve strength and beauty. Then came pages of plates showing the ravishing model doing the exercises, wearing only tight-fitting shorts. Alec gazed and gazed. At closing time, he decided to steal the pamphlet.

However, for the hour or more he'd been worshipping his newfound god, his prick had been throbbing under his knickerbockers. When he leaned over the table to pick up his copybook, said prick got pressed between the tabletop and his belly; on encountering warm flesh, albeit his own, it started to spasm, overwhelming him with exquisite pleasure. He sat back down and closed his eyes while this euphoric, if ill-timed, event went on and on and on. When the spasms stopped at last, he glanced around to be sure his deep breathing had drawn no eyes. Then he tiptoed out of the library with the pamphlet tucked into his copybook, which he carried in front to hide anything that might have leaked through.

"How flooshed you are, Licky, all red in the face," Aderyn said when her boy came home. "Let me feel for fever."

"No, Ma, it's only this tight collar the school makes us wear."

"Well, you appear quite the gentleman in it."

"A gentleman might buy hisself one that don't choke. Or send his valet to buy one. I'll just take it off now," he said and skittered away.

In the cramped bedroom he shared with his brother, he sat on his cot. With grown-ups around, he'd been too scared even to peek at the pamphlet on the tram back from Dorchester, but now he took the prize out of his copybook. He touched the image on the cover as tenderly as he might have touched the model himself. Here was Alec's ideal, the one he wanted both to possess and to become.

He soon learned that dumbbells like those recommended by Professor Attila were not to be had in Osmington. What he did find was a rusty pair of heavy plow-horseshoes in the shed by the old outhouses. He figured they must weigh about five pounds apiece. He cleaned them and made grips from rags. For half an hour each day, between school and sweeping up at the butcher shop, he'd sling them around in accord with the professor's regimen. There was barely enough room between his cot and his brother's iron bedstead to do so. If he stood on Fred's bed and crouched, he could just see himself in the tarnished mirror screwed to the top of the chest of drawers and gauge his progress.

Alas, he could see none—no Olympian shoulders or arms, no deep manly bosom. Sometimes he thought maybe he discerned a new ripple in the mirror, but then the mattress would shift under his feet and it would prove only a shadow. The regular practice did however produce two undeniable, if invisible, results. First, his appetite became bottomless, requiring Aderyn to pile on more chops and liver and to try to fill in the gaps with puddings. It made no sense to her that, much as he ate, his school clothes and Sunday trousers were getting loose in the waist.

"I wonder could it be tapeworm?" Aderyn said to her husband.

"The boy's growing, my dear," was all Elwood said.

The second was this: At night, Alec was entirely fagged, too tired to roil on his cot, think degenerate thoughts, or quietly hump an imaginary beloved while trying to keep his hands off himself and not wake Fred. Thanks to Professor Attila, once under the covers, he was fast asleep till morning.

He needed his sleep, because in this last term of school, there was a grave matter to reckon: What would he do with his life? In Osmington, sons of working families by custom followed in their father's line, the way his brother was doing. Fred had been training for years now alongside Elwood and was becoming a skillful butcher. But since the senior Scudder did not own the business, he could not name his elder son his successor. So Fred planned to work a few more years as a hireling and then take his trade to the New World. He would emigrate to Argentina with its enormous cattle ranches, and set up shop in that land, where he'd find no contemptuous ruling class playing high-and-mighty with him. His sweetheart was already stockpiling goods for the home they would make there.

Though Alec hated the uncertainty about his future, he was glad enough to escape the life of a butcher. Not that he was squeamish, but on trips to the slaughterhouse to choose the big carcasses, he thought he recognized some of the cattle and sheep from the farms of his schoolmates' families. Too bad the animals were so good to eat, because he preferred them alive, or at least when they had a sporting chance, like the rabbits and birds he hunted sometimes with Freddy and Da. Besides, a butcher stayed indoors, day in and day out, waiting on people, always the same housewives or the gentry's uppity servants, who expected a man to grovel to them the way they did to their masters.

In fact it was one such servant who proposed the answer to Alec's big question. The housekeeper of the nearby manor usually sent a maid to the butcher shop, but once each month she herself came after closing (with a footman to carry her parcels) to settle the account. On inquiring politely about Mr. Scudder's wife and sons, she learned that young Alec would soon finish school and was about to start seeking work. This she found interesting because her brother-in-law—the game-keeper at the grandest estate, she claimed, in all of Dorset—had recently been authorized to hire a boy as his assistant. Knowing the Scudders to be a respectable family, she would be pleased to mention Alec for the post, if Mr. Scudder wished her to do so. Indeed Mr. Scudder so wished.

"A *sarvant*?" said Alec (aghast) at supper. "Deliverin' me into bondage, yer own son?"

"Oh, the high dudgeon," said Elwood, rolling his eyes. He turned to his wife: "That's from your side."

"If so," Aderyn quipped, "then it comes with good looks and quick wits."

Alec pled, "I'm to bow down to toffs and kiss their patent-leather shoes?"

"Now, Alec, a gamekeeper's different—you'll be out in the healt'y fresh air all the day, not dancin' attendance at table."

"How far away is this place?" said the mother. "Whenever will we see the boy?"

"I wouldn't do it, not me," said Fred. "I treat no man as my better; it degrades the whole family."

Elwood looked askance at his elder son. "Thanks, Fred, for your learned opinion."

The younger one groaned: "It's the twentieth century, Da—no more peasants and serfs; mankind's evolved."

"I'm aware of the date, and we've not yet evolved out of eating."

"But *sarvitude* . . . ," Alec said. "It's come to that? After all me hard work in school, even stoodyin' Latin . . ."

"A noddin' acquaintance with Caesar won't feed you—
which, these days, God love ya, has become no paltry expense. What skills have you, son? Learn a skill for yourself, as
our Freddy has butchery, and then take it wherever you will.
You're always a free man. You might even go overseas some-
day and join your brother."

"Not Licky too!" said Aderyn.

"Don't fret for your baby, Ma," said Fred. "There's no *gamekeepers* in the Argentine—it's only toffs have gamekeepers,
and there's no toffs there."

"Frederick!" Elwood said, smacking the table. "Ain't it
time you go visit your sweetheart?"

After many such conversations, wherein Alec invoked both
Magna Carta and the Rights of Man; after scrounging with
no luck for work in Osmington and losing all hope when his
mother suggested he might go north to join her distant cousin
near Leeds (where he pictured himself expiring, consumptive
and half-blind, in a windowless sweatshop); after many tests
of his father's long-suffering Alec agreed to give service as a
gamekeeper's boy a try.

2

But before Alec left school and home, Osmington had one more lesson to teach him. On what he knew would be his last visit to the library, he saw a notice for a theatrical event of particular interest to him to be held in Dorchester: EPIC PHYSIQUE CONTEST. The poster featured a clichéd strongman, swiped from a circus ad, but the copy promised a contest of strength, artistry, health, and muscular development, to be judged by William L. Murray of Nottingham, winner of the 1901 Grand Competition in Royal Albert Hall, produced by Eugen Sandow. There would be the substantial prize of twenty guineas.

Sneaking into the show on the next Saturday afternoon proved easy enough among the crowd. He figured that if he wore his school clothes, he could pass for a shopkeeper's son. The trick worked: he slipped unnoticed under the nose of an usher who'd been handed several tickets at once. Inside, he found the house full to overflowing. He weaseled down a side aisle and stood close as he could to the stage.

The MC called for quiet; then he spoke about the friendship of King Edward with the great Sandow. His Majesty loved all sport and held that the health and strength of Englishmen were key to the might of the empire. The king himself had deigned to patronize the first Grand Competition in London. Now Dorchester was honored by the champion of that contest, who would judge today's contest. The criteria were as follows: general muscular development, strength, symmetry, health, and tone of the skin. To begin this athletic display, Mr. Murray himself would give a short exhibition of his award-winning physique. The crowd applauded as Murray entered, his red robe bound with a sash. He untied the sash and let the robe slide to the floor: he was naked except for a loincloth and sandals laced up to his shins. Everyone clapped and whistled.

Thanks to the footlights and his well-rehearsed posing, Murray did resemble the Farnese Hercules—massive chest, arms, thighs; flesh shaved smooth and oiled. He rippled his glistening midsection like a belly dancer. The audience admired and murmured. When he pivoted to show his back, they grew silent, as though they were witnessing something scandalous: the loincloth was cut away to a mere string behind, so he seemed nude. He displayed his equine buttocks as proudly as his arms and shoulders, shifting his hips left to right, resting his weight first on one leg then the other in voluptuous contrapposto. He pivoted halfway around, untied one side of the loincloth, and pulled it forward, covering his sex in his hand, so they might enjoy a sideways view of his undraped physique top to toe. The crowd cheered. Murray, pleased and disdainful, refastened the loincloth and exited.

Then the competitors entered—barrel-chested, chastely covered in tights and leotards. They showed their strength in conventional ways by lifting weights. They were applauded lukewarmly. Alec was disappointed: their burly physiques struck him as commonplace. And not one was from Dorset. This particularly annoyed the crowd. A man yelled from the audience, "They're all practiced showmen! Where's the sport in that? Can't a regular fellow compete? How come we've no one from Dorset?"

Hubbub ensued. Meantime, a young man walked up the

steps from the audience to the stage and talked privately to the MC, who then held up his hand for order. "Wait, wait," he said. "Here's a lad from Osmington asking if he might show. What do you say?"

Of course the crowd hollered in favor; onstage, the competitors smirked. The newcomer was trim and fair, with a youthful bit of a beard, dressed in well-worn rustic tweeds. Alec's eyes widened: he knew the man. Rowena Blunt's brother, the one with the risible name, Ivanhoe. Van, as they called him, was some years younger than Fred; the two used to go about together, until their lives turned old and serious, Fred with his girl and Van with his family's farm. But Alec liked Van: he was thoughtful and calm (unlike Fred), and when Alec had started to notice the beauty of men, he'd admired Van's straight eyebrows and smooth, strong neck.

Van behaved matter-of-factly, unlacing his shoes, removing his tie and collar, even whistling softly while the audience chattered and joked. They quieted down as his stripping progressed. When he was standing before them in singlet and drawers, they murmured: Here was a splendid man. Nature had graced him with narrow hips, wrists, and ankles in pleasing contrast with the shapely muscles; his proportions, height to shoulders, arms to legs, were just. He pulled off his singlet and showed them a torso honed to tautness. His drawers were tight and transparent enough to reveal his sharply defined middle zone (the Belt of Apollo, as Professor Attila called it): he lowered them to display the lines of muscularity carved there (incidentally uncovering the stem of his cock and, when he turned around, the top of his buttocks). His legs were particularly fine, thighs and calves swelling, knees supple. His skin had a golden cast to it. Alec's heart was thumping.

Murray, dressed now, came back onstage and reviewed

the contest's criteria. He awarded the prize to a man from Gloucester, which evoked a round of booing. He then said that he was making a second prize from his own pocket to the young man who had stepped forward impromptu and shown how the benefits of physical culture and hygiene were within reach of all.

A half hour later, Alec was waiting for the tram back to Osmington, rereading the contest's fly sheet, kept for a souvenir. Behind him a familiar voice called, "Young Scudder, is it? Fred's little brother?"

Alec blushed so deeply he broke a sweat. "That's right," he answered. "Just Alec."

Van noticed the flyer. "Been to the show, have ya? Devotee of physical culture?"

Alec had to swallow before he could speak: "Uh-huh . . ."

"Do you practice yourself?"

"Some."

"Good for you, then!" said Van.

They sat side by side on the tram. Van made little of his prize: he hoped the money at least would quiet his father, who'd complained about his taking the afternoon off from the farm. Rather than boasting, Van drew Alec into a conspiracy of laughter about their siblings, staid Fred and foulmouthed Rowena. "Poor little Wee-wee Cunt. But how can you blame the child?" Van said. "That family she comes from! What kind of people call their kids Rowena and Ivanhoe and their workhorses Thomas and Sally?"

The more Alec tried not to picture Van's valiant thighs under his trousers, the less he could think of anything else. Besides, the ride kept jostling them closer together, and Van stretched his arm across the back of the double seat, frequently marking their chatter with a squeeze of Alec's shoulder. He told Alec he'd mail-ordered some dumbbells and set them up in the barn, where no one disturbed him.

When they were parting at the Osmington stop, Alec ventured to ask if he might try Van's dumbbells sometime. "How about now?" Van said. "There's still a good two hours till supper and evening chores."

"Uh . . . all right."

Van had left his bicycle at the station. He lifted Alec onto the crossbar and pedaled the two of them through the countryside in the May afternoon. "This here's the secret of prizewinnin' legs," Van yelled into the breeze.

Inside, the Blunts' barn was higher than St. Osmund's nave, with sunlight streaming aslant through the loft's open shutters. The horses' stalls adjoined. The place smelled of them a little, pleasantly, to Alec's nose—Van was fastidious about keeping the livestock clean. He offered Alec a ladle of water, then poured the rest of the bucket into the trough. He patted the horses' necks. They whinnied. "With me out of the way all afternoon, you've had a good rest?" he said to them. "And here's a friend come to visit." He beckoned Alec to stroke them. He nodded toward a sunny corner. "Yonder's the shrine of manly pulchritude."

There among bales of hay were three pairs of dumbbells, an old wooden bench, and an even older wardrobe mirror, all cracked and crazed. Alec picked up a pair of dumbbells, feeling their heft and curling his arms. Van laughed and said, "Just like Professor Attila the Hun!" In the mirror Alec could see that, behind him, Van was taking off his clothes. He splashed water from the trough on his face. He met Alec's eyes in the mirror and said, "I'll show you some moves I've made up myself."

He demonstrated: he leaned with one hand on the bench

while with the other he raised and lowered a dumbbell, then changed sides. "That's for the upper back," he said. He sat on the ground with his back to the bench, pushed with his legs till his back arched and his shoulders rested on the bench, reached overhead with a dumbbell gripped by both hands, and raised and lowered the weight. When he sat back on the ground facing Alec, he was breathing hard. He said, "Broadens the chest, I believe." But Alec had been speechless since seeing him nude. When Van spoke to him, Alec avoided his eyes in shame. "Have a go at it now, why don't ya?" Van said. "Get out of them woolens and collar."

In silence, Alec obeyed. He turned his back as he slipped off the knickerbockers. His hard-on made him too embarrassed to take off his drawers; he tried shifting it to one side so at least it didn't stick straight out. When Van saw him out of his clothes, he said, "Well, look at you, now! How fine you've grown, a sturdy example of our Dorset architecture." He felt Alec's arms and shoulders approvingly; Alec smiled and shied away, but Van drew him back. "Yes, very nice," Van said, then mussed his hair and turned him to face the mirror. "See what I mean? Look. Don't tell me you're modest. It's only just me and yourself."

Alec saw in the long mirror what he couldn't see in the bedroom at home: his body had changed, mostly by nature, but also encouraged by Professor Attila's art. His childish waist had grown firm; his thighs sinuous, chest wider, arms rounded. Unlike Van, who was tawny, Alec was very white, with a hint of blue veins under the skin where his pectorals swelled.

Van guided Alec through some exercises. To adjust Alec's form when he was curling the dumbbells, Van had him face the mirror again and stood close behind. He slid his arm around Alec's waist and told him to shift his weight back up against him. "So it's your arms doin' the work, not your back." Alec, weak-kneed from the pleasure of Van's holding him, closed his eyes. He faltered. Van mistook the wobble for loss of balance and said, "It's all right, you can't fall, I've got hold." When Alec said nothing, Van asked, "What, have you hurt yourself?"

"No, I'm not hurt," said Alec. He stepped away from Van, turned to face him, and looked guiltily down at his drawers: full front and center, his hard-on, now leaking, would not be denied.

Van chuckled. "Well, what's to expect?" he said. "Sure we're stiff day and night at sixteen, that's nature's way, no matter what the vicars might tell ya. And trust yer aged pal here, at twenty I find it's no different at all. Look at me now, startin' to grow, just seein' you spunky."

Alec was too naïve to take heart from Van's arousal. He felt even more anxious, so much that he trembled. "It's more than that," Alec said.

Van felt his arm: "You're shivering. What, are you cold?"

"Not cold, no. It's more, I'm tellin' you."

Van looked puzzled.

Alec said quietly, "It's me . . ."

Van was quiet for a moment; then his face turned gentle. "Ah," he said, "yeah . . . that's all right . . ." Again Alec avoided Van's eyes in shame. "But don't I know how it is?" he said, seeking Alec's gaze with his own. "I know . . ." He reached out his hand: "Will you come here to me? Come." Alec accepted his hand. Van drew him closer and embraced him. "How's that, now?"

In Van's embrace, Alec believed he was realizing his deepest longing. Their warmth and the streaming-down sunlight; their breath and the spring breeze through the wide-open barn; the scent, the pleasure of their flesh together. It was glorious, a fulfillment of all of his senses, but Alec, who was favored by love, was mistaken about the depth of the feeling. He would one day know a joy even deeper, when he would accept not only another's embrace, but his mind and spirit as well, and give himself in return.

"Better?" said Van.

"Yeah."

Van tugged Alec's drawers: "Now kindly remove these damn things." Van wanted to play, and that playfulness helped put Alec at ease. Van snatched the drawers, sniffed them, declared them "ambrosial," and tossed them aside. He opened his arms and ordered, "Here. Stand on my feet." Alec was shorter, so when he stood on Van's feet, they met eye to eye. Van squeezed Alec's backside till he giggled and squirmed. "Now do me the same and wiggle your toes on my instep . . . Ah, yeah, that's how . . ."

Locking eyes with Alec, he grew a bit serious. He reached down to position their pricks; his, upright against Alec's belly, and Alec's between his own thighs. He held Alec close. "Comfy?" he whispered.

"Oh yeah . . . ," Alec said.

Van flexed his thighs tighter. "And how's that?"

Alec moaned with the pleasure.

"Do ya like that?"

"Uh-huh."

"Are ya sure you're not joshin' me?"

"Uh-huh . . ."

"Thrust a bit back and forth."

"I'm gonna—"

"Good, let me help."

Van licked two fingers, reached around behind, and

chucked Alec's prick under the head. "Aw fuck!" Alec said as he tensed and shot, spattering hay, dumbbells, mirror. Then Van tightened his embrace. Alec felt a warm spurt on his belly up as far as his chin. He gasped, let out a long breath, and relaxed. They held each other in silence, Alec resting his face against Van's neck. He said, "I . . ."

"Sshh," Van said, "I know, I know . . ."

The next time they saw each other, their amorous flesh was confined in their black Sunday best at St. Osmund's. The vicar preached on a passage from 1 Corinthians: "When I was a child, I spake as a child, I understood as a child, I thought as a child: but when I became a man, I put away childish things." At the end of the service, he announced the first banns of marriage for Mabel White of Wool and Ivanhoe Blunt of Blunt Farm, Osmington, who were to be wed at the bride's parish of Holy Rood three months hence. The congregation tittered with approval.

Outside, Fred was congratulating Van on his good match. Alec joined them. He shook Van's hand and earnestly wished him health and happiness in his life to come. He also said goodbye. School was finished; Alec was leaving the village.

3

When Michaelmount Priory, the Benedictine monastery for women, was founded in 1391, the cloister attracted families of good name but limited means, those who could afford (or were willing to pay) a fetching dowry for only one or two of their daughters; the others they consigned, with a modest bequest and a servant or two, to a celibate life of prayer. The house's first superior, famously elegant, kin to the Duchess of Cornwall, was said to have been Chaucer's model for the coquettish prioress in *The Canterbury Tales*; this lady led her canonesses to renown for their erudition and eccentric mission of educating girls. The mission ended on February 11, 1531, when Henry VIII declared himself head of the Church of England, dissolving the priory and claiming its wealth for the crown. The canonesses went back to their families with neither bequests nor servants.

As a secular estate, Michaelmount was bought and sold among generations of titled families who overwhelmed the original building with additions and decked the park with follies—the most famous among them the Temple of Reason (1783), an arch of a ruined Roman aqueduct (while Byron was fighting for Greece), and a Burmese pagoda (when Victoria was hailed Empress of India). Now the priory was in its fifth year of ownership by the Wentworths, a couple with no title but unlimited means, thanks to holdings in the B&O Railroad and Cunard and White Star, plus the new Anglo-Persian

Oil Company. They wanted to smarten up the old place. To that end they were hiring more staff, like young Alec Scudder, the gamekeeper's assistant.

Alec was of two minds about his new life. He liked being out from under his parents; he liked having money, little as it was, without needing to beg every penny. He liked much of his work—raising the birds, stocking the streams; he especially liked his own particular charge of taking care of the boathouse on the big pond, where he could cool off in the summer. He also felt somehow he'd entered the world: although Michaelmount was no closer to London than Osmington was, the great house kept its eyes on the metropolis as the village never had.

But he hated being a servant. Back home he'd had nothing to do with the upper classes. He despised them, of course; everybody did. They'd take the first pews in the church, so the commoners could admire their well-tailored backs by the hour on Sundays. He was taught to show respect by making way and doffing his cap, which he did grudgingly, though he found such gestures merely annoying, not painful, because it was no different from how you showed decent manners to elderly neighbors. But now it irked him to call those his own age—or even younger—*sir*, while they called him Scudder or *hey there*. He tried rationalizing: After all, didn't everybody, even the king, have to do what other people wanted? At heart, though, he knew servitude was different. It was all about pride bought for the price of somebody else's degradation. This was a new phase of his education—learning how the world worked.

His discontent, though, was more a matter of head than heart, because at this time of life it was difficult for Alec not to be happy. He was young and healthy; well-fed, clothed, and sheltered; and he spent his days mostly outdoors. He even discovered a certain asset to his queerness: it kept him out of trouble with girls. At nearly eighteen, his looks were maturing: his face, once round, was leaner and strong; his lips, once pretty, were sensual. Work kept his pale skin ruddy, and his coloring was set off to advantage by his habitual shirts of homespun flax or wool. He'd grown a couple of inches taller; faithful to Professor Attila's discipline (with his first month's wages he mail-ordered a pair of dumbbells, which he wrote to tell Van about), he was becoming more fit and shapely day by day. In short, Alec was a pleasure to look at ("A near occasion of sin," quipped the Irish laundress), a pleasure by no means lost on the thirteen girls and women in service at Michael-mount.

The young ones vied for his notice; the older ones mothered him and urged their favorites on him. If Alec had been made in the usual manner, he no doubt would have succumbed to such bounty and been husband and father before he was out of his teens. But he was not made in the usual manner. He was still young enough to treat the women's matchmaking as teasing. As for the girls, he played along with their flirting, but hoped that by keeping a certain distance, he might avoid hurting anyone's feelings or betraying his own lack of attraction. The matrons thus ruled he was virtuous (and therefore all the better a catch); to the girls, he was fetching but dull, aloof, and spent too much time reading. As for Alec himself, he accepted, grudgingly, that at this time and place there'd be no love for him, not the kind he craved. He wondered if there ever would be such love, union with a like-minded man. Or maybe Van by his marriage was teaching Alec a lesson about manhood. If that were the case, he asked himself, if like Van he was fated one day to marry, then surely when the time came, when he was older, wouldn't he (as Van did, he imagined) feel the appropriate urges? Meanwhile, he lived his young life.

Of his employers, the best he could say was that he rarely saw them. The Wentworths stayed mostly in the city, in an apartment in a showy new building near Kensington Palace. They dined in restaurants; they traveled for pleasure, often to France or the States, and separately: a London daily reported that a certain Mrs. W. had sailed the Caribbean for a week on a yacht given by an admirer to her friend, the movie star and "most beautiful woman in America," Anna Q. Nilsson, while Mr. W. visited Paris.

When the Wentworths did stay at Michaelmount, it was for weekends, house parties of several days to which they brought two kinds of guests. Mr. W. invited "business-people," as the butler disdainfully called them, and their tightly corseted wives. On the other hand, Mrs. W. invited an odd lot. Her women appeared either mannish or exotically femi-nine, affecting styles Alec learned were called Oriental, in-volving shawls and asymmetrical hems; the men looked pasty and spoke demonstratively. Both her men and her women smoked cigarettes endlessly, sometimes scented with spice or perfume.

During these house parties, Mr. W.'s men went shooting in the mornings. Alec would guide them, betraying his quails and bright-quilled pheasants to their clumsy aim. Sometimes Mr. W.'s huntsmen were joined by one or two of Mrs. W.'s women (often better shots than Mr. W.'s men), but never by their own wives, nor by Mrs. W.'s men (who preferred to talk and smoke indoors).

One such party fell at midsummer of 1912. Alec had worked hard all morning: up before dawn, he fed the birds, prepared the guns and trails. He guided the hunters and de-livered the shot-ridden fowl to the kitchen; finally, he cleaned the guns before storing them. At midday he ate a good dinner and was getting ready for afternoon chores when the game-keeper announced the best kind of surprise, a half holiday to honor the season. One of the gardeners told Alec about the fair at nearby Brenford, so the two walked over together.

In a field the villagers had set up canvas tents, open-sided, festooned with garlands of ivy. These sheltered tables with cheeses and jams to taste and for sale, as well as a makeshift pub with barrels of beer. Little kids gotten up like sprites in face paint and paper wings scampered all over the place. There were games—quoits and ninepins, and a jackboot-toss for the prize of a piglet. While Alec was enjoying a second friendly pint, a young blacksmith slapped him on the back and invited the visitor to run in their St. John's race.

"All right, then, why not?" said Alec. He guzzled the rest of his beer before they set off to the starting line. There, to his shock and delight, Alec saw that, honoring a quaint tradition, the Brenford Midsummer Footrace was run naked. He and the blacksmith joined the scores of youths, stretching, jogging in place, their clothes folded and stacked on tables provided. The whole village was watching, including women and girls, with an awning and chairs for the gentry, and nobody thought it was queer.

Alec was glad he was tipsy; it helped to disarm his shame, not to mention his terror of springing an erection, which he hoped the public circumstances would inhibit. As he set his clothes aside, a parson, eyeing him up and down, lifted his tankard in salute and winked. Alec joined the blacksmith among the runners. The starting pistol fired.

Two pints of beer drunk quickly, he learned, are poor

preparation for a half-mile sprint; he also learned that an actual race run naked is nothing like the picture on an ancient
Attic pot. The beer sloshing inside him undermined his footing on the damp grass, so much so that he could hardly pay
due homage to the array of lovely boys' backsides. After the
first quarter mile, though, he found his balance and rhythm.
He even lifted his head to take in the bright sky and exult in
running full-speed in the fresh summer air.

He finished the race in the middle of the pack. While he
was dressing, his blacksmith found him, crushed him with
a hug, and insisted on standing him a pint at the pub tent.
There a man with a concertina was playing "Alexander's Rag-
time Band" as the crowd sang along. Alec felt a tug at his
sleeve from behind. He turned and saw no one till he looked
down: there was a child of four or five, a little boy made up
as a brownie in some gauzy muslin, absurd and completely
enchanting. Alec (who, as the priory's cook approved, had "a
way with children") understood that the child wanted to tell
him something but couldn't make himself heard over the din.
He opened his mouth to yell; Alec put his finger to his lips to
signal he should not do so and knelt down beside him.

"We can talk now. Alec's my name. What's yours?"

"Muthtardtheed."

"Pleased to meet ya, Sir Mustardseed," Alec said and
screwed up his face.

The child laughed at the silliness. "Here," he said, "I made
one for you too." He held out a circlet of ivy and flowers, like
the one he wore in his hair, fastened in back with a profusion
of motley ribbons.

Alec was touched. "Why, thanks very kindly." He wanted
the child to understand that he was sincere in his gratitude,
so he took his time admiring the little wreath, engaging the

boy's eyes as he did so. "Oh yes, amazingly intricate . . . I think
this must be quite magical, as are you."

Mustardseed beamed at the praise.

"Now would you please show me how best to wear it—just
like you?" Alec sat back on his heels so the child could reach
his head better. Mustardseed settled the circlet in place and
vanished into his forest of grown-up trousers and dresses.

Sylvan-crowned, Alec stood. The runners howled; women
applauded. The blacksmith called out, "Behold our young lord
of the elves!" and a girl kissed him full on the mouth.

Someone behind him called, "Sutter."

He knew he was being addressed, but disliked the tone,
the one used by certain house servants with the outdoor staff,
so he chose not to answer till the blacksmith nudged him: "I
believe you're wanted."

It was Mrs. Wentworth's maid, Agnes, turned out in a
picturesque hat and hobble skirt. Alec said, "Oh. Afternoon,
miss."

"Didn't you hear me?"

"Name's Scudder. Thought you wor callin' another."

"I'm sure," she said. "Here. From Mrs. Wentworth." She
gave him a large, heavy coin. "She was pleased with your
showing in the race."

"I came in thirty-fourth."

"Still, she was glad to see you run—as a man from the
priory. I'll tell her you thanked her." She walked off. Heads
turned to follow the mincing steps required by the skirt
that caused her hips to sway fetchingly. Alec glanced at the
money—more than a month's wages. He slipped it into his
pocket.

Now trays of sausages were passed around, and the tent
was cleared for dancing. Two fiddles, a drum, a banjo, and a

flute joined the concertina, their sound irresistibly merry. Alec liked dancing; he led the girl who'd kissed him in a quick one-step to "The Washington Post March," then, even quicker, to the "Horse Trot" cakewalk. She wore lots of petticoats—that was part of the fun; their weight lent momentum to the giddy twirling. But when the tempos slowed, and the tunes turned lovey-dovey, Alec courteously stepped aside so she might favor another partner: his companion from Michaelmount, the gardener.

Alec slipped away for more ale among the runners. Being near them tantalized him, as did their easy affection toward one another. The blacksmith made room on the end of a bench, slipping his arm around Alec's waist so he wouldn't fall off. It seemed natural for Alec to rest a hand on the fellow's thigh to balance himself. Relaxed by the beer, warmed by his desires, Alec moved his hand higher. The blacksmith took no notice.

Later, at sunset, the latest one of the year, someone shouted from out on the field, "It's ready!" Everyone rushed to where brush and logs were piled on a makeshift scaffold. A torch was touched to the tinder: cheers rose with the flames as St. John's bonfire roared into the darkening sky.

Next afternoon at Michaelmount, the gamekeeper came to the boathouse to summon his assistant. He found Alec morose and hungover, at work with a plane and shellac on a leaky rowboat.

"Hullo, Mr. Prentice," Alec said. "I should finish this up in an hour."

"Put it aside now, lad," Prentice said. "You're called to the house."

"Me? Whatever for?"

"Not about shootin', all's I know. That snotty maid of the missus came to call. I thought maybe the gentlemen changed their mind about havin' a shoot, so I ast Agnes wouldn't the lady rather see me? She said it wor you in particular. I said I hoped you'd caused no trouble. She said not at all, only Mrs. W. wanted a word." He wiped a smudge from Alec's cheek. "So wash your hands now and get a clean shirt that don't smell of turpentine, and your Sunday shoes too, not them muddy boots, and go to the house for your word."

When Alec reported to the kitchen, the housekeeper looked him over, pushed his hair back from his forehead, and whisked his trousers with a clothes brush before sending him up to the music room. He stopped in front of a pair of tall double doors, one of them ajar. He overheard fragments of talk:

A man said, ". . . the choicest fruit on the noblest tree in the garden. To taste it would be worth the loss of Eden."

A woman said, "Such raptures at that distance—I trust you thanked God for my field glasses . . ."

Alec knocked. The woman called, "Yes, come in."

Though it was as big as a ballroom, Mrs. W. used the music room for her private parlor: two crystal-swagged chandeliers hung low enough almost to touch; the woodwork was painted ice-blue and gilded; a row of arched windows pierced one wall; arched mirrors reflected them. Piano and harp stood covered with canvas; otherwise, the space was empty but for a delicate couch and a pair of chairs at the far end, bracketed by screens, where she now sat with her guest. Behind them, on an easel, was a painting of a nocturnal city.

Mrs. Wentworth beckoned him. His bulky shoes squeaked on the waxed parquetry; the noise, enhanced by the room's perfect acoustics, humiliated him. Was this why the lady had called him? To make fun of his awkwardness? She was not yet dressed for the day—she wore makeup, rings, and a dressing gown figured with peacocks. He remembered the cook's complaint about serving two breakfasts: for Mr. W.'s guests on the sideboard at 8:00 and for Mrs. W.'s in their bedrooms at noon.

"Mr. Risley wants to see the park," she said. "Please guide him."

"Yes, ma'am," Alec said. "Will the gentleman care to shoot?"

Both hostess and guest chuckled at the question. Risley protested, "I come to praise nature, not to bury her." His voice was loud; his diction overprecise. He was younger than his hostess, twenty-six or so, but his beard made him seem older, his face and long slender hands pale as a moth.

"Two o'clock, then, darling?" she said to Risley.

"Yes. Let's say I'll be back by four—for tea, or lunch, or whatever you call it here."

"We shan't worry if you're late." Then to Alec she said, "Meet Mr. Risley by the garden gate in twenty minutes. That's all."

"Yes, ma'am," Alec said; he hesitated. "Ma'am—?"

"What is it?"

"Only I thank you . . . for bein' generous with me yesterday—the race, you know, I'm meanin'—the money . . ."

"What? What did Agnes tell you?" she said. "Never mind. She got it wrong. You can thank Mr. Risley."

Risley was lighting a cigarette.

"Then thanks, sir," Alec said. "But I'm not quite easy acceptin' so much—for only just horsin' around like we wor."

"Keep it," Risley said, exhaling the clove-scented smoke. "That race inspired me."

In their tour of the woods, they'd walked only as far as the boathouse before Risley got to the point: he wanted sex and would pay. He began his proposal with highfalutin praise, comparing Alec's face to those in paintings by Giorgione and his form to Mercury's in Botticelli's *Primavera*.

"Sir, your speech is quite learned, and mostly over my head, as I'm sure I've no need to say," Alec said.

"Guilty as charged, but one has to say *some*thing," Risley said. "Seems that's all my crowd ever does—talk, talk, about the Sacred Band of Thebes and Phaedo and Socrates and David and Jonathan and the Myrmidons and *formosus Alexis*. Then they bat their eyelashes and retire, each to his own chaste bed. As for getting down to business, nothing. I do hate pussyfooting. I mean, what's the point, among men?"

"What makes you think I'd be that way inclined?"

"I go on my hunch—sometimes I'm wrong. But frankly it's not your 'inclination' that interests me, it's your . . . well, perfection . . ."

"I heard you and the lady, earlier, inside . . . about field glasses and all."

"Then you know!"

"She don't mind you sayin' unspeakable things?"

"Unspeakable to whom? Florence Nightingale? Trust me, the lady don't mind, though that husband of hers might call for smelling salts. Truth be told, she's rather fond of boys who like boys."

"That's what you told her? I'm one of those? That's why she called me? For a close look at the pervert?"

"No, no, you've got it all wrong. She was just taking care— she thought you might find it awkward if I approached you out of nowhere."

"So you've shamed me before my employer."

"But I'm telling you, there's no shame—"

"Word gets around—you don't know. People hear things, servants, they do, like I did. Have you no fear of the law?"

Risley sighed. "I fear living in fear. That's not living at all."

These words of courage took Alec off guard. Risley put aside his impatience and cynicism. He even smiled. He had a good set of teeth, and the new expression brightened his eyes and made his face seem less stony. "Come on, now," he coaxed Alec, "no one's about. There, in the boathouse. You need do nothing, only relax and enjoy yourself, as I promise you will."

Though he might not admit it, Alec was flattered by Risley's admiration. Being desired was a kind of power, and after last night he'd felt he had none. Too timid to make a play for the blacksmith or anyone else, he'd moped his way back to the priory at midnight alone. (His pal, the gardener, got lucky with the girl they'd both danced with and stayed later.) In his bed, his mind flashed through the day: the naked runners, some sinewy, some fleshy, and that one demigod who'd gazed at him sweetly. He imagined joining with them, in pairs or in orgies, embracing and kissing, giving, receiving, time after time. He jacked himself; it wasn't enough. Twice more. Then he was able to doze for a bit, but soon he woke in a lather—so again. And once more at dawn.

Now today he was spent and full of self-loathing and pity. Why not let this rich gasbag have what was left of him? What harm? Let the gentleman service the servant for once, who'd take his damn money and tell him, *That's all, you may go.*

"No," Alec said, "I don't fancy you."

"What's that?"

"I'm certain you heard me."

Risley's smile turned uneasy. "*Fancy?* But that's like incli-*na*tion, it doesn't matter."

"Except for your fancy, we'd not be havin' this conversation."

"Let me just show you," Risley said. He reached to fondle Alec. Alec gripped his wrist to stop him.

Risley said, "It's perverse of you to refuse, when I could give us both great pleasure."

Alec said nothing.

"It's those runners at Brenford you fancy, I know. See how far you'd get with them. They'd knock out your teeth."

Risley might have been right about teeth-knocking, but Alec hated him for saying it. If there had been any chance of his changing his mind, it was gone now. "In fact I've had several," he said out of spite, "and they, me. No money involved, I assure you."

Risley lit a cigarette: "I'll find my own way back to the house."

"Take back that money you gave me."

"Keep the money, I told you, you shit." He started off.

In the boathouse, Alec sat in a corner and sulked. Did they all see through him? Risley, Mrs. W? This was something new about being queer, this innuendo and subterfuge, and it sickened him. He wished he could leave Michaelmount. But where to? No matter—he knew he'd be sacked for sure.

4

Not long after, Alec was indeed informed of his dismissal, but Risley had nothing to do with it. Rather, the housekeeper announced that the Wentworths, who were divorcing, had sold the priory to the Anglo-Persian Oil Company. At APOC's behest, the imperial family of Persia would be moving to England; their country seat was to be Michaelmount (where soon ground would be broken for Arabian stables and a cour d'honneur in the style of Persepolis). The emperor's own staff would replace most of the junior servants. Every effort would be made to find suitable positions for those being let go.

So during the following winter Alec moved from Dorset to Wiltshire, to a house called Penge, where the head gamekeeper was retiring. The under-gamekeeper, Mr. Ayers (himself not young), was succeeding the retiree, and Alec, now with two years' training and experience, would be filling the vacated post. It was a promotion for him, with an annual salary of twelve pounds.

Penge was nothing like Michaelmount. It was truly a family's home, not a stage set—a small enough family, for sure: just the old widow, Mrs. Durham, and her son, Clive, who had recently finished legal studies, and his new bride, Anne. There was also the widow's married daughter, who lived in the city and visited often, whom her mother called Pippa.

At Michaelmount there'd been no end of money; at Penge there was little enough. Maintaining the place was a duty, not a show, for the Durhams. House repairs were put off till they could be no longer, then done as cheaply as possible. They considered the land much more important, since it supported not only themselves but also many others, so they used their available funds chiefly for upkeep of the woods and the farms. At Penge a second gamekeeper was by no means an ornament, as he had been for the Wentworths. Local hunters, issued a license, were allowed to shoot in the park in season. It took the work of two men to care for the game, defend them from polecats and ferrets, manage the licensees' quotas, chase poachers. Alec was given charge of the dogs: two spaniels, a brood of tuneful beagles, plus a dachshund called Bruno, hardly more than a puppy yet the terror of badgers twice as big. In addition, he was assigned the care of the boathouse, in light of his experience at Michaelmount. Though he worked longer hours and was often called on to help with general chores, he took satisfaction in the greater responsibility. He also approved of how the Durhams cared for the land entrusted to them.

If only he'd not been a servant. He was nearly nineteen now. Servitude troubled him more than when he was younger, and more still in this new place. The Wentworths, with their untellable wealth, had been distant, almost unreal, easy to ridicule. Here, in a house smaller than any wing of Michaelmount, the Durhams were always close at hand. Alec judged the widow a decent woman, and this sharpened the insult of her not knowing his name, even after months of employment.

Little as she must have cared about her servants' names, she took great care to manage their souls. She insisted on churchgoing. And the squire's young wife proved worse than the old lady. She had a new vicar appointed, Reverend Borenius, who brought High Church pomp to little St. Simon's in the village, where he caused candelabras to blaze on the reredos, bells to jangle at weekly Communion, and incense clouds to rain odors of sanctity on all the faithful, Durhams and others alike. Alec didn't mind the theatrics: they made the service less boring. Borenius, however, was a stickler not just about ceremony, but about policing the morality of his flock as well, which meant nosing into their business.

And Penge's isolation irked Alec. The place was remote, the village dismal—no lively fairs, let alone an annual footrace for naked boys. As he matured, his loneliness was growing more urgent. He saw no one for himself, nothing. There were others of his kind at Penge, to be sure, Clive Durham for one, he was certain. The squire had been busy at his desk when Alec arrived for his interview. Clive set down his pen and looked up: his eyes widened on seeing the candidate. He reddened, lowered his gaze, pretended to reread the recommendation. Alec knew immediately; his knowledge was confirmed within his first month on the job. Simcox, the valet, filled Alec in on the gossip: Hadn't one of the maids walked in on the squire, two years ago, before he was married, while he was caressing his friend from Cambridge, the fellow with the dashing black hair, in a most affectionate manner in the bedroom adjoining his own? And hadn't others seen the two of them lying among ferns in the woods, embracing? Simcox was reliable in this matter: he was certainly one of them himself.

One evening after supper, Alec sat in the boathouse and smoked the briarwood pipe his mother had sent for his birthday. She had written in her note, "As a young wyfe, I woud so injoy the cent of your father's tabaccoe . . ."

A generation had passed. Now he himself was on the cusp of manhood. What did Penge hold for him? A promotion to head gamekeeper when Ayers retired? A small pension after

a solitary lifetime serving the Durhams? Couldn't he do
better elsewhere? Argentina . . . ? He let the idea take shape
in the pipe smoke: the immense scale of that western land—
mountains, rivers, plains, a seacoast stretching toward the
world's end. Maybe he could work with Fred awhile and then
strike out on his own. And what about love? Surely he'd find
one like himself in such a wide-open place, an honest, passion-
ate man. Free from scowling gentry and vicars and the law,
they'd share their lives, their bed . . . The nicotine made Alec
woozy. When he stood, he stumbled over the sleeping spaniel
that had followed him and now yipped and needed soothing.

Next morning, though, clearheaded after a strong pot of
tea, he did not find the idea of emigrating absurd. He wrote
to Fred, who responded by inviting his little brother to join
him and his bride on their journey, scheduled to begin on
August 30, 1913, with the departure of the SS *Normannia*
from Southampton.

Alec accepted. Fred broke the news to their parents. Elwood received it with equanimity; not so their mother, who,
Fred wrote, "cryed that her heart was cloven in two." Nonetheless, the brothers pressed on. Fred offered to help with
funds for the ticket. And Risley's guinea, saved along with
most of Alec's earnings, went a long way toward outfitting
him with a kit of cheap ready-made clothes. He felt he'd
taken hold of his life.

As part of his plan he decided that since (like Van) he
might one day need to marry, he ought to make some effort
with girls. There were two cousins in service at Penge, both
seventeen and both named Mildred after their grandmother.
One called herself Mill; she worked in the dairy. The other,
called Milly, worked with the cook. The girls had trim figures
and pretty skin; they took pride in their grooming and liked

to laugh: that was attraction enough for Alec. And they were happy to play along when the handsome under-gamekeeper started to pay them more notice. Because they were three altogether, the girls understood that it was about fun, not serious courtship.

When they were alone, there was kissing. (Once, the girls even kissed each other to show Alec how a brigand would ravish a lady. That demonstration brought on all three a falling-down fit of giggles.) In the shadows there would be groping and fondling: breasts, privates, etc. Alec discovered that when the girls touched him a certain way, he'd become aroused. It was nothing like the spontaneous overpowering rush of excitement he felt for certain men, but it sufficed to encourage him: if need be, he believed, he could perform the duties of husband.

He also started to open his mind beyond the limits of rainy Wiltshire. The Working Men's College was offering courses at nearby Wilton. The teachers, young idealists with degrees from Cambridge and Oxford, were advancing the founder's vision of university-style learning for men of the working classes. The scholars made regular trips from London to regional towns to deliver the goods.

Most of the men who came to sign up for school sought practical training in mechanics or drafting, with an eye to getting ahead in business. They were disappointed to find that those subjects were taught only in the city. Rather, the Wilton extension offered courses for "enrichment" in the humanities: literature, history, art, and political philosophies. Alec chose two classes that met on Tuesday evenings—The English Poetic Tradition and Italian City-States.

Harrison Grant's course in poetry was crowded with clerks with ink-stained fingers, who spent their days copying

contracts, their backs hunched over desks. Word had gotten
out that this particular teacher was a genuine Cambridge don
volunteering his service pro bono. He was older than the other
instructors—fifty, Alec guessed—nice-looking, with brown
hair going gray and clean-cut features. At the first meeting,
he mapped their course of reading, emphasizing Milton and
Shelley, and introduced the men to the college's mission: they
were to acquire knowledge through hard work, but he hoped
they would also form friendships, essential to education, with
their teachers and one another, by meeting outside the class-
room and enjoying sports together.

The men liked the message and they liked him. As the
room grew stuffy, he removed his jacket, inviting them to do
likewise, loosened his collar, rolled back his cuffs, showing
a figure not just trim, but fit and strong. Here was a man for
whom learning was by no means at odds with virility, a man
for his students to admire and to imitate.

He gave the assignment for next week—they were to read
Milton's "Lycidas," make notes, including questions, and be
prepared to discuss. If they had time they might look ahead to
their second pastoral elegy, Shelley's *Adonais*, with an eye to
contrast. He also announced that, to encourage their forming
friendships through sport, he would offer basic instruction in
boxing on several consecutive Sunday afternoons. The men
applauded him when class was dismissed.

Italian City-States met next in the same room. All but two
of Grant's students left—Alec and a lumber-mill worker. "I'll
stay for the first meeting," the lumberman said. "No one says
I have to come back."

A haberdasher's clerk joined them. He told them that his
shop "caters to a cultivated clientele," many of whom traveled

abroad, and he hoped having some knowledge of the Continent might impress the customers and thus his boss.

The instructor, named Morgan, was much younger than Grant, thirty or so, and seemed unfazed by the size of his class. Rumor had it that he had been the older man's student at Cambridge. He was therefore acquainted with his dashing teacher's allure and aware he possessed little himself. His face was triangular, broad forehead tapering to a narrow chin; his figure was triangular too, but in the wrong way—shoulders narrow, hips wider. Still, Alec found his manner appealing. When he spoke or listened, which (unlike Grant) he did in equal parts, Morgan made you feel that he wanted to know you more than he imagined you could want to know him (or maybe more than he wanted you to know him). This self-effacing quality, mixed with his kindly demeanor, assuaged his homeliness. Plus, Alec judged, his mustache was excellent.

He explained that their course would draw on several disciplines: history, literature, politics, philosophy, but particularly art and architecture in Milan, Venice, and Florence. He opened a portfolio of art plates. He proposed to "read" the images for what might be discerned about each city's character. He beckoned the students forward to join him at the teacher's desk, where he spread the pictures: from Milan, Leonardo's *Last Supper*; from Venice, Giorgione's *The Tempest*; from Florence, Botticelli's *Primavera*.

In these latter two, Alec saw the figures that Risley had cynically compared him to. But there was nothing cynical in Morgan's appreciation. When he analyzed the compositions, revealing their underlying geometry, the men were first amazed, then gratified. In order to view the images more closely, the lumberman and Alec leaned over the desk together. Engrossed, they knocked heads, and everybody laughed.

Through the spring and early summer, Alec's spirits rose. The secret knowledge that he'd soon give notice lent him power over the Durhams and raised himself in his own eyes. Tuesday nights brightened his week. After Morgan's class, the haberdasher would go right home, but Alec and the lumberman and their teacher would go for a pint together. Morgan seemed so at ease in the pub among workingmen that Alec found himself reevaluating the upper classes, or at least admitting there might be one or two decent folks among them. Mr. Grant, on the other hand, for all his preaching about friendship, could not dismount his Cambridge high horse. Still, Alec managed to attend three of his Sunday boxing lessons, where, for the small price of getting his nose bloodied, he learned how to land a fair uppercut. He also enjoyed the poetry, which, but for the requirements of Grant's course, he might never have discovered.

But just as important to his education was Alec's understanding that both of his teachers were like him. This enriched his knowledge of himself and his kind: of himself, because he found he possessed this particular insight by nature; of his kind, because he now saw there were many of his sort, throughout all livelihoods and social classes, as different from one another as were folks who called themselves normal. Both these men, he likewise intuited, were trapped. That understanding was also part of his education. He hoped he would avoid their mistakes. Clearly Mr. Grant became aroused when his students stripped down to spar at his Sunday gatherings; yet he seemed to disapprove of himself on their behalf for doing so. He'd try to disguise Eros as sportsmanship by showing them some new punch or footwork, but what the man truly craved was their touch and affection. Alec figured he was too knotted up inside to admit the desire, much less to act on it. Alec wished he could say, *It's all right, sir, go ahead, feel us up—we all think you're grand and we'd feel you right back.*

In contrast, Morgan, whom Alec deemed genuinely kind, seemed shackled by this kindness, or a misunderstanding of it. He seemed to fear that he might somehow harm others if he pursued his own desires.

"May I write to you, sir?" Alec said to him in the pub after the last meeting of Italian City-States, after the lumberman had said goodbye to them, leaving the two by themselves.

"I'd be very happy to hear from you! Yes, please write and tell me everything—about your adventures in the Argentine, about the loves and triumphs, and when there's nothing to write about, well then just write about nothing."

This warmth, this effusiveness, was what Alec liked best about Morgan. In the months they'd known each other, his lively humor had emerged from his reserve. Alec was also gratified that such a learned man as Morgan would care to know him. "Truly?" he asked.

"Truly."

There were things he wanted to say but did not know how to, or even if he should. He loved Morgan, and felt his love reciprocated, but he was not attracted to the man sexually. Alec sometimes wished it might be otherwise, because he knew that Morgan was attracted to him and would have liked to please him, but there was no forcing or faking such feeling, least of all with someone as insightful as his teacher. Did the man understand his quandary? Yes, Alec believed, and the tension was fruitful for both of them, allowing Alec to love him without the entanglement of sex; at the same time making their friendship, tinged with Eros, tolerable for Morgan, whom Alec sensed had no sexual experience and (for reasons more complex than he could fathom) might not wish it.

"Except for my folks," Alec told him, "there's few people I'll miss when I leave England, and none more than you."

So in due time, in the last week of July, Alec gave a month's notice at Penge. He was promptly called to the squire's study. It had been less than a year since their first and only meeting, yet he was surprised by the change in Clive Durham: he was losing his blondish hair and gaining fat in the middle. With his blue eyes and his rosy cheeks going plump, before long he might serve as a model for a "country squire" in Staffordshire china, made to squat on the mantel in Granny's parlor.

"Leaving us, Scudder?" Durham said.

"Yes sir, emigrating."

"Seems sudden and drastic."

"P'rhaps Mr. Ayers told you about my brother, sir . . . He was goin' abroad by hisself with his bride, but then invited me."

"The three of you? Odd. No girl of your own?"

"No luck that way yet, sir. Perhaps I'll find someone there."

"Not a Spaniard, I hope, or some half-breed. Best seek your own kind, a good English girl to settle you down. Though please don't make off with one of our maids." He laughed, then assumed the manner of older man to younger. "Marriage, believe me, improves us men immeasurably."

"Yes sir."

"We've been satisfied with your work. You're a sharp fellow. You ought to have given more notice."

"Without meanin' offense, sir, I couldn't risk it, gettin' dismissed early, if you'd got unhappy about me leavin'."

"Now, that's low thinking. Have you ever known any servant to be treated unfairly in this house?"

"No sir."

"If you were patient, one day you might follow Ayers as head keeper. You know what life holds for you here, but you've not a clue about the hardships you'll face overseas. It's like trying to build civilization all over again. Consider the lives of your children."

"Yes sir."

"Think about what I'm saying."

"I'll do that."

"Good luck to you, then, and here." He gave Alec an envelope. "It's a reference about your work and character."

"Thank you, sir."

Alec closed the door behind him. He'd been dreading this meeting, as if the squire had the power to hold him back. Now that it was over, he felt he was truly advancing toward his future.

The next weeks were the busiest of his life, what with his work to keep up while getting ready to go. Mill and Milly, saddened at first by his news, soon turned to playacting heartbroken maidens who vowed to throw themselves into the sea after his ship. One day, near the back road to the train station, the three of them found a quarter hour to practice dramatic farewell kissing. But their play was interrupted when a car drove by, bringing a guest to the house, who scowled at them from within. The girls snickered and turned away.

Alec locked eyes with the man, a handsome fellow with black hair and a mustache. He felt a sudden charge. Just as suddenly—and to his surprise—he understood it was mutual. The guest's expression softened, unwillingly, it seemed, from anger to mildness. What was Alec seeing? Desire, loneliness, longing, even helplessness? The man's lips parted, as if to speak, but he did not. When Alec realized they were staring at each other, he lowered his gaze and touched the brim of his cap. The car continued on toward the house.

II

KINGFISHER

5

Their fun spoiled, the dallying maids went back to their duties, but not Alec. Although his chores likewise needed doing (before he was free to tend to his own pressing business of preparing to leave England), he could make himself do nothing. What had just happened?

In some ways, the silent exchange had been familiar. How many (uncountable) times he had noticed a fellow, undressed him with his eyes in a flash, then, in another flash, forgotten him. Nearly as often the game was a contest, the two players dawdling and dithering between steamy stares and feigned indifference to see who would back down first. These fantasies always came to nothing. Was that what had just happened?

If so, then why was he dumbfounded?

What had he seen in the stranger? The motorcar, the angle of the man's chin, and what could be seen of his clothes expressed privilege. Was that what had attracted Alec? Wealth and what comes with it? Could he be so small-minded? He had reason to hope not, because (to give himself credit) Risley's money and trappings had held no allure for him, nor, for that matter, did Clive Durham's.

Could it have been the man's appearance, then, that beguilingly handsome face? Alec's head would have turned to look after him had he passed by anywhere, no denying that. Yet it was the rare face and form that could surpass Van's or excite a more urgent desire. For certain the pleasure they'd shared back home was ravishing, but it went no further than that for Alec: an unforgettable pleasure enjoyed with a friend.

This was something new. It had to do with the change in the man's expression from sternness to tenderness, from power to humility. Alec felt he could have walked through his gaze into the future.

For days he'd been avoiding the manor house. Reverend Borenius, who often visited, had stepped up his solicitous questions now that Alec was getting ready to emigrate. But on this rainy afternoon, he risked the vicar's prying. He lingered near the house, outside the drawing room windows. He was rewarded with a glimpse of the newly arrived stranger within, talking with Borenius and young Mrs. Durham. The man's figure was athletic, as he had sensed it would be. Alec haunted the kitchen, where he learned that the guest was one Mr. Hall, Cambridge classmate and intimate friend of Squire Durham. He remembered the gossip he'd heard from Simcox.

The news of his identity gave some validation to the desire that Alec believed he'd seen in the man's face. It also tantalized him. He grew jealous of the one he worked for. Durham and Hall. Cambridge had been theirs, where teachers like Grant and Morgan coddled them and where the work of servants like Alec gave them the leisure to love. Maybe they still were lovers.

He chatted around the kitchen till he learned that Mr. Hall would be sleeping in the Russet Room; then he posted himself in the shadows below its window, where parted curtains showed a lamp burning. Maybe he would pass the window, and Alec could see more of him. Durham, however, had just returned home from a day of political canvassing. Would the squire go to Hall's room?

Hall himself appeared above, alone, looking out at the rain. Soon the face, handsome, troubled (and lonely, Alec told himself), withdrew. The maid closed the curtains. He heard the beagles baying, off in the kennels. For the first time in all his service he'd neglected to feed them on schedule. He walked back toward the gamekeeper's cottage, still puzzling.

That morning, when he had been planning his day, he'd intended to spend the evening in his room reading about Argentina. Now he wanted only to get back to the main house as soon as he could. After tending the dogs, he changed his wet clothes and, though he'd shaved in the morning, he did so again. The rain had curled his hair; he was about to tame it with a comb when he recalled that the Mildreds said it was pretty that way—like that of a prince or a pirate. So he left it, and even encouraged the curl with his fingers. The effect pleased him in the mirror: maybe he did resemble Giorgione's young soldier. But when he remembered Risley's flattery, he frowned at his image, judged the curls unmanly, and tried combing them flat. He was more confident about his chest, smooth and broad; he unbuttoned the top of his shirt to show it off some. He was glad his spare trousers were old corduroys, worn thin and revealingly tight. He didn't know how, but he planned to put himself in Hall's way tonight.

At the house, after the meal was cleared upstairs, Alec stayed on in the kitchen, contrary to his habit. Milly asked why.

"Hopin' the rain might ease up," he said, drying the pots.

He learned that Simcox would be looking after Mr. Hall as his valet. Piqued, he wished he could think of how he himself might be closer to Hall. Then he got lucky.

The drawing room bell rang on the board. The parlormaid,

whose duty it was to answer, was in the toilet. As it rang once
again, she rushed out of the loo and up the stairs cursing. She
returned immediately to fetch dry rags and a basin. "It's leakin'
again up there," she said, "the roof over the window bay. Come
on, Simcox—we're to shift the piano out of the drip."

"I'll give a hand," Alec said too quickly and loud. When
the others looked at him in surprise, he added, "A piano takes
two men, don't it?"

"It's on casters," said Simcox. "We'll manage."

"Still, it's heavy; miss might injure herself."

"Yes, Scudder, come along," the parlormaid said. "I've got
my hands full."

"But they're in evening clothes up there," Simcox said, "and
this one looking like Will Scarlet."

"Didn't the ol' trout just give me the stink eye for them
ringin' twice?" she said. "Come on, now, you two."

Upstairs, candlelight touched the drawing room's shabbi-
ness with bleary glamour. For Alec, though, it all served as a
foil for Hall, a striking figure in his black and white clothes
among the faded colors. Talking with Archie London, the
squire's brother-in-law, Hall took no notice when the three
servants entered together. The old lady did, though. She muttered, "*Le délai s'explique. C'est toujours comme ça quand*—we
have our little idylls belowstairs too, you know."

She spoke French no better than his village schoolteacher,
so Alec understood every word. Still going on about the de-
lay. The smutty trull, did she imagine that he and Simcox,
two poofs, had been fucking the parlormaid on the kitchen
counter? Couldn't be simple as the girl's taking a piss? Meantime, how about the old lady's son and his lover boy playing
willy-grab under her dinner table?

The leaking ceiling was merely a symptom: Penge House

was falling apart. The servants got down to work quietly, hampered by the threadbare rug under the piano, soaked through and jamming the casters. And Anne Durham had mucked things up further by trying to dry the piano wires with blotting paper, now all shredded and stuck. She left that problem for the maid to fix.

"You men, what do you want to do tomorrow?" Durham said to his guests. "I must go canvassing. Don't come too. It's beyond words dull. Like to take out a gun or what?"

"Very nice," said Hall and London.

"Scudder," said Durham, "do you hear?"

Alec heard, but, struggling with the piano, did not answer quickly enough. The old lady muttered another insult, "*Le bonhomme est distrait.*" Distracted was right. But not by the parlormaid.

"What—?" Alec whispered to Simcox.

"Scudder," Durham repeated, "the gentlemen'll shoot tomorrow—I'm sure I don't know what, but come round at ten. Shall we turn in now?"

"Early to bed's the rule here, as you know, Mr. Hall," said Anne Durham. She bade good night to the three servants and led the way upstairs. Hall tarried. The servants were now on their knees: the parlormaid drying the floor, the men trying to yank the rug smooth. From under the piano Alec could see the gentleman walk to the bookcase.

"Damnation," Hall muttered, "isn't there anything, anything?"

"What's that?" Alec whispered to Simcox.

"Sshh," Simcox said, "he's not talking to us."

Hall found a book and left. Alec and Simcox maneuvered the piano away from the leak. The parlormaid dismissed them; she stayed on, complaining to herself, to put the room in order.

Alec was glum. Hall had never once looked at him in the drawing room. Had their meeting of eyes that morning, so momentous to Alec, meant nothing to him? Then he took heart, allowing that maybe Hall was being cautious. Anyway, Alec would be near him tomorrow for shooting. When he went back out into the night's heavy rain, he intended to return straight to his room in the gamekeeper's cottage, but, unable to help himself, he detoured by the Russet Room window. Just as he did so, the curtains parted above, and there was Hall.

The man stared off into the park, into the rain. As before, he seemed troubled. He sighed. Then he did something strange: he slapped his own face with his right hand, as if trying to startle or even punish himself. Was something wrong? Should Alec call out? Would he be angry? Then the curtains closed, and Hall was gone.

For the second time that day, Alec was soaked. He did not return to his room, though. Instead he went to the boathouse. It was leaky, much worse than the drawing room, but he thought of the place as his own. He wanted only his solitude. He took off the wet clothes, wrapped himself in the blanket he'd bought for Argentina, and huddled in the corner that he'd padded with cushions from the old rowboat. The blanket dried him and contained his warmth against his flesh. He listened to the rain—on the roof, on the pond. There was no reason for hope, but reason was beside the point.

Next morning, during two hours of shooting rabbits, Hall said no more to Alec than he would have to a cabbie in town. Sometimes their eyes met, but Alec saw none of the fire of yesterday's gaze; Hall merely gave him a vacant little smile that cemented the barrier of class, while Archie London never shut his damned mouth—rarely hitting his mark, often miss-

ing, always bragging. Despite the rain, London coerced Hall
into shooting again after lunch. The showers let up and fog
came in their place. Hall seemed even more distant than he'd
been in the morning, as if preoccupied, though sometimes
Alec caught the man staring at him, not unkindly, nor quite
present, like a daydreamer.

Near four o'clock, Alec spotted a ferret and aimed. London,
without warning, fired first. He missed, and the ferret dashed.
Before Alec could contain his disgust, he said, "Damn—that
pesky thing's been raiding the quail." London was peeved at
the servant's implying that the miss was his fault, but Hall
chuckled.

That was the end of their outing. The gentlemen returned
to the house for tea.

The hours of nearness had sharpened Alec's attraction. He
found Hall's voice mellow and gentle, his eyes beautiful—
greenish, flecked with brown like the woods. While they
were shooting, Alec, whenever he could, stood where he
might better admire Hall's body, sometimes so close that he
could feel the man's warmth. Once, when he'd whispered over
his shoulder, "There, sir, between the spruce and the oak,"
Hall turned to Alec and their faces nearly touched. Neither
flinched. Alec guided Hall's eyes back to the quarry with his
own: Hall fired and hit his mark.

For a second day, Alec had put off packing. Instead he
moped in the boathouse. And again after dinner, he lingered
in the kitchen. The rain resumed. When at last he went back
out into the wet night, he stopped under the Russet Room
window.

He saw a play of two men's shadows on the closed curtains.
He recognized Hall at once, but who was up there with him?
Simcox? Then Alec knew it was Durham. Again, jealousy

took hold of him. Would they embrace? Alec thought to fire his rifle. That would startle them apart. The shadows drew closer to each other. Alec aimed toward the sky. But before he pulled the trigger, they separated, and then Durham's shadow was gone.

Alec lowered the shotgun. He was weeping and did not know why. The rain washed the salt of his tears back into his eyes, stinging them. Then immediately the curtains upstairs were pulled open, the sash thrown wide, and Hall appeared, the downpour soaking his hair. He looked wild, troubled. "Come!" he suddenly yelled toward the sky. Just as suddenly he drew back, slammed shut the window, and closed the curtains.

The outburst shocked Alec more than his gunshot would have shaken the night.

He walked away—not to his room, but to the boathouse, to stay alone again. Last night there'd been hope, but tonight his emotions were desperate, his lust urgent, fired by the day's close contact. His senses—sight, hearing, smell—could conjure Hall now. He imagined his eyes, his voice, his warmth.

Toward dawn a plan took shape: He'd suggest that Hall come to the pond to swim. He'd accompany the gentleman there, as he had others when they swam. But he'd strip naked himself as he'd never done and join Hall in the water. Surely the man would like what he saw. And if not, so what? In ten days Alec would be aboard ship, out of reach of disappointment and disgrace.

But at breakfast he learned from Simcox that Mr. Hall would be leaving by the early train, returning to the city with Mr. London. Alec got up from the kitchen table without a word. He went around to the front door, where he found Hall, pacing by the motorcar in the rain, preoccupied, impatient to leave. His eyes widened when he saw Alec.

"Ah, Scudder," he said, "here we are, for yesterday's shoot." He offered a tip. Alec, tongue-tied, refused the money silently. Hall shrugged and went into the house, where, through the open door, Alec saw him speaking with London, who then came out and likewise offered a tip. Alec, confused, muttered thanks and, without looking at the money, accepted it. London went back and spoke again with Hall, who called to Alec familiarly from the doorway, "Hullo! So my five shillings aren't good enough! So you'll only take gold!"

Humiliated, he could have grabbed Hall by his lapels, shaken him, and yelled, *I am* not *your servant!*

Instead he attended in silence as Anne Durham, joined by the squire, bade goodbye to her guests: "Best of luck!" Then, to her husband, but intending for Hall to overhear: "Now, a woman in love never bluffs—I wish I knew the girl's name. I imagine her a lively brunette with bright brown eyes."

A girl in the city. That's why Hall was leaving. Alec snatched the gentleman's suitcase before Simcox could and carried it to the car. "Stick it in, then," said Hall to him coldly.

The auto backfired and pulled away. Without hesitating or thinking why, Alec ran off across the park. Not far from the house the road took a steep hairpin climb through some dog roses. Days of rain had gouged it with ruts—he was sure the mud would slow the car down. He ran through the wet grass and woods faster than he had raced at Brenford; the strain and his madness made his heart pound. He caught up to the car near the top of the rise. He chased it alongside the roses, thorns snagging his skin and his clothes. Hall leaned his head out of the window. On meeting the forest-green eyes, Alec abruptly stood still. Now it was Hall who was dumbfounded by their silent encounter, not Alec. Before it had gone on many yards, mist and rain turned the auto to shadow in Alec's sight.

He watched the rain rinse the blood from his scratched hands. What had happened to him? he wondered. Two days ago he'd been eager to start his new life, ready for freedom from the likes of Durham and Hall and their feeble old world, the one that kept them on high at the price of his degradation. But now? Muddy, bleeding, chasing a car in the rain like a wet hound . . . For what? A crush on a man who despised him?

He walked back to the keeper's cottage, to his room. He'd not slept in his bed, he realized, for two nights. He felt exhausted and duly chastened. He slapped his own face; he laughed when he remembered how he had seen Hall do the same. He pressed the heels of his hands into his eyes and yelled, "Go!"

The gamekeeper's wife poked her head in at the door. "Alec, what's wrong?"

"Sorry, Missus—tryin' to scare off that ferret I saw out the window—"

"Well, dry yourself now, before you get sick; they're counting on you for cricket tomorrow." Closing the door after her, she muttered to herself, "In the rain with their guns for hours on end. Why don't these men stay in and play cards . . . ?"

Alec cleaned himself up. He also took stock of his folly and declared it behind him. He resolved to get back to business, his own. From the boathouse he fetched the blanket along with some books he'd left, and packed it all away in his trunk for the trip—he'd spend no more nights there. He sorted and rechecked the papers for embarkation. He was determined to sleep soundly tonight in his own bed and wake up ready for the next day, when he'd help roll the pitch for the match and play well, a last bit of fun before leaving Penge and Wiltshire and England. Hall was gone, also his madness.

And the rain too, at last. The clear evening sky promised a bright day tomorrow. Feeling healthy again, like getting over a nasty but short-lived virus, he was walking toward the main house for supper, past clouds of evening primroses in plentiful bloom after whole days of soaking, when he saw Hall among the flowers, touching them, sniffing them. Alec stopped dead; his throat went dry; he wanted to duck away. But if he did so, he would attract notice and questions. Instead he approached the guest, touched his cap, and said the first thing that came to mind, "Evenin', sir. Will you be shootin' tomorrow?"

"Ah, Scudder, good evening—you know there's the match in the morning—they've asked me to play for the park."

"Yes sir, of course. Forgetful of me to ask . . ."

Hall, it struck Alec, was paying him full attention. He felt his face redden when he recalled this morning's reprimand about the money and then his chasing the car. But the man's frank regard conveyed no reproach. Alec fumbled for something to say. "I'm sure I'm very sorry I failed to give you and Mr. London full satisfaction, sir."

"That's all right, Scudder." Then Hall gave a conciliatory smile and turned to go into the house.

Before he could stop himself, Alec called out, "Glad to see you down again so soon, sir."

"That's all right, Scudder," Hall said again and went in. Alec, regretting he had spoken out of place, watched him go.

At supper in the kitchen the others noticed that Alec was lost in thought. Simcox said, "He's off to the moon."

"Dreamin' about Argentina," Milly said, "all the money he'll make and wooin' some rich rancher's daughter."

Alec smiled. He said to Simcox, "Only three upstairs at dinner? Just Mr. Hall and the vicar with the ol' lady, and she's withdrew?"

"Lively company for the young gentleman, eh?"

"Might you go ask him, then, before the gents rejoin the missus, if he'd care to swim in the pond tomorrow, after the match? I've bailed out the rowboat since the rain let up. He might like to dive—them Cambridge types all like to."

"Go on, Simcox," the parlormaid said. "Maybe it'll hurry them along and we can finish."

"All right." Simcox yawned and straightened his shirtfront. He went off and reported back promptly, "Mr. Hall won't be swimming, Scudder. He said he saw you before dinner. Nothing new since." Then he added slyly, "On the other hand, the vicar requests a meeting this evening. Asks if you'll kindly tarry a bit so's he can speak with you."

Alec groaned, the parlormaid rolled her eyes, Milly shrieked with laughter, then covered her mouth just as the Reverend Borenius appeared at the open kitchen door and rapped quietly on the frame. The servants all stood at their places, Milly so quickly she knocked over her chair. "Pardon the interruption," said the vicar, "but I was hoping to speak briefly with Mr. Scudder—his departure is so fast approaching."

"Yes sir, I just told him," said Simcox.

"Perhaps in the pantry, sir," the parlormaid said, "where you can be private. Milly, set a chair for the vicar in there."

When they were alone, Borenius began, "I'd like to get things in order for you before you set sail—churchwise, I mean, Mr. Scudder, as pertains to your Christian life."

"Most thoughtful of you, sir," Alec said.

"Not at all. I was certain you'd find it useful to have certain documents available in your new home, so last week I wrote to your home parish in Osmington. They've sent a record of your baptism. But they find none of your confirmation. Perhaps if we could supply them the date or even the year, that would help them."

"Yes, well, sir, I don't recolleck as I've been confirmed."

"Ah . . ." The vicar tried not to frown.

"The parents did not insist," Alec felt obliged to explain. "Mum leaned a bit toward the Unitarians."

"And you?"

"Unitarian? No sir, as those things go, I rather enjoy the traditional music. I was a choirboy till the voice changed."

"I see. Of course, I noticed you didn't communicate last Eastertide, but I assumed that was a matter of choice—not an unusual choice, I regret, among young men . . ."

"Like the squire hisself, sir," Alec said quickly, in defense against the clerical scowl, then added, "who don't even go to church—"

"If one *chooses* not to communicate, that's a matter of conscience, as it is for Squire Durham, whose opinions are informed. But to be held back by a canonical impediment—well, I take that as the Church's neglect. I do wish I'd known. How long exactly till you leave?"

"Week from Saturday, sir."

"So soon? I doubt there's time for the necessary instruction; still, I'll ask the bishop. You're approaching an age when it's best to be settled, with a helpmate, to start a family. Confirmation readies young people for all the Church's benefits as adults. In most dioceses they insist before marriage—though I'm uncertain of customs in the Argentine . . ."

This conference, endured as a nuisance at first, was starting to anger Alec. Writing to his village church, that was cheeky . . . Why should any man believe he had the right to hound another about religion? Servitude, there was the reason. In the eyes of the Durhams—and Borenius too—the lower classes (embodied in their servants) were children, prone to misbehavior and not to be trusted with their own lives. Alec thought he should set the vicar straight and tell him he attended St. Simon's on Sunday mornings not for his own sake or his employers' demands, but because Mr. Ayers, whom he liked, had said it would please him. He found it easier to accommodate the honest old fellow than to let him down. As for confirmation—that was something else, a matter of will, of active consent on his part as an adult. Holy Mother Church was free enough with her abominating and execrating the likes of Alec. Confirmed in such beliefs? The rabid old sow could fuck herself first.

"Sir," Alec said, "I'm to unpack the cricket things and clean them for tomorrow's match, if you might excuse me just now."

"Yes, go; I'll see what can be done and we'll talk again soon."

Alec left quickly. The evening had rattled him. First, meeting Hall in the garden, where the man's gentleness had undone his resolve. Then, inviting him to swim and setting himself up for rejection. And now Borenius, trying to snag him just before he was about to break free . . .

Alec was hurrying through the front shrubbery when he walked smack into someone and caught hold of his elbows for balance: it was Hall. Alec was startled not just by the run-in, but also by Hall's appearance. Golden pollen from the evening primroses clung to his black hair, adorning him eerily, beautifully, like some woodland god. Their eyes locked; Hall's lips parted in surprise. Alec wanted to kiss him, fiercely. Instead he rushed out through the gate without a word.

In his confusion, Alec had forgotten his rifle in the kitchen, so he hurried all the way around the house and took it from just inside the door. Alone in the herb garden, he leaned against the wall to steady himself. As soon as he did so, he saw two men walking toward him: Hall again, now with Borenius. Dark as it was, Alec could tell they recognized him. "Good night, sir," Alec muttered, trying to include them both as they passed.

Feeling pursued by those he most wanted to avoid, he went back around front to the shrubbery, where he hoped he might be alone. But there was Hall, having seen the vicar off, dawdling again, his nose again in the primroses. Once more Alec said, "Good night, sir."

"Good night, Scudder," he said, and then: "They tell me you're emigrating."

His interest surprised Alec. "That's my idea, sir."

"Well, good luck to you."

"Thank you, sir." He expected Hall to go now, but the man lingered in silence, as if waiting for their talk to continue, so Alec ventured to say, "It seems rather strange."

"Canada or Australia, I suppose."

"No sir, the Argentine."

"Ah, ah, fine country."

"Have you visited it yourself, sir?"

"Rather not, England for me," said Hall. They'd taken a few steps side by side and bumped in the dark. Alec watched Hall go on back into the house.

England for me. True enough: England was for Hall and his like, no one else, only them. Alec knew he ought to go to his room and forget about him. He ought to get into bed and be still; think about cricket, or nothing; or read from the anthology on his bedside table: a dose of Tennyson would put him to sleep. In spite of himself, rifle in hand, he walked toward the Russet Room.

The window was dark, like those of the rest of the house at this hour, but tonight a ladder leaned against the wall, its top resting on the stone sill. The roofers must have left it; they were repairing the leaky bay of the drawing room below. But what if Hall had placed it there himself? Alec was certain he'd done no such thing; nonetheless he put a foot on the ladder's first rung, testing his courage as much as its strength. He pulled back. Maybe Durham was up there with Hall. His heart sank; he started to walk away. Just then, the curtains upstairs were pulled open. At the window was Hall, who was looking out over the park, where the just-risen moon turned the mist in the grass all smoky white. Hall was shivering—the night had grown chilly. He gripped the top of the ladder with both hands and shook it. Was he testing it? Did he want to descend, to escape whatever was troubling him? As he had the night before, again he called out crazily to the sky, "Come!" Then he let go of the ladder and was gone again from sight. Despite the cold, he left the window and curtains wide open.

At once Alec knew what he must do. He climbed the ladder quietly, then through the window and into the room. Hall was in bed, watching in silence. Alec leaned his gun carefully against the windowsill.

He went to Hall, knelt beside him, and whispered, "Sir, was you calling out for me?"

Hall said nothing, but his gaze was gentle, even grateful.

"I know, I know . . . ," Alec said and touched him.

6

"Had I best be going now, sir?" Alec asked. It was about two o'clock.

As if he had not heard the question, Hall said, "We mustn't fall asleep, though, awkward if anyone came in." He laughed a pleasant blurred laugh. "You mustn't call me sir," and the laugh sounded again, brushing aside such problems as class with charm and insight. "May I ask your name?" he said awkwardly.

But Hall's well-intended words served to remind Alec of the problem rather than dispel it. He answered, "I'm Scudder."

"I know you're Scudder. I meant your other name."

"Only Alec just."

"Jolly name to have."

"It's only my name."

"I'm called Maurice."

They talked quietly, intimately—about when they first saw each other, about Alec's kissing the girls ("those people," Maurice called them—jealously, to Alec's delight), about his watching two nights at the Russet Room window.

"Do you mean you were out in all that infernal rain?"

"Yes . . . watching . . . Oh, that's nothing, you've got to watch, haven't you . . . See, I've not much longer in this country, that's how I kep' putting it."

"How beastly I was to you this morning!"

"Oh, that's nothing—excuse the question, but is that door locked?"

"I'll lock it."

Hall locked the door; when he returned, he stood at the foot of the bed, naked, aroused, unsure. He looked at Alec shyly and in silence, seeming not only to offer himself, but to seek permission, even approval. The sheet was tangled across Alec's middle; he pulled it away. Maurice smiled at the welcome, lay beside him, warmed him with his embrace, and nestled his face against Alec's neck, his breath like a wordless whisper. He touched the head of Alec's cock and showed him the droplet on his fingertip. He wiped it on his own cheek. Alec found Maurice's lips with his own and parted them gently, the way Van had taught him, with the edge of his tongue.

Later, spent again, they slept. At first they rolled apart, as if their newfound intimacy harassed them, but toward morning a movement began, and they woke deep in each other's arms. Off in the distance, the bell of St. Simon's struck. Maurice's head lay heavily on Alec's chest. Alec remained still, as much to cherish his own contentment as to protect his lover's repose. When he could wait no longer, he caressed Maurice's hair and said, "Sir, the church has gone four, you'll have to release me."

"Maurice, I'm Maurice."

"But the church has—"

"Damn the church," Maurice said, half-asleep, kissing his nipple. Alec writhed with the pleasure.

"I've the cricket pitch to help roll for the match . . ." Still, Alec did not move, except to fondle Maurice's hair. He was very happy that Maurice wanted to keep him there. More to himself than to Maurice he said, "I have the young birds too—the boat's done . . ." and then went mindlessly on about Archie London diving into the water lilies. As he spoke, he slipped out of bed.

"Don't, why did you?"

"There's the cricket—"

"No, there's not the cricket—you're going abroad."

The tone was petulant, but his face was sincerely pained. The words ambushed Alec. In his daydreams about this night, he had not pictured the sadness of parting, much less that the gentleman might regret his leaving England. Gathering his clothes, he said, "Well, we'll find another opportunity before I do."

"If you stop," Maurice entreated, "I'll tell you my dream . . ."

While Alec stepped into his trousers, Maurice told him his dream about his eccentric late grandfather, who claimed to believe that God dwelled invisibly within the sun, as the human soul did within the body. "I wonder what you'd have made of him . . ."

The closeness implied in those words, the social parity—that Alec should have met Maurice's grandfather and been asked an opinion—disarmed him further. Harried, confused, he said, "I dreamt the Reverend Borenius was trying to drown me, and now I really must go, I can't talk about dreams, don't you see, or I'll catch it from Mr. Ayers."

"Did you ever dream you had a friend, Alec? Nothing else but just 'my friend,' he trying to help you and you, him. A friend," he repeated, sentimental suddenly. "Someone to last your whole life and you, his. I suppose such a thing can't really happen outside sleep."

The words, giving voice to Alec's own feelings, stopped him still. He ached to lie with Maurice for another hour. But then it would be morning and impossible for him to leave unnoticed. They'd be found out; there'd be trouble. For both their sakes he stepped quietly away from the bed. When he reached the window, Maurice called: "Scudder . . ."

Alec stopped and turned to him.

"Alec, you're a dear fellow and we've been very happy."

"You get some sleep, there's no hurry in your case," Alec said and climbed down the ladder. Dawn was breaking. He went out through the gate dividing the garden from the park. It was so quiet that he was sure Maurice could hear the clink of the latch upstairs.

Back in his room, Alec lay down on the bed where he realized he'd not slept for three nights. His flesh glowed—satisfied, pleasantly sore. The two of them were little experienced— Maurice, to Alec's surprise, even less so than himself. At moments they were clumsy or rough: they bruised each other with their passion. No matter, even the awkwardness made him happy. In his own eyes he had acted with courage, maybe for the first time since becoming a servant. He was the one who'd pursued, kept watch, climbed the ladder, risked getting caught, or worse—rejected, punished, disgraced. He was the hero of their night together. And he was very happy with Maurice, with the beauty his face revealed when close to his own, with his strength, his ardor, his wish to keep Alec in his arms, to please him: *You mustn't call me sir . . . I'm called Maurice.*

You're going abroad . . . Alec now asked himself why. Surely not for "getting ahead," like Fred. Wasn't it rather for the kind of freedom he'd just tasted? To be one with a man of his choosing, who, like him, wanted a friend, *Nothing else but just "my friend," he trying to help you and you, him. A friend, someone to last your whole life and you, his . . .*

In the distance, St. Simon's bell struck five. The hatchlings were squawking in their coop. He got up to tend them. Later, after the birds were fed, and the dogs, and the kennels swept and the spaniels brushed, after he'd helped the gardeners smooth the cricket pitch, when it was time for him to get ready to play, there was something nuptial about Alec's happiness. He was going to see Maurice; they would meet in the daylight, in the eyes of the park and the village; they would play together on the same team, these two who had spent the night breaking the law by loving each other. *Did you ever dream you had a friend, Alec?*

Morgan had made him a gentlemanly gift for his trip: a box of sandalwood soaps from Fortnum & Mason. He'd stored them away, but now he unpacked a cake and, rather than wake up the household by filling the bathtub, went to the boathouse to bathe. When he took off his shirt, he still could smell Maurice. He inhaled deeply, happily. And he smiled when he saw their spunk, dried on his belly and legs, on his chest and shoulders, plenty of it, all mixed together. He hooted and jumped into the pond where the stream fed it fresh, scrubbed himself from head to toe, then again, imagining what wicked fun they'd have if Maurice was here with him.

Walking back to the keeper's cottage, he went out of his way to pass by the Russet Room window. The ladder was still there. The workmen, like Alec, would be playing cricket today. If only they'd leave it! Tonight he'd climb that ladder with no hesitation. He and Maurice would wear themselves out with love, and sleep again in each other's arms, and wake with their lips not inches apart.

In his room, he dressed in the flannels. The Durhams had splurged on correct white clothes for Penge Park. This was Alec's first year in the match: the outfit was new, the trousers

made to order, cream-colored, snug in the waist, roomy in
the seat and thighs. When he'd showed them off to Mill and
Milly, they squealed and pinched his bum. He hoped Maurice
would like them as much.

The park team was gathered at the field with Mr. Ayers,
who always kept score, about a dozen yards from the shed
where the dowager and young Mrs. Durham sat with their
guests. Meantime, Simcox, on the servants' behalf, had gone
to the Russet Room to ask Mr. Hall to captain in the absence
of the squire, who was campaigning. They were surprised to
hear that he had declined and requested that Alec should
captain.

"Mr. Hall claims he's no cricketer—" said Simcox to Alec,
"a bit of well-bred modesty I'm sure—and asked me who's our
best bat. I told him we have no one better than the under-
gamekeeper. So he said, 'Make the under-gamekeeper captain.' I ventured to suggest that things always go better under
a gentleman, but he'd have none of that and said you should
put him in deep field. Also he won't bat first, he'd rather
eighth. Start without him, he said, as he won't come down till
it's time. Frankly, he looked rather ill to me."

Alec took Simcox aside. "Ill, is he, Mr. Hall?"

"Lovesick, that's what they're saying."

Alec went suddenly queasy and hot.

"Now what's wrong with you?" Simcox said. "You've just
turned all peaked yourself."

"No, it's only too bad for the team."

"Didn't I suspect something when I woke him this morning? He's usually quite chatty when I bring him his tea, but
today he hid under the covers and had not a word for me.
And the bedclothes—a shipwreck! Like he'd been thrashing
around all night long. It's some girl in London, they say; she

must be one fussy brat, stringing him along, a fine catch like him." Then, lowering his voice, he said, "Unless maybe she heard rumors of him and the squire . . ."

Alec wanted to go to Maurice, to know the truth, to hold him, to be held and reassured. Instead he did as instructed: he captained. The park won the toss. Maurice came down from the house fifteen minutes later. He sat apart from the rest of his team (all of them servants) in the shed at the feet of the ladies and their guests, who often yawned. Alec, though busy blocking the vicar's lobs, could see that Maurice was disturbed. Sheltered there among his own class, did he regret last night?

But when Maurice joined him to play, his fear was calmed. It was a new over; Alec received the first ball. Abandoning caution, he swiped it into the ferns. He met Maurice's eyes and smiled. He was untrained, but had the cricketing build, and the game took on some semblance of competition. Maurice played up too. Alec watched him running, reaching, stretching; the sport engaged him fully, mind and body. They were dressed alike—in their whites, as teammates, equals! A win would belong to them both; they were against the whole world—not only Mr. Borenius and the field but the audience in the shed and all England were closing around the wickets. They played for the sake of each other—if one fell, the other would follow. They intended no harm to the world, but if it attacked they must respond, they must stand wary with full strength. And as the game proceeded it connected with their night.

But Clive Durham's arrival ended Alec's joy easily enough. When he came to the pitch the lovers were no longer the leading force; people turned their heads, the game languished and ceased. Alec resigned from play. It was only fit and proper that the squire should bat at once. Without looking at Maurice, Alec receded. He stood in front of the shed with dignity, and when Durham was done talking with the ladies, Alec offered his bat, which the squire took as a matter of course, then flung himself down by old Ayers, among the other servants. Durham continued to hold up the match by chatting with Maurice, whose face, earlier honest with the effort of play, now smoothed itself into a genteel mask. Alec imagined their banter frosted with "my dears" and "frightfuls." How he hated Durham. And he was peeved that Maurice was going along. A nudge from the village's socialist schoolmaster parted the Cambridge gents, who at long last shut their yaps and returned to the game. Maurice went out first ball and abruptly walked away from the field.

"Wait for me," Durham called after him.

Maurice ignored the request and went straight for the house. As he passed the servants, they stood and applauded him frantically—but not Alec. He knew Maurice was looking at him, and kept his eyes down. He would not behave like a fatuous lackey. Instead he loosened the top of his shirt so Maurice might see the bruise on his neck, a trophy of last night's passion.

The squire soon called Alec back into the match and left the field for the house, "to resume his campaigning," as the park team was told. Was he inside now with Maurice? Alec wondered. Then, when he was fielding, Alec saw Durham's motorcar on the drive that skirted the field. *Safe trip, Clive, deary,* he said to himself, *and do fuck the fuck off!* He felt reckless and strong. He stamped his foot on the ground as the auto passed by.

The park went on to win the match. Alec was praised, and both teams feted with an outdoor meal.

He overheard Milly saying to Simcox, "Took ill somefin'

awful, all of a sudden, green-like in the face. Too much sun, they're sayin'."

"It's that wench in town," Simcox said. "Now, didn't I know? He told the young missus that he'd gotten a letter, but there was no letter, I'd have seen it. He's brokenhearted, the gentleman—"

"The squire hisself motored him to the train. Frankly, I think he's a darlin', takin' it so hard. That's what a girl wants, a man fallin' to pieces for her—it's a sign of true love. She'll come round, you'll see."

Alec immediately lost his appetite. He collected the cricket things in silence. He said privately to Simcox, "Might you write down Mr. Hall's address for me?"

"What on earth for?"

"He asked about one of the rifles; I told him I'd look up the factory number and such. Now that he's gone so sudden, I'll not likely see him before I leave England—I'll just send a note." On his way to store the equipment, Alec passed the Russet Room window. The ladder was gone.

He went to the boathouse. He opened the slats of the shutters: sunlight patterned the floor like fish bones. He read the address Simcox had given him, not knowing what he would do with it. He lay back in his corner and watched the dust float in the sunbeams. *We've been very happy . . .*

One of the spaniels nosed through the door and came to him. He stroked her silky head. Reason admonished Alec: he'd already been too wild, stealing into the manor last night, to the bed of a man who could have rejected or even betrayed him. It would be still more reckless to write Maurice at his home in that haughty suburb. To write would test their relationship. Could it survive outside a moldy bedroom in a decrepit country house? To write would also test Maurice, and himself even more. The pain of rejection would belong only to him, since Maurice held the power to hurt, accorded not only by money and class, but also by Alec's own yearning. Why risk it? Why not cherish the memory of their night together, keep busy for the next ten days, and set sail?

Still in his white cricket clothes, the trousers now stained reddish on the right leg, where he'd rubbed the ball, he walked to the village with the spaniel. There he sent Maurice this wire: COME BACK, WAITING TONIGHT AT BOATHOUSE, PENGE, ALEC.

7

The weather changed. A cold night followed the sunny day, and Alec, having packed his blanket away, had only his clothes for warmth in the boathouse. The chill kept him mostly awake. When he did doze, the rustle of a twig would rouse him because it might signal Maurice's coming. But Maurice did not come. At dawn, Alec told himself he had sent the telegram too late. The message likely missed the last post to Maurice's house, but he would surely receive it this morning. He went about his work quietly and apprehensively, hoping he might hear from Maurice, fearing he would not. He avoided the younger servants, who were eager to josh him about the game. When the Mildreds offered a prize for victory, he said he hadn't the time, too busy getting things ready for his trip.

At day's end, still no word. He reasoned that Maurice had not replied because a message addressed in his hand to Alec might attract attention. He'd best come unannounced. At nightfall, he returned to the boathouse to wait. Chance, or nature, had mated the young men so perfectly that, even after one night together, their separation was painful to Alec; his flesh remembered Maurice's, vividly, palpably, as if he were actually present. When he turned onto his belly during his fitful sleep, he came so hard that it hurt and he woke up groaning.

Before dawn, desolate, he wrote again:

> Mr. Maurice, Dear Sir. I waited both nights in the
> boathouse. I said the boathouse as the ladder is taken
> away and the woods is to damp to lie down. So please
> come to "the boathouse" tomorrow night or next,
> pretend to the other gentlemen you want a stroll, easily
> managed, then come down to the boathouse. Dear Sir,
> let me share with you once before leaving Old England
> if it is not asking to much. I have key, will let in. I
> leave per Ss Normannia Aug 29. I since cricket match
> do long to talk with one of my arms round you, then
> place both arms round you and share with you, the
> above now seems sweeter to me than words can say . . .

Writing those phrases, he remembered how passion had
humbled Maurice, or had led him, willingly, to humble himself. Alec did so now in turn:

> I am perfectly aware that I am only a servant that
> never presume on your loving kindness to take
> liberties or in any other way.
>
> Yours respectfully,
> A. Scudder.
> (gamekeeper to C. Durham Esq.)
> Maurice, was you taken ill that you left, as the indoor
> servants say? I hope you feel all as usual by this time.
> Mind and write if you can't come, for I get no sleep
> waiting night after night, so come without fail to
> "Boathouse Penge" . . .

He carried the letter to the village for the first mail; the
postmaster assured him it would be delivered by noon. On

turning away, he immediately regretted sending it. Why had he groveled? Why call Maurice "Mr." and "Sir"; himself "only a servant"? Maurice had left him without a word, to shiver in the damned boathouse alone. And now? Too good to answer the menial gamekeeper? "Loving kindness." Damn! Maurice was worse than Risley, who at least called a servant a servant and would pay for what he wanted.

"Might I have it back, my letter?" Alec asked the postmaster. "I just recalled I left out something important."

"Ah no, lad. I'd be breaking the law to give back a letter once posted; that could cost me my pension. Write again, why don't you, to say what you left out."

On his way home through the park another kind of anxiety overtook him: Could Maurice truly be ill, too sick to write? At the keeper's cottage, he found Mrs. Ayers in her kitchen pouring tea for Reverend Borenius.

"Here's young Alec now, Vicar," she said.

"Good morning, Mr. Scudder," he said with a friendly smile. "Out and about first thing?"

"Yes sir—the birds and the animals, you know, they're quite early risers."

"And won't they miss you when you leave us—as will we all," she said. "The vicar's come to speak with you, so I'm just setting the pot on the table."

After the door closed behind Mrs. Ayers, Borenius said, "I was hoping to catch you before you began your day's work—to take up our conversation of two nights ago. Have you a few minutes? I've asked Mr. Ayers's permission."

There was no escaping. "Of course, sir."

"I inquired at the cathedral about confirmation. As I feared, it can't be arranged before you go."

Alec tried to keep from sneering; he wasn't sure he succeeded.

"Please don't trouble yourself, Vicar," he said. "I'll take care of such things overseas when I'm settled."

"Will you?" Borenius pulled his chair closer to Alec, lowered his voice, and continued more confidentially, "It seems I have more reason for concern. When we couldn't find you earlier, Mrs. Ayers knocked on your door. The bed was clearly unslept-in."

Alec, speechless, drank from his cup to give himself a moment before answering. He swallowed and said, "You see, sir . . . I fell asleep in the boathouse."

"Working late?"

"Sometimes I go there to read."

"This is not the first time she's found your bed so, Mrs. Ayers let slip. Several mornings recently, in fact."

"Yes, well, sir, it's a big trip, I'm stayin' up late gettin' ready and all—"

"As the good woman herself suggested—she's very protective of you." Borenius leaned closer still. "Mr. Scudder, some have noticed your keeping company with two of the girls here in service . . ."

"Beg pardon?"

"Certainly such attractions are all quite normal, and I would have dismissed it as gossip, but the unslept-in bed suggests something disturbing. You're at an age when a man seeks a mate. As one who cares not only for your salvation, but for your earthly happiness in the true, deep sense of that word, I take it as my duty to remind you that what it suggests is more than unseemly—"

"Sir, I—"

Borenius cut him off: "It's perilous, even deadly, I'm not exaggerating. Promiscuity undermines a man's suitability for wedlock, to say nothing of the consequences to the girls. Two of them? Cousins? It's shocking. It degrades us; it corrupts our search for true love, which is of course a good and holy thing; not to mention the risk of disease."

Alec got up from the table. "It's nothing like what you're saying—"

"I'm not trying to interrogate you. I'm speaking to you in Christian friendship. Will you accept that? If not, then I've failed."

Alec was too flustered to answer.

"Sometimes," the vicar went on, "as the poet says, 'the world is too much with us.' 'Getting and spending,' the business of our lives. Spiritual matters seem unnecessary, even a luxury, and believe me, not only for you. But as much as emigrating is a wonderful enterprise, I'm sure it's an upheaval as well, and such change is often distressing. Anxiety might lead a young man to seek comfort in the wrong places; it's then we most need the strength our faith affords us . . ." Borenius approached him, but stopped short of placing his hand on Alec's shoulder. He went on, "While there's no time for confirmation, perhaps you'd care to be shriven before you sail."

"Sir?"

"To confess."

"To you?"

"To God. Come, come, you know right from wrong. We're all of us sinners. The sacraments can be a great comfort in times of change. It's a first step. Set sail with a clean heart and conscience."

Alec said nothing.

"You'll think about it, won't you?"

"You've given me lots to think about."

"Good. Call at the vicarage anytime." Borenius turned to go.

Alec spoke up with a hint of defiance, "Sir, if Mrs. Ayers

should find my bed not slept-in again, please know I'll likely
be spending a night with my folks in Osmington."

After Borenius left, Alec, his breath quick and shallow, sat
at the table and stared at his folded hands. He didn't know
what to do or even to think, only that he felt humiliated. He
dropped his head forward, raking his hair with his fingers.
The touch recalled the way Maurice had crushed Alec's hair
in his hands and told him how good it felt and smelled. The
memory made him sadder still. "Maurice," he said aloud.

You know right from wrong . . . Two days ago he did know.
He knew that the Church and the law were wrong and that his
own desires were right because they had led him to Maurice.
Their night of happiness had vindicated him, redeemed the
loneliness and confusion, proven the truth, the goodness, of
his desires. But now, if these same desires could lead to the
despair he was feeling today, maybe they were indeed wrong,
as everybody said. Maybe he ought to ask for forgiveness.

On the lampstand by the door to his room Mrs. Ayers had
left a letter. His heart pounded at the sight, but it was from
Fred, not Maurice. In his new life abroad, his brother had
determined to "move up" from the trade of butchering into the
clean-handed world of business. Much as he scorned those he
refused to call his betters, Fred believed that with his brains
and gift of gab he belonged among them. He was ashamed of
Alec's being in service, especially of his rough outdoor work.
Fred had found a job with an insurance company that was
opening an office in Buenos Aires. His letter gave news that
he'd negotiated a place for Alec as well—as a filing clerk. "So
you'll put to good use that sharp new suit of clothes," he wrote.
"Practice wearing your bowler till you can do so with ease."

A filing clerk. Like his brother, Alec had a high opinion of
his own talents—too high to settle for a life of sorting papers

in that magnificent unbounded land. He would go along for now. Once in Argentina, he just might set out on his own.

At the midday meal in the kitchen, Milly was chattering away about the religion class the vicar was starting for servants not yet confirmed. He'd talked to them about confessing their sins. "I think he tends toward the papists. And you know what Romish priests do to girls in confessional boxes."

Simcox sat at the table with a newspaper and scowled at her over his glasses. He changed the topic by reading aloud, "'Old people stooped with suffering. Middle age courageously fighting. Youth protesting impatiently. Children unable to explain. Baby crying, can't tell why.'"

"What's that," the parlormaid said, "another revolt in Bulgaria?"

"Listen and learn," said Simcox. "'All is misery, from their kidneys.'"

"'Kidneys'?"

"Sshh. 'Only a little backache first. Comes when you catch a cold. Or when you strain your back. First sign of kidney trouble—urinary disorders, stone, gravel, rheumatism.' It's an advertisement for Doan's Backache-Kidney Pills. They claim it's from catching a cold. Anything to sell their pills."

"Are we so dull in Wiltshire?" the parlormaid asked. "Nothing more exciting in all the *Police Court News*?"

"Here's an item from Wilton. A bellboy at the hotel, charged with lewdness involving a guest, a traveling *gent*, no less—and they discovered a note from the boy threatening exposure."

Alec choked on his soup.

"Oooo . . . lewdness and buggers; they'll both hang themselves," Milly said. "It always ends that way with poofters. Like last May. Germans, weren't they? Spies! Dressin' like mollies and all. I seen the pictures. Remarkable, really, the illusion."

"Austrian, not German," Simcox said to Milly. "Just one, Colonel Redl. He shot himself—no rope. The emperor said he was sorry the man died in mortal sin, which is what suicides do, and therefore would go to hell, according to your papists. How might the vicar handle *that* in confirmation class?"

"Well, pardon me that unlike some I'm unschooled in perversion."

"Perversion has nothing to do with it. One couldn't avoid the story, all over the press, a great international scandal, eh, Scudder?"

"Huh? Yeah, I'd heard somethin' about it—not what you said of the emperor, though." Alec finished his soup and got up to leave. "'Scuse me now, please; don't mean to be rude, but I'm behind in my chores."

"There's cold roast from last night," the parlormaid said.

"Thanks, miss, the soup filled me up."

Afternoon passed and evening followed, and nothing from Maurice. Why did this hurt so badly? Such risk he'd taken to offer himself to Maurice! He'd been welcomed eagerly, even gratefully. Now shunned. Why? In body and mind, in their passion for each other, they were equals. The force of this pain shocked him: he could feel it just there in his gut. Would it ever ease? Could he do nothing to help himself?

He started another letter:

> Mr. Hall, Mr. Borenius has just spoke to me. Sir, you
> do not treat me fairly. I am sailing next week, per s.s.
> Normannia. I wrote you I am going, it is not fair you
> never write to me. I come of a respectable family, I
> don't think it fair to treat me like a dog. My father is a

respectable tradesman. I am going to be on my own in the Argentine. You say, "Alec, you are a dear fellow"; but you do not write.

It felt good to chide Maurice, but still his words had no force. He wrote and underlined:

I know about you and Mr. Durham.

Let Maurice squirm. Yes, that was good. Still, he could feel tears rising as he wrote:

Why do you say "call me Maurice," and then treat me so unfairly?

He wiped his nose with the back of his hand. He was resorting to helpless reproaches again. Then he was inspired. Why wait upon Maurice, like a lackey, when he could take action himself:

Mr. Hall, I am coming to London Tuesday. If you do not want me at your home say where in London, you had better see me—I would make you sorry for it.

There—yes! Let him try to explain why this servant had come to call at his house as boldly as a client or friend. Why not go to London? Why should his life be stalled in this help-lessness? He would compel Maurice to see him.

Sir, nothing of note has occurred since you left Penge. Cricket seems over, some of the great trees has lost some of their leaves, which is very early.

Has Mr. Borenius spoken to you about certain girls? I
can't help being rather rough, it is some men's nature,
but you should not treat me like a dog. It was before
you came. It is natural to want a girl, you cannot
go against human nature. Mr. Borenius found out
about the girls through the new communion class.
He has just spoken to me. I have never come like that
to a gentleman before. Were you annoyed at being
disturbed so early? Sir, it was your fault, your head was
on me. I had my work, I was Mr. Durham's servant,
not yours. I am not your servant. I will not be treated
as your servant, and I don't care if the world knows it.

He had finally got to the heart of it. I AM NOT YOUR
SERVANT. I WILL NOT BE TREATED AS YOUR SER-
VANT. He concluded:

I will show respect where it's <u>due only</u>, that is to say to
gentleman who are gentleman. Simcox says, "Mr. Hall
says to put him in about eighth." I put you in fifth,
but I was captain, and you have no right to treat me
unfairly on that account.

Yours respectfully, A. Scudder.
P.S. <u>I know something.</u>

He'd lost himself in the letter, moving his lips as he wrote,
as if declaiming a speech to Maurice (and to himself) in a way
impossible in person, when the words were in the air and you
could take them back and stammer and break down. He felt
excited while writing, like chasing prey in the woods. He read
it over, but it did no good, because it was too soon to catch the

errors or to understand that the threats were vile and destructive. He was angry; now Maurice would know. He posted it quickly, before he could change his mind.

Later, at tea in the kitchen, Simcox was reading the evening edition of *Police Court News*. "Aha," he said over his specs. "Now, look at this. That snipe of a bellhop at the Wilton hotel, turns out the gent he touched for cash is quite aboveboard and well-connected. The little blackmailer's facing six months' hard labor . . ."

"Blackmail?" Alec said.

"What else would you call it? 'Extortion,' I suppose one might say to be polite."

"Maybe he was just fightin' back, the lad I mean; maybe the gent took advantage."

"'*Lad*'? Says here he's twenty; he knows what's what."

"Hard labor," said Milly, "that's what he needs. He'll hang hisself behind bars, wait and see."

Alec finished his tea quickly and rose from the table.

"Oh, here, Scudder," the parlormaid said. She handed him an envelope. "By the midday post."

Outside, he went into the alley of primroses to read the note by himself:

A.S. Yes. Meet me Tuesday 5.0 p.m. entrance of
British Museum. B.M. a large building. Anyone will
tell you which. M.C.H.

8

Alec asked Mr. Ayers for Tuesday off to visit his parents in Osmington in advance of leaving England. Permission granted.
He then wrote to his father to say that he would be unable
to visit on Tuesday, as they'd previously planned, because
Mr. Ayers was unwell and needed him that day at Penge, but
he would come Wednesday instead.

For the most critical day of his life, he put on the blue
worsted suit he'd bought for Argentina. The ready-made
jacket and trousers were stiff, the cheap fabric scratchy, the
fit awkward and uncomfortable, but Alec, unaccustomed to
business clothes, believed that was the price of wearing them.
Instead of his cap, he took the new bowler. He wished he'd
remembered to get his hair cut, because, as usual, the damp
weather bewitched it: the lustrous ringlets and waves poked
fun at the hat's sober dome. He crammed it on as best he
could and set out.

Much as he thought himself worldly, in truth Alec's acquaintance with the capital was mostly vicarious, gleaned
from chitchat and newspapers. He'd paid careful attention
when Morgan, who lived in London, talked about culture
and landmarks, and when Simcox (who, Alec believed, had a
lover in town or was seeking one) mentioned certain locales.
Thus he'd put together that the British Museum was not too
far from St. Pancras Station, which he therefore chose for his
destination; likewise he mentally noted the name of a pub the

valet liked and a hotel where he'd stayed—"nothing grand, of course, but perfectly clean."

He marveled that three years had already passed since his own most recent visit to the city. That had been in 1910, shortly before he'd started at Michaelmount, the twentieth of May precisely: his father decided that the two of them should "witness history" and took his son to view the funeral procession of King-Emperor Edward VII, the Peacemaker.

On that day, the imperial pageant had awed the crowds lining the streets into an eerie silence. Nine monarchs of Europe, helmeted, plumed, walked behind the gun carriage bearing the double-crowned coffin, pulled by hundreds of sailors in lockstep. Entire brigades marched by, fusiliers, grenadiers, royal guardsmen with swords drawn and tucked under their arms in mourning. Courtiers, maharajas, heads of state—the pomp went on for miles, the vast scene set to the music of muted horns and thudding muffled drums.

Now, passing through the countryside, then suburbs that grew thicker as the train approached London, Alec recalled the naïve sixteen-year-old he'd once been and smiled. Three years later, he was wiser, having tasted some of life's bitterness. He tried to keep his rage against Maurice burning. But when he closed his eyes and rested his head, instead of feeling anger he'd recall the tenderness of their night together, his lover's kind eyes and touch, their embracing, kissing . . .

His nerves tensed when London itself first appeared. As the train drew into the station under the iron skeleton with its sooty glass skin, he felt charged with the energy of seven million people, all with their hearts pumping seventy times a minute. The city was drawing his pulse into its own.

On the platform, crowds rushed, somehow merging, the vast spaces hardly able to hold them, their motion seeming to

carry him with no effort of his own along the concourse. This
was not how he remembered the city from three years ago.
But then London, holding its breath for the king's funeral,
had not truly been London. Now the city was itself, driven by
the vying hungers of those millions of mouths.

Dazed by the hubbub, he had to orient himself before he
could start out for the museum. He walked toward a constable
to ask the way. But he was busy, posing for a tourist's Kodak.
The photographer's pal, a stocky young weight lifter, his shirt-
sleeves rolled high, was flexing his biceps for the bobby to feel
and mug his awe for the camera. The tableau was slapstick and
bawdy. Certain men stared voraciously, the way they stared at
Alec. They'd scan his form with a practiced glance, catch and
hold his eye. He marveled at how openly they dared to show
their desire. Or maybe it only seemed so to him because he
shared it.

He found a big map behind glass: he saw he was little more
than a mile from the British Museum. He decided to walk
rather than risk getting lost in the Underground. Besides, the
city's onslaught had unbalanced him, and he wanted to re-
gain his footing before meeting Maurice. Walking calmed his
thoughts. But outside, all was traffic, noise, pelting rain. Afternoon was already dim as twilight under the dense cloud cover,
the humid air stinking of petrol fumes, horse shit, and urine.
He didn't walk so much as dodge other people maneuvering
through the nastiness as fast as they could, like ropewalk-
ers with umbrellas aloft. Everybody looked repulsive—pasty,
blotchy, damp, and cross, because the rain required more
clothes than did the August heat. When he skipped out of
the way of a fast-rolling cab, its filthy wake spattered the new
trousers intended for sunny Buenos Aires.

On Bloomsbury Way, he found himself in front of what

struck him as the funniest-looking church ever, with a kind of ziggurat for a steeple, growing out of a belfry made to look like a little Greek temple, where a lion of stone seemed to be chasing a plump unicorn, who twisted in terror. When Alec asked a passerby about the museum, he pointed to the next corner.

So dark was the afternoon that some of the lights had been turned on inside, and the great building suggested a tomb, miraculously illuminated by the spirits of the dead. It was quarter to five. He was glad of the extra time. Here, on the portico, out of the rain, he could finally be still and collect his thoughts. *Blackmail.* A hateful word. When he'd written the letter, in his hurt and his wish to hurt back, he'd grabbed for any weapon. But surely Maurice would not take his threat seriously . . .

And soon there he was. Maurice climbed out of the cab on Great Russell Street at three minutes before the hour. How very handsome he was, how much at ease in this city, whose aggression deferred to his stride. Alec despaired. He hated his damned new suit; it was vulgar and ugly, and, comparing himself to the one he loved, he felt that way too. He wanted to be back in Wiltshire, in the woods, at ease in his soft corduroys. But he had no choice now: he must go forward.

"Here you are," Maurice said, raising a pair of gloves to his hat. "This rain's the limit. Let's have a talk inside."

"Where you wish."

Maurice was friendly, his voice calm. As soon as they entered the building, Alec raised his head and sneezed like a lion.

"Got a chill? It's the weather."

"What's all this place?"

"Old things belonging to the nation."

Which nation? Alec asked himself. *Surely not this one.*

They paused in the corridor of Roman emperors. Alec recognized some of the marmoreal Caesars from the books in the Dorchester library. Here they were, with their Mediterranean profiles and draperies, perpetual captives of the barbarians they had sought to conquer.

"Yes, it's bad weather. There've only been two fine days," Maurice said; then added mischievously, "And one fine night."

Alec's heart leapt at the words, but he turned his face away, because it wasn't the opening he wanted. He was waiting for signs of fear. He pretended not to understand the allusion, and sneezed again. The roar echoed down vestibules . . .

"I'm glad you wrote to me the second time. I liked both your letters. I'm not offended—you've never done anything wrong. It's all your mistake about cricket and the rest. I'll tell you straight out I enjoyed being with you, if that's the trouble. Is it? I want you to tell me. I just don't know."

Since he neither defended himself nor attacked, he gave Alec no opportunity to advance. *You've never done anything wrong . . . I want you to tell me.* His tone was conciliatory; he was attentive to Alec himself, not to the trouble he was causing. Disarmed by his manner, Alec tried to provoke him:

"What's here? *That's* no mistake." Alec touched his breast pocket. Maurice looked puzzled, not angry. Did he think Alec was pointing to his wounded heart? He clarified: "Your writing. And you and the squire—that's no mistake—some may wish as it was one."

"Don't drag in that," said Maurice, but without indignation.

Alec pushed at him harder: "Mr. Hall—you reckernize it wouldn't very well suit you if certain things came out, I suppose."

Again Maurice seemed puzzled by the words, not annoyed,

as if he sought to understand the emotion that drove them. His forbearance exasperated Alec, who kept on trying to provoke him: "What's more, I've always been a respectable young fellow until you called me into your room to amuse yourself. It don't hardly seem fair that a gentleman should drag you down." He surprised himself with the prissiness of his complaint (sounding like Milly, he thought, parroting her journals for young ladies). And worse, he was demeaning his courage: he had gladly risked his safety that night of his own accord.

Growing desperate to goad Maurice, he lied outright: "At least that's how my brother sees it." He faltered as he spoke these last words. "My brother's waiting outside now, as a matter of fact. He wanted to come and speak to you hisself, he's been scolding me shocking, but I said, 'No, Fred, no, Mr. Hall's a gentleman and can be trusted to behave like one, so you leave 'im to me,' I said, 'and Mr. Durham, he's a gentleman too, always was and always will be.'"

Now it was Maurice who'd turned away, toward the bust of Hadrian. He rested his hand on the pedestal and studied the calm bearded face. "With regard to Mr. Durham," said Maurice, "it's quite correct that I cared for him and he for me once, but he changed, and now he doesn't care anymore for me, nor I for him. It's the end."

"End o' what?"

"Of our friendship."

So it was only by mentioning Durham that Alec had gotten through to Maurice. His lament about being dragged down by a gentleman and the threat of a menacing brother outside had failed to reach him at all. "Mr. Hall, have you heard what I was saying?" Alec stepped closer, next to the bust of Hadrian's beloved, the melancholy Antinous.

When Maurice turned to face Alec to answer, he was struck by the likeness between the gamekeeper and the beautiful carved image. "I hear everything you say," Maurice said thoughtfully, and continued in exactly the same tone: "Scudder, why do you think it's 'natural' to care for both women and men? You wrote so in your letter. It isn't natural for me. I have really got to think that 'natural' only means oneself."

Alec had forgotten that part of the letter; besides, it was irrelevant to his business today. During their night together, it was clear to Alec that Maurice had been jealous of seeing him with the girls, so he mentioned them in his letter to irritate him. Natural? Hadn't the vicar himself said, "Certainly such attractions are all quite normal"? Alec sensed a weakness, an implied doubt about manhood, and exploited it. "Couldn't you get a kid of your own, then?" he asked.

"I've been to two doctors about it. Neither were any good."

"So you can't?"

"No, I can't."

"Want one?" Alec asked, as if hostile.

"It's not much use wanting."

"I could marry tomorrow, if I like," he bragged, though he was certain now, after his night with Maurice, that he never would. While speaking, he caught sight of a winged Assyrian bull, and was distracted by his naïve wonder. "He's big enough, isn't he? They must have owned wonderful machinery to make a thing like that."

"I expect so," said Maurice, also impressed by the bull. "I couldn't tell you. Here seems to be another one."

"A pair, so to speak. Would these have been ornaments?"

"This one has five legs."

"So's mine. A curious idea." Standing each by his monster, they looked at each other, and smiled. For a moment, their conflict evanesced; it was sweet for both young men to be exploring this strange timeless place together. Then Alec hardened himself again. "Won't do, Mr. Hall." Having created the fiction of his big brother's presence, he tried to make it less flimsy by repeating it: "I see your game, but you don't fool me twice, and you'll do better to have a friendly talk with me than wait for Fred, I can tell you. You've had your fun and you've got to pay up."

Maurice looked into his eyes gently but keenly. Nothing resulted from the outburst at all. It fell away like a flake of mud. Murmuring something about "leaving you to think this over," Alec sat down on a bench. Maurice joined him there shortly. And thus it was for twenty minutes: they kept wandering from room to room as if in search of something. They would peer at a goddess or vase, then move at a single impulse, and their unison was the stranger because on the surface they were at war. Alec recommenced his hints— horrible, reptilian—but somehow they did not pollute the intervening silences. He failed to make Maurice afraid or angry. Instead Maurice seemed to regret that any human being should have gotten into such a mess as the one that Alec was making for himself. When he chose to reply to some remark and their eyes met, he would smile, Alec's heart would melt in the warmth, and he would smile back. He was beginning to sense that the actual situation was a practical joke, almost— and concealed something real, that they both desired. Serious and good-tempered, Maurice continued to hold his own. If he made no offensive, it was because he felt no anger. To set it moving, a shock from without was required, and chance administered this.

Maurice was bending over a model of the Acropolis with his forehead a little wrinkled and his lips murmuring, "I see,

I see, I see." A gentleman nearby overheard him, started, peered through strong spectacles, and said, "Surely! I may forget faces but never a voice. Surely! You are one of our old boys."

Maurice did not reply. Alec sidled up closer.

"Surely you were at Mr. Abrahams's school. No, wait! Wait! Don't tell me your name. I want to remember it. I will remember it. You're not Sanday, you're not Gibbs. I know. I know. It's Wimbleby."

Maurice replied, "No, my name's Scudder."

Scudder? Alec realized that Maurice did know the old man and did not want to be recognized. "It isn't," Alec said, "and I've a serious charge to bring against this gentleman."

"Yes, awfully serious," remarked Maurice, and he rested his hand on Alec's shoulder so that his fingers touched the back of his neck. The touch stirred Alec, as did Maurice's taking his name for his own.

The old man gave a friendly nod, as though he understood that these two young fellows were sharing some joke. To Maurice he said, "I'm extremely sorry, sir, it's so seldom I make a mistake," and then, to show he was not an old fool, addressed the silent pair on the subject of the British Museum—not merely a collection of relics but a place round which one could take (with a glance at Alec)—er—the less fortunate, quite so—a stimulating place . . .

A patient voice called from a few yards off, "Ben, we are waiting," and the old man rejoined his wife.

Alec jerked away from Maurice and muttered, "That's all right . . . I won't trouble you now."

"Where are you going with your serious charge?" said Maurice, suddenly formidable.

"Couldn't say." He looked back at Maurice, whose coloring stood out against the stone heroes, perfect but bloodless, who had never known such bewilderment or infamy as Alec did now. He realized what a fool he'd been to imagine this splendid man could care for him, and more of a fool to plot to force him to do so. "Don't you worry—I'll never harm you now, you've too much pluck."

"Pluck be damned," said Maurice, with a plunge into anger.

"It'll all go no further—" He slapped his own mouth, as Maurice had done in the rain at the Russet Room window. "I don't know what came over me, Mr. Hall. *I* don't want to harm you. I never did."

"You blackmailed me."

"No sir, no . . ."

"You did."

"Maurice, listen, I only—"

"Maurice, am I?"

"You called me Alec . . . I'm as good as you."

"I don't find you are!" There was a pause before the storm; then he burst out: "By God, if you'd split on me to Mr. Ducie, I'd have broken you. It might have cost me hundreds, but I've got them, and the police always back my sort against yours. You don't know. We'd have got you into quod, for blackmail, after which—I'd have blown out my brains."

"Killed yourself? Death?"

"I should have known by that time that I loved you." With these words, the rows of old statues seemed to totter before their eyes. Maurice added quietly, "Too late . . . everything's always too late . . . I don't mean anything, but come outside, we can't talk here." They left the enormous and overheated building, seeking darkness and rain. On the portico Maurice stopped and said bitterly, "I forgot. Your brother."

"He's down at Father's—doesn't know a word—I was but threatening—"

"—for blackmail."

"Could you but understand . . ." He pulled out Maurice's note. "Take it if you like . . . I don't want it . . . never did . . . I suppose this is the end."

Assuredly it wasn't that. Unable to part yet ignorant of what would come next, they strode raging through the last glimmering of the sordid day. Maurice recovered his self-control. In a deserted square, against railings that encircled some trees, they came to a halt, and he began to discuss their crisis.

But as he grew calm, Alec grew fierce. It was as if that old gentleman, Maurice's teacher, had established, or reestablished, the infuriating inequality between them, so that he struck as soon as the other had grown tired of striking. He cried out to Maurice from the depths of his anguish, "It rained harder than this in the boathouse, it was yet colder. Why did you not come?"

"Muddle."

"I beg your pardon."

"You've to learn I'm always in a muddle. I didn't come or write because I wanted to get away from you without wanting. You won't understand. I even got myself hypnotized to see if I could change. But in the trance you kept dragging me back and I got awfully frightened. I knew something was evil, but I couldn't tell what, so I kept pretending it was you."

"What was it?"

"The . . . situation."

"I don't follow. Why did you not come to the boathouse?"

"My fear—and your trouble has been fear too. Ever since the cricket match you've let yourself get afraid of me. That's why we've been trying to down one another, and still are."

"I wouldn't take a penny from you. I wouldn't hurt your

little finger," he growled, and he rattled the bars that kept him from the trees.

"But you're still trying hard to hurt me, in my mind."

Alec failed to stifle his rising tears: "Why do you go and say you love me?"

"Why do you call me Maurice?"

"Oh, let's give over talking. Here——" and he held out his hand. Maurice took it, and they knew at that moment the greatest triumph an ordinary man can win. They saw now how natural it was that their abandonment to each other at Penge should have led to peril. They knew too little about each other—and too much. Hence fear. Hence cruelty. They held and they held: their gaze at each other was steady, firm, warm as the grip of their hands.

Alec rejoiced in Maurice's victory over him, because now his soul was free of its torment. Presently he spoke. Spasms of remorse and apology broke him; he began to tell his friend everything, no longer ashamed. He spoke of his relations. No one knew he was in London—Penge thought he was at his father's, his father at Penge—it had been difficult, very. Now he ought to go home—see his brother with whom he would travel to Argentina, his brother connected with trade, and his brother's wife. He came of a respectable family, he repeated, he bowed down to no man, not he, and he was as good as any gentleman. But while he bragged he took Maurice's arm. They both deserved such a caress—the feeling was strange. Then words died away, and they stood still.

In the silence and the stillness, Alec was afraid. Then he found his courage and said, "Stop with me."

Maurice swerved to face him. By now they were in love with each other consciously. Alec's heart was beating violently. He said, "Sleep the night with me. I know a place."

They were silent again, with eyes downcast. Alec was shivering, he didn't know whether from the rain, from fear of rejection or terror of being accepted, or from his fierce longing. He glanced up at Maurice, likewise shaken, who pleaded, "I can't, I've an engagement." A formal dinner party awaited him of the sort that brought work to his firm and that he couldn't possibly cut. Yet, with Alec beside him, he had almost forgotten its existence. "I have to leave you now and get changed. But look here: Alec, be reasonable. Meet me another evening instead—any day."

"Can't come to London again—Father or Mr. Ayers will be passing remarks."

"What does it matter if they do?"

"What's your engagement matter?"

They were silent again. Then Maurice said, "All right. To hell with it," and they walked on together in the rain.

9

"Alec, wake up."

An arm twitched.

"It's time we talked plans."

Alec snuggled closer, more awake than he pretended, warm, sinewy, happy. Happiness overwhelmed Maurice too: when he tried to speak, having Alec in his arms made him forget what he wanted to say. Light drifted in upon them from the outside world, where it was still raining. A strange hotel, a casual refuge, protected them from their enemies a little longer.

"Time to get up, boy. It's morning."

"Git up, then."

"How can I, the way you hold me!"

"Aren't yer a fidget, I'll learn ya to fidget," Alec said in his best parody of his own Dorset accent. He tickled and nibbled till his lover squirmed. He wasn't deferential anymore. The British Museum had cured that. This was 'oliday, London with Maurice, all troubles over, and he wanted to drowse and waste time, to tease and make love.

Maurice wanted the same, but years ago his father's death had made him—the oldest child, the only boy, with two younger sisters and a mother to protect—feel like the head of a family, a habit of mind he'd held on to. Now the oncoming future preoccupied him. Alec, attuned to his mood, tamed himself. The brightening light through the window began to make their coziness unreal. Something had to be said and settled. O for the night that was ending, for the sleep and wakefulness, the toughness and tenderness mixed, the sweet temper, the safety in darkness. Would such a night ever come again?

"You all right, Maurice?"—for Maurice had sighed. "You comfortable? Rest your head on me more, the way you like more . . . that's it, more, and Don't You Worry. You're With Me. Don't Worry."

Alec had redeemed himself. Since throwing off the poisonous intentions, he'd been himself, honest and kind, loving and merry. "Nice, you and me like this . . . ," he said, their lips so close now that it was scarcely speech. "Who'd have thought . . . First time I ever seed you I thought, 'Wish I and that one . . .' just like that . . . 'wouldn't I and him . . .' and it is so."

"Yes, and that's why we've got to fight."

"Who wants to fight? There's bin enough fighting."

"All the world's against us. We've got to pull ourselves together and make plans, while we can."

"Why d'you want to go and say a thing like that for, and spoil it all?"

"Because it has to be said. We can't allow things to go wrong and hurt us again the way they did down at Penge."

"Don't talk to me about Penge. Oo! Mah! Penge, where I was always a servant and 'Scudder do this' and 'Scudder do that' and the old lady, what do you think she once said? She said, 'Oh, would you most kindly of your goodness post this letter for me, what's-your-name?' What's-yer-name! Every day for six months I come up to Clive's bloody front porch for orders, and his mother don't know my name. She's a bitch. I said to 'er, 'What's yer name? Fuck yer name.' I nearly did too.

Wish I 'ad too. Maurice, you wouldn't believe how servants get spoken to. It's too shocking for words. That Archie London you're so set on is just as bad, and so are you, so are you. 'Haw, my man,' and all that. You've no idea how you nearly missed getting me. Near as nothing I never climbed that ladder . . . 'He don't want me really,' and I went flaming mad when you didn't turn up at the boathouse . . . a place I always fancied . . . got the key on me still, as a matter of fact . . . looking over the pond . . . very quiet, now and then a fish jumps, and cushions the way I arrange them . . ."

Having chattered himself out, he was silent. His voice died away into sadness, as though truth had risen to the surface of his pond and was unbearable.

"We'll meet in your boathouse yet."

"No, we won't," Alec wailed, like a child. He pushed Maurice away; his chest heaved mournfully; then he pulled him close, pressing their hearts together with violence, and embraced him as if the world were ending. "You'll remember that anyway." He got out of bed and looked down out at the grayness, his arms hanging empty. As playful as he'd been when they woke, now he was bereft. "I could easy have killed you," he said quietly, thinking he knew not what—that death would hurt less than parting?

"Or I, you."

Yes, of course it was true . . . They were as well matched for fighting as for love. Yesterday, when Maurice talked about shooting himself, his mortal rage had scared Alec. Today Alec felt it too: "Where's my clothes and that gone?" He was dazed. "It's so late. I h'aint got a razor even, I didn't reckon staying the night . . . I ought—I got a train to catch at once or Fred'll be thinking things."

"Let him."

The calm voice stopped Alec's rummaging. He gazed at Maurice reclining on the bed, his skin glowing from their hours of love. He looked serene, confident, and satisfied, and indeed he was. His manner had changed. As Alec no longer deferred to him, so Maurice no longer patronized; rather, he spoke frankly, one friend to another. This new equality was more than Alec could endure; he went back to poking around for his clothes.

"My goodness, if Fred seed you and me just now," he said, sounding prissy again.

"Well, he didn't."

"Well, he might have—" He knew he was making no sense. "What I mean is, tomorrow's Thursday, isn't it, Friday's the packing of the ship, Saturday the *Normannia* sails from Southampton, so it's goodbye to Old England."

"You mean that you and I shan't meet again after now."

Pierced by Maurice's sadness, Alec could not bring himself to face him, so he played cocky. "That's right. You've got it quite correct."

And if it wasn't still raining! Wet morning after yesterday's downpour, wet on the roofs and the museum, at home and on the greenwood. Maurice said, "This is just what I want to talk about. Why don't we arrange so as we do meet again?"

"How do you mean?"

"Why don't you stay on in England?"

Alec felt the floor drop away from under his feet. Terrified, he whizzed around and snarled, "Stay? Miss my boat, are you daft? Of all the bloody rubbish I ever heard. Ordering me about again, eh, you would."

He was struggling to escape to someplace familiar and safe, where Maurice was a toff who believed it his birthright to command such a menial as Alec and was therefore worthy of contempt. But Maurice would not follow him there, indeed could not, because for him such a place no longer existed: "It's a chance in a thousand we've met, we'll never have the chance again and you know it. Stay with me. We love each other."

Alec closed his eyes. *We love each other.* Not a confession, but rather a statement of fact. Maurice was speaking for both of them with an authority Alec had no wish to deny. He tried to escape once more, to argue from reason, or at least practicality, but it all sounded childish and false: "I dessay, but that's no excuse to act silly. Stay with you, and how and where?" He picked up the hideous blue suit. "What'd your ma say if she saw me, all rough and ugly the way I am?"

In fact he appeared especially graceful at the moment, the pale light silhouetting his taut figure and glorious hair. There was a natural elegance about Alec, a refinement in his features and the shape of his limbs, not the mere vestige of adolescence, but rather a quality that would be his all his life. His beauty took Maurice's breath now—like that of the carved image on the column from the temple at Ephesus they'd seen yesterday, Hermes guiding the soul of Eurydice to the underworld. But his beloved was infinitely more beautiful because he was alive with a bright, bright spirit. "She never will see you," he said. "I shan't live at my home."

"Where will you live?"

"With you."

"Oh, will you? No, thank you. My people wouldn't take to you one bit, and I don't blame them. And how'd you run your job, I'd like to know?"

"I shall chuck it."

"Your job in the city what gives you money and position? You can't chuck a job."

"You can when you mean to," said Maurice gently. "You

can do anything once you know what it is." Nothing surprised Maurice in this talk, not his own brashness nor Alec's resistance. But who could conjecture the outcome? "I shall get work with you."

"What work?"

"We'll find out."

"Find out and starve."

"No. There'll be enough money to keep us while we have a look round. I'm not a fool, nor are you. We won't be starving. I've thought that much, while I was awake in the night and you weren't."

There was a pause. Alec had already decided he must refuse, so he went on more politely: "Wouldn't work, Maurice. Ruin of us both, can't you see, you same as myself."

"I don't know. Might be. Mightn't. 'Class.' I don't know. I know what we do today. We clear out of here and get a decent breakfast and we go down to Penge or whatever you want and see that Fred of yours. You tell him you've changed your mind about emigrating and are taking a job with Mr. Hall instead. I'll come with you. I don't care. I'll see anyone, face anything. If they want to guess, let them. I'm fed up. Tell Fred to cancel your ticket, I'll pay for it, and that's our start of getting free. Then we'll do the next things. It's a risk, so's everything else, and we'll only live once."

His words electrified Alec. He wanted to respond by crushing their hearts together again. But he would not succumb. He laughed cynically and continued to dress. His manner, driven by fear and mistrust, resembled yesterday's. "Yours is the talk of someone who's never had to earn his living," he said. "You sort of trap me with 'I love you' or whatever it is and then offer to spoil my career. Do you realize I've a definite job awaiting me in the Argentine? Same as you've got here.

Pity the *Normannia*'s leaving Saturday. Still, facts is facts, isn't it, all my kit bought as well as my ticket and Fred and wife expecting me."

Maurice saw through the brassiness to the misery behind it. But what did it matter? No amount of their misery would prevent the *Normannia* from sailing. Alec buttoned the jacket of his damned scratchy suit. He looked at his sun-browned hands. They'd grow pale, he imagined, with office work abroad. "Well, I'm off," he said, and then added, flippantly, to seal the barrier between them, "Pity we ever met, really, if you come to think of it."

"That's all right too," said Maurice, looking away from him as he unbolted the door.

"You paid for this room in advance, didn't you, so they won't stop me downstairs? I don't want no unpleasantness to finish with."

"That's all right too," said Maurice again, still looking away.

In the corridor, after he'd closed the door behind him, Alec felt Maurice hoping for his return. He hurried downstairs and told the front desk that he was leaving now and the gentleman in #9 would be checking out shortly. Back out on the street, in the rain, he looked up at their window. Then his eyes began to smart, and he knew from experience what was coming. Head down, he walked as fast as he could back to St. Pancras.

10

On this particular Wednesday the Scudders opened their home to visitors; Aderyn laid her sideboard with shortbread and jams and two kinds of cordials; Elwood set out whiskey and stout. Neighbors were calling to say goodbye to the boys and Fred's bride, Jane Atkins. Aderyn explained to her guests that her younger son, expected last night, had postponed his arrival till morning because he was needed at Penge. "Conscientious to a fault," she bragged, with no doubt he'd be joining them shortly. But when Alec at last did appear, he was hardly looking his best: bedraggled, wet, and (granted his beard was sparse) in need of a shave. She feared he was ill. Fred frowned at his little brother's mud-streaked trousers and unbarbered hair. Elwood took his youngest aside to ask if he'd been drinking. When Alec protested he'd had not a drop, his father suggested that perhaps a tot of rye might then be in order. Alec disappeared into his old bedroom to tidy himself. He swallowed the whiskey and made up his mind to show the villagers he could not be happier about the limitless horizons of his new life overseas.

The clouds were breaking just as the Blunts arrived—Ivanhoe, Mabel, and Phyllis, aged six months, arrayed in a satin blanket in her mother's arms. The baby's presence turned the cottage into an aviary of feminine chatter. The men drifted outdoors. Van and Alec strolled off together. Van slipped his arm around Alec's waist and squeezed slyly. "You don't seem quite yourself," he said. "Homesick before you've set sail?"

"Nothin' like that."

"What's eatin' ya, then?"

Alec sighed.

"Oh no, no—not love! Now, that's too bad. Tell your old pal. Some handsome boy breakin' your heart? We're cads, ain't we all, the entire masculine half of the human race."

"No, Van, it's no boy . . ."

"A girl! That makes things simpler. They don't jail you for kissin' a girl. She can join you abroad. And if she's draggin' her feet, there's others who'd jump at the chance, mark my word. You're too clever by far, and good-lookin', ever to fret about findin' a wife."

Alec could not go on with the banter; he was worn out from the battle within. He wanted to confide, to unburden, to rest in his friend's strength. "Please—this goes no farther?"

Van raised his right hand.

"It's a man, not a girl."

"Oh . . . ," he said, more seriously. "Older, then?"

"Like you—just turned twenty-four."

"That old, eh?"

"A gentleman."

"Ah . . . and have you—?"

"Yes."

"Like we did?"

"It's different . . ."

"I see: 'love.'"

" . . ."

"But you're leavin' Saturday."

"That's right."

"If he's a man of means, he can visit you overseas. That would show his good faith."

They stopped in the lane. Clouds were threatening again.

"He's asked me to stay here with him."

Van faced Alec, took firm hold of both his arms, and said sternly, "Don't you be a great goat-fuckin' fool."

"No, no—I told him no . . ."

"Good." He relaxed his grip. "Because it's all fakery, love this and love that. When lads have eyes for each other there's nothin' sweeter than sharin', and don't we know how sweet, we two? But *love*? It's a lie of the upper classes, a fancy for them with too much time on their hands, tartin' up for their own delectation what for most of us couldn't be plainer. It's family holds folks together, property, land, not 'love.' Stay with him? What, here? As a servant? When so much could be yours overseas? If he truly cared for you, he'd never ask such a thing. Alec! What happens when he tires of you, or you of him?"

"Yeah, you're right . . ."

"Course I am. You're all topsy-turvy now—about this big trip, leavin' behind what you've always known. But you're such a fine fellow—who knows better than I how very fine? Once out at sea, you do as I say: take a sailor-boy in your arms for the nonce; before you touch shore, I promise, you'll have forgotten this gentleman's name."

The clouds were sputtering rain yet again. They hurried back toward the cottage. Van kept his arm around Alec's shoulder, as if to shelter his young friend from the weather, or perhaps to press home his advice. Van's physique had grown thicker, more substantial, since he'd assumed the run of the farm, and Alec took comfort in his warm strength. This was a man to be trusted, a kind man, of his own people, who understood the realities of his life as Maurice could not. Though three years of living away from the village had exposed Alec to manners and objects and ideas that made Osmington seem backward, still this was rightly his home.

But now he must escape. To avoid getting caught in his lies, he told one more, that Mr. Ayers was still out of sorts; he also mixed in some truth, that his trunk was at Penge and he needed to move it thence to Southampton to stow on the ship. He promised to return no later than noon on Friday; he would spend his last night in England at his parents' home.

Alone with his thoughts on the little train back to Wiltshire, he marveled at how much life had been crammed into twenty-four hours! Only yesterday he'd been riding to London—a blackmailer about to confront his victim. Could he have been so callow, so stupid? It was all different now, and so was he. He'd faced Maurice and acknowledged his wrongdoing. They'd shaken hands. It would have been easier if they'd parted with that handshake, but he could only blame himself for what had followed.

He tried not to dwell on the happiness of their night in London, their second night together, richer than the first, of deeper emotion, more intimate touch, but his lover's words, tender and brave, kept calling him back: *I'll see anyone, face anything. If they want to guess, let them . . . We love each other . . .* He whispered aloud, "Maurice." Then he banished the thought.

For all his complaining about Penge, he was glad to return there at last. By nature Alec was solitary. He craved love, of course, and companionship, but when it came to work or to thinking, he did best on his own. At Penge he'd always had plenty of time by himself. In the gamekeeper's cottage, Mrs. Ayers offered to sponge and press his new suit (now woefully crushed) and caught him up on things. In his absence, her husband had spent the morning with Alec's designated replacement, acquainting the new boy with the routine and supervising him as he undertook chores. She found the youngster quite pleasant. She trusted he would do well.

The news saddened Alec. When he was making his afternoon rounds, he wished he might find something amiss, but all was as it should be. So the park would thrive without him, no returning to the safe old ways.

Next day was leave-taking. He used his morning call at the door of the manor to pay his respects to the Durhams. The young missus conveyed the squire's best wishes—he was busy with campaign speeches. She also managed to prompt her mother-in-law discreetly with Alec's name. At the servants' midday meal, the cook brought out his favorite Blue Vinney and knobs. Later, the two Mildreds strolled with him along the road toward the station. Apparently Communion class was reforming them: instead of kisses, they gave him their hands to shake and promised to pray for his well-being. After, when nearly everything was locked in his trunk, he packed what was left—spare shirt and drawers, razor, pipe, his anthology of poets, and a cake of Morgan's sandalwood soap—into a satchel to carry by hand. He visited the kennels to pet the beagles farewell, hug the spaniels, and rub the dachshund's belly. In the hatchery, he let the young birds nibble a finger. He gazed one more time at the woods and the pond and his boathouse.

Early Friday morning, Mr. Ayers took him and his trunk to the train stop. At Southampton he met up with Fred in his borrowed lorry. The two brothers together brought Fred's household goods and furniture, plus all the trunks, to the wharf to be loaded onto the *Normannia*. Then back to Osmington. Soon after supper with the parents, Fred left to stay the night with Jane's family; the three other Scudders then retired to their beds.

Next morning when Alec was buttoning his trousers, he found in his left pocket the key to the boathouse. He'd meant to leave it at Penge yesterday when he'd locked up for the last time. What to do? He could send it by post to Mr. Ayers or entrust it to his father to deliver later, but his was the only copy, and he'd always felt protective of it, since it granted access to his own private realm. The ship would not sail until nearly sunset: he had the whole day free. If he told his parents he wanted to take the key back himself, he knew they'd insist that he let them do so tomorrow, which was sensible. But Alec was in no state to be sensible. So at breakfast he lied, saying he'd forgotten something essential at Penge, a book with one of his traveling papers tucked in it. He said he knew just where he'd left it and could scoot back and forth by himself in no time. His parents chided him but were persuaded to go ahead to Southampton as planned with Fred and Jane and her folks. Alec would join them directly from Penge; he assured them he'd arrive at the port before they did. When he picked up his satchel on his way out the door, they offered to carry it to the ship with them instead. "Ma and dad luggin' my bag for me? What kind of son would I be?"

The little train did its duty. At Penge he walked from the station through quiet fields. He entered the estate at its lower end, through a gap in the hedge. Squirrels scuttled above in the trees. He hoped to meet no one who might ask why he was there.

The morning was gray, but quick-moving clouds signaled change. The sun had broken through by the time he reached the pond and the water reflected its splendor. In these last days, the park seemed more silent to him than it had before his visit to London. Even the songbirds, their mating season long past, were quiet. Light pierced the gaping shingles of the boathouse, which stood dark against the water and derelict, like all the buildings of Penge. Yet here was where love (he could call it so now, freely) had taught him to suffer. The trysting place, he'd once hoped, whose only key he, for no particular reason, always carried. He would return that key now. *We'll meet in your boathouse yet . . .*

He opened the wide double doors. Light scattered the shadows inside. There in his corner were cushions from the rowboat, as he'd placed them just so, waiting long nights for Maurice. The air was warm, damp, steaming in the sun. Silence and solitude had quieted his mind. He became aware that his skin felt strangely delightful, but he could not name the cause of the sensation. He hugged himself and closed his eyes.

He opened them on what he would remember all his life as a vision: there, in the water, perched on a floating branch, a bird hardly bigger than a sparrow, yet brighter than the sunny ripples, so radiant that she seemed at once to absorb and shed light—the very center of creation. Magical color beamed from her wings, her head and beak of brilliant blue spangled with silver, throat white, breast a luminous orange. A kingfisher. He had only ever seen her kind on the wing, as a swoop, a flash of iridescence, an afterglow; now she was close and still. He held his breath lest she fly off. She did fly, but then alit even closer to him, on the railing of the little dock, a few feet away. She eyed him, opened her beak, and called—and, in a blink, flew off over the pond.

Alec ran down the dock after her, pulling off his clothes and jumping into the water, as if to follow. He slipped below the surface and for the first time ever opened his eyes underwater. He'd always feared the water would hurt his eyes, but it didn't, not at all. It was wonderful, the wavering light—and the sound, what was it? His own heart and lungs? He burbled and watched the bubbles rise. Then he saw he was not alone. The kingfisher had returned, also underwater now, almost next to him: she'd caught a minnow. In an unbroken arc she swam up, broke the surface, and took flight toward her nest as he followed her up into the light. Just as his head emerged from the pond, rain fell again, suddenly, in torrents. He stumbled and slipped onto the boathouse's deck, stood up, opened his arms to the sky, and let it all wash over him.

After drying and dressing, he walked to the village on those secret bypaths he knew through the woods. From there he sent two wires. Then back to the boathouse, where no one would find him because no one ever came. All afternoon he did nothing but watch the water, watch the sun and clouds come and go. The hours passed. He thought about what might be happening at the wharf in Southampton. The ship's loading, his family's arrival, their waiting, Fred's ranting about his lateness, Jane's fretting, his father's concern, his mother's unspoken relief that her youngest was not on board the ship that would have carried him away from her, as death had taken three of her other children. What would he tell the folks? Little enough. *Of course he finally couldn't bring himself to leave his homeland*, they'd say to the neighbors, or, *At the last minute, a certain Mr. Hall offered a better position than any he'd find overseas.*

But there might be no Mr. Hall. To date, their love had been a contest. Now it stood at a draw and might prove a stalemate. Each had failed the other, Maurice abandoning Alec at Penge without a word, Alec threatening blackmail in London. *You've had your fun and you've got to pay up.* Christ, had he truly said that? Like the battle-ax "dame" in a Christmas panto! Yet Maurice had not laughed at him (as he deserved), had shown no disgust, not even impatience. Was that what it meant to be a gentleman? No, that's what it meant to be Maurice. And still, still, even after Maurice had opened his heart and confessed his fear, Alec had given in to his own cowardice and left with the cruelest goodbye: *Pity we ever met, really* . . .

Why should Maurice come now? Why should this excellent man, who endured his childishness and forgave his treachery, why should he not be done with such a troublesome mistake as Alec had shown himself to be?

He gave up asking himself questions he couldn't answer. Of this much he was sure: no matter by what name he might call it, a real power had seized him when he'd locked eyes with Maurice two weeks ago on the road from the station. It was why he'd kept watch in the rain at the Russet Room window, why he'd risked climbing the ladder, why he'd disgraced himself by suggesting blackmail. It was why he'd said, *Stop with me*, when they were about to part in London, why his heart ached in Maurice's absence and thrilled at his sight. He knew this as well: the saddest thought he could think was not to see Maurice again. To do so by his own choosing was beyond his will or his strength, therefore he was giving the choice to his lover. Not as a hero, but as a friend, Maurice had stood up to his bluster and discerned the fear behind it, and behind that, something else. He had seen Alec's suffering, and therefore his love, and loved him in return. And *that* was the strange delight he felt in his skin today, the knowledge of being loved.

But now would love fail them as they had failed each other? He marked the time the *Normannia* would be pulling out to sea. Bells would clang, whistles shriek, crowds bustle. Here at the pond all was silence. The afternoon had broken into glory. White clouds glided above the water and the woods. Already sunset was beginning to transfigure the sky with the kingfisher's colors, orange and silver and blue.

But Alec's spirits sank while the radiance soared on high, because Maurice did not come. Alec couldn't blame him. *Wouldn't work . . . Ruin of us both, can't you see, you same as myself . . .* His friend was taking him at his word, as an equal.

The sudden heartbreak revealed to him how entirely exhausted he was, ravaged by every sort of emotion. For many days now he'd lived with no relief from the intensity: sorrow, rage, thrill, fear. He'd been rushing around southern England: Wiltshire, London, Dorset, Southampton. What to do now? He ought to go to the village for something to eat. Instead he flopped facedown on the old cushions and slept.

In the last dying of the day, he opened his eyes. His lover was kneeling beside him. Half-asleep, he fondled Maurice's arm between his hands before he spoke. "So you got the wire," he said.

"What wire?"

"The wire I sent off this morning to your house, telling you . . ." He yawned. "Excuse me, I'm a bit tired, one thing and another . . . telling you to come here without fail." And since Maurice did not speak, indeed could not, he added, "And now we shan't be parted no more, and that's finished."

III

IDYLL

11

Without another word, they made love—Maurice in tears, Alec bursting with thankfulness, their ardor stoked by their ordeal. Afterward they murmured and sniffled and laughed. Alec's midday wire had never reached Maurice at home; he'd spent the morning in his office, then gone to Southampton to see Alec's face once more before he sailed. He confessed he'd had no hope of speaking to Alec, much less touching him, but only wanted to see him. "I love you. I couldn't help myself."

"How rotten I acted toward you in London!" Alec said.

"It's no matter now. When I saw you weren't on the ship, I'd have done anything for you. I'd have jumped over the moon."

Only instinct had led him to the boathouse. He'd called out to Alec twice from the pond. When there was no answer, he'd begun to despair and nearly turned back, but there, inside, he had found his beloved asleep in the last light of day. Suddenly he stood up and started to dress. "We've got to go."

"Wha—? Right now?"

"This place belongs to Clive Durham."

"But he don't know we're here."

"But I do."

"Well, of course you do—"

"Please, Alec, let's have no more to do with him or his house. Come on, get dressed."

Alec hugged a cushion. "Not just yet. Come back over here."

Maurice grinned. "Oh, we'll have plenty more—tonight, a whole lifetime. We'll go to the inn, get supper—I'm so hungry! Aren't you hungry? Then tomorrow—I don't know—we'll figure it out. I'll be back in twenty minutes."

Alec sat up abruptly. "Wait—where are you going?"

"To tell Clive goodbye."

His unexpected visit perplexed Clive, as did Maurice's re-fusing, without saying why, to enter the house. They talked outside among the shrubs, where shadows cast by the moon-light hid Maurice's face. When he announced that he loved the gamekeeper, Clive at first thought he meant old Ayers's wife; a ridiculous mistake, really, but that's how far he had left behind not only his love for Maurice, but any thoughts at all of love between men. Then the squire tried to talk sense to him, telling him that Scudder had that very day emigrated. Maurice said no, that Scudder had changed his mind and stayed in England. Then Maurice said something about hav-ing "shared" with Alec, as he'd called the servant.

"Shared what?"

"All I have," Maurice said. "Which includes my body."

It was nonsense; it was disgusting. Clive asked Maurice to meet him for dinner in town the following week, where they might work through this madness reasonably. But no one an-swered him. He extended his hand to shake. No one took it. He was speaking to no one. He could never say exactly when, but Maurice had disappeared into the night.

By the time Alec collected himself, dressed, and closed up the boathouse, Maurice had returned. They'd swapped places emotionally, Maurice now beaming, Alec clinging and sobbing.

They left the key in the lock. The blue moon of August lit their way through the woods to the village. Since it was Saturday night, the inn was still serving supper, which they ate as heartily as oarsmen after a race. They registered under their own names.

"We don't mind sharing a room," Maurice said to the innkeeper.

She hesitated slightly as she wrote in the ledger. "Oh." She looked up at Maurice. "Don't I know you from Penge, sir," she said, "the cricket match?"

"That's right," Alec answered, "we played for the park—together."

"He captained," Maurice added. "Our best bat."

Upstairs, they made love and dozed. On opening a drowsy eye, Alec was met with a sight that provoked a conflict of lust and tenderness: his sleeping lover's rump, smooth and shapely in the moonlight, dimpled, pale, and muscular. It looked luscious. He succumbed to temptation and gave it a bite—a sweet little bite for sure, but enough to cause Maurice to yelp. A pillow fight ensued, which elicited pounding on the wall from the next room and a cry: "That's enough in there!"

They covered their mouths to keep from laughing out loud. Alec wagged a forefinger at Maurice and whispered, "Bad doggy."

Maurice hung his head. He giggled: "Woof." He lifted Alec back onto the bed, where they enjoyed each other again, quietly now, and then slept for nine hours in the deepest contentment, hearts at rest in each other at last.

Thus began their life together as outlaws.

12

Under the law they were criminals; outside it, merely young lovers. For them to live by the law would mean—what, separation? Marriage to others? Furtive meetings? No, the law was unjust. To subject themselves to it would make them complicit with its tyranny. So they would live outside it. But how?

Alec's possessions, even his clothes, were on their way to Argentina: a reminder to Fred, if he needed reminding, of his little brother's fecklessness. As for his parents, they must surely be baffled, angry as well, but at least not in a panic. His second wire yesterday had been sent to their home; they would have read it when they returned from Southampton: DON'T YOU WORRY I'M FINE. DECIDED TO STAY. EXPLAIN TO-MORROW.

Tomorrow was now today, Sunday, so Maurice was reprieved from reporting to his office. He phoned his mother and told her that he'd been unexpectedly called out of town on business late yesterday afternoon and stayed the night; he apologized for having missed supper; he'd come home later. The day's first task would be to make peace with the Scudders, whom Maurice had met yesterday at the ship. That meeting complicated matters because if, as the lovers contrived, Alec was staying in England to work for him, why would Maurice have gone to Southampton to see him off?

Such questions they discussed on the train, where they decided they would neither lie outright nor say any more than was necessary. Alec would speak with his parents first; Maurice would wait outside the cottage till the groundwork was laid. This scheme was promptly dashed when they met the Scudders in the lane on their way home from the late morning service at St. Osmund's.

"My Licky!" Aderyn cried out on seeing them, and rushed to embrace her son. Alec was ready for her tears, but Maurice was moved by them, because tears had been forbidden in his house. He'd shed more in his love for Alec than since his earliest childhood. Over tea in her parlor, Mrs. Scudder apprised them of the villagers' shock when she told them after church of Alec's disappearance. "And none more upset than young Vanny Blunt," she said. "By nature he's most placid, yet he smote his palm with his fist and muttered such language under his breath as I'd rather not understood."

Maurice spoke up, "Well, you see, Mrs. Scudder, Mr. Scudder"—nodding respectfully to each—"it did come about so very quickly, this change of heart. Alec had turned down my offer. He'd said he intended to go through with his plans to emigrate."

"That's right," Alec said. "I told Mr. Hall thanks kindly, but our family's respectable tradespeople and I'd my fill of servitude, and a job waitin' abroad for me same as he's got in London."

"Not that I'd, um, I mean, I hope I'd made it clear I wasn't seeking to hire a servant—"

"I'd not even have listened, that been the case."

Elwood said, "What's this work you've proposed for him, sir?"

"Yes, sorry—got ahead of myself, didn't I? I'm planning to buy forest land."

"Indeed!" said Aderyn. "How very lovely . . ."

Maurice rewarded her sentiment with his most ravishing smile, at which she blushed.

"Ah, and whereabouts have you in mind?" the father asked.

"Bit north—not too far. Nottingham, I hope, depending on what's available."

"Why, that's just round the corner, these days," the mother said, and then to her son, "You can come home for dinner on Sundays."

"Ma, the man's not yet purchased a sapling, and you're already reelin' me in for meals?"

Maurice went on, "I thought we'd raise game . . . to supply hotels and restaurants," improvising details to develop this plan for himself as well as his audience, "and perhaps harvest a little timber as well. New buildings are going up on every corner in London, so the market's quite good for construction materials."

"Interesting," Elwood said.

"Da, Mr. Hall wants me to manage the woodland's game," Alec joined in.

The parents' eyes widened: "Manage . . . ," they said together.

"Exactly," Maurice went on. "When we met at Penge, Alec and I, when I was visiting there, he guided us guests shooting. His work was first-rate, I can tell you. Knowledgeable, courteous—he made a very favorable impression—"

"As he always does, Mr. Hall," said Aderyn, growing more pleased with this stranger at his every word.

"I thought, 'That's my man.' Granted, he's young, but still, he's got—what is it now, three years' experience?"

"Goin' on four," Alec said.

"He can grow with the business. So I was delighted when

I learned last evening that he'd changed his mind and was accepting my offer."

"I'd only just wired him when I wired you," Alec explained.

Now Maurice felt obliged to explain, "Yesterday afternoon, since I'd not yet seen his message, I came to the ship to assure him I bore no hard feelings—about his choice, the earlier one I mean, turning me down—and to wish him good luck abroad."

"Like a true gentleman," said Aderyn, bestowing her supreme compliment.

"Tell me, son," Elwood said, "what caused you to change your mind out of the blue?"

"What does it matter?" the mother said. "He's here with us."

"Please let Alec speak for himself, my dear."

"Well, Da, it was thinkin' about it, when I had time to myself, that changed my mind . . ." Knowing his plausibility was at stake, Alec chose words that would appeal to his father. "How often's a man offered such an opportunity, in his own backyard, so to speak? To build on a skill he's already learned, the way you advised me . . ."

His father nodded.

"The Argentine will always be there. If it don't work out with this enterprise here, then I might go abroad next year, as I'm sure Mr. Hall would understand . . ."

Maurice nodded.

". . . but to turn down this chance without even tryin', it seemed foolish to me. You can see for yourself the gentleman's sincere in his intentions, willin' to come talk with my family today. Besides, he's offerin' better wages than they're payin' clerks overseas."

With word of more money, the senior's eyes brightened.

"Well, it does my heart good to hear you finally talkin' some sense, for I had my doubts you possessed any at all, watchin' that ship sail off yesterday. But now what about Freddy? Did you give your brother no thought? He was furious, rightly so."

"Fred's always furious," Aderyn said.

"Sir, if I might," Maurice interceded. "That's understandable, very—young Mr. Scudder's annoyance, I mean. I've offered to advance Alec the money to repay his brother the price of his passage. We can do that much at least."

"Most considerate of you, sir," said the mother; then to her husband, "It's clear Mr. Hall holds our Alexander in high regard, as he deserves. I couldn't be happier. At last I can say how terribly sad I was feeling—"

"Now, Aderyn—"

"I'm allowed to say to my son—since he's chosen to stay of his own free will—that leaving for halfway around the world was no source of joy to his mother. Losing them both at once! I was heartsick. We're getting no younger, Elwood. Whenever would we see them? Oh for heaven's sake, shoot me at sunrise if I'm such a traitor."

So far, the conversation was covering ground Alec and Maurice had prepared together. Then Aderyn said, "And won't it be good to have one of the boys in the cottage again?"

"What's that, Ma—?"

"Where else would you stay but here in your home till things are settled in Nottingham? You said yourself the land's not yet been procured."

The lovers exchanged an uneasy glance.

"Have I said something wrong?"

"Not at all, Mrs. Scudder, no, of course not . . . Only . . . I've asked Alec to start right away—"

"Tomorrow," Alec said.

"So soon?"

"Yes, he's agreed to stay in town—"

"What, in London! All by himself?"

"Ma . . . ," Alec protested.

"Near our office," Maurice said, "while we get things off the ground—at my expense, of course. Believe me, I'll be keeping him busy. Likely we'll be working some nights and he may need to travel with me. I hope to teach him a bit about business in advance of starting up. But when it comes to the forest, he'll be the teacher."

"I see . . . ," she said with little conviction.

Side by side again on the train, the lovers pressed their thighs together. Maurice let out a long breath of relief and rested his head on the back of the seat. "Got any gin in that satchel of yours?"

Alec likewise leaned his head back and faced Maurice. When they locked eyes in public this way, they found the intimacy especially sweet—secret, transgressive. "She was flirtin' with you," Alec said, "shamelessly, right there in front of her husband, eyelashes aflutter and all."

"Of course she was. Didn't I rescue her darlin' from them dragons that dwell over the sea? I enjoyed the attention. Mrs. Scudder's quite pretty—I can see it runs in the family."

"Hmmph."

"She loves you," Maurice said with sudden tenderness, "they both do, as I do. You don't know how much you're loved." Then he leaned closer to whisper: "Licky . . ."

They checked back into the hotel in Bloomsbury where they'd stayed last Tuesday. Now for the day's second order of business: Maurice's mother. "I'm going to need a few hours," he said to Alec.

"Is that all? I figured you'd stay the night."

"Why? There's no place I want to sleep tonight, or any night, except in your arms. I'll ask no one's permission, only yours. Nothing keeps us apart anymore, not the Church or the law, much less your family or mine."

Love had breathed clarity into Maurice along with mettle, qualities Alec admired. This confidence was no magic of birth, he discerned, but rather acquired by education, going to school with those who would become society's leaders. Alec decided he must acquire some himself. "Ought I come with you? I could wait somewhere."

"Thanks, but I'll do better by myself. It's my own private snake pit, you've no idea. Mother's friends with Mrs. Durham, the elder . . ."

"Wha—! Your mum and Clive's?"

"That's right. And my sisters know his."

"Who, Pippa? That's married to damned Archie London?"

"'Fraid so."

"Well, for fuck's sake . . ."

While Maurice set off for the suburbs, Alec explored the blocks around the hotel. The scene was disappointingly quiet. Sunday afternoon, last weekend of August, everyone gone to the country or seashore: shops closed, of course, pubs closed or restricted in hours. The lovers had agreed that Maurice would have tea and supper with his family, so Alec should find something to eat on his own. He decided to do so soon, before places shut for the night. On the corner of Morwell Street he passed a pub whose name he recognized, one Simcox had mentioned: OPEN TILL 19:00.

Inside was smoky and friendly enough, even respectable: when the glass doors (discreetly frosted) of the snug-room swung open, he could see ladies within, sipping from little steins. He asked for the ploughman's lunch, along with a pint of porter. A few sips put him in a reflective mood. This upheaval of his plans, of his life . . . could it be possible, in less than two weeks? Each day some drastic about-face. And now? The *Normannia* was already hundreds of miles at sea, breasting the waves of the mid-Atlantic, guided by sextant and stars. Yet instead of boldly confronting the winds of his fate, he sat munching pickles and cheese in a pub in Bloomsbury. And even more worthy of marvel was the scene at his parents' cottage this morning, no less than a capsizing of England's ironclad social order. Mr. Maurice Christopher Hall II, drinking tea not from china but from thick earthenware, fired by the potter of Osmington, at a table covered with calico, in sight of that warped and rickety spinet, once Grandmother's treasured emblem of respectability in Cardiff; Maurice, with his flawless manners and looks and speech, striving to win the approval of the village butcher and his wife. *You don't know how much you're loved* . . . He guessed not, not if Maurice was willing to squirm for him. He smiled at the thought, shaking his head in disbelief. "Maurice," he said to himself, but aloud.

"What's that?" said a man with his back to Alec, who was chatting with others, among them a sportive fellow in leather trousers and a helmet with the goggles pushed back. As the man turned to face him, two pairs of eyes widened. It was Simcox, who opened his mouth in amazement: "Scudder—?"

Alec swallowed his mouthful of porter. "Hullo. What brings you to town?"

"Me? You were the one going off to the Pampas for a cowboy."

"Yeah, well, changed my mind—last minute, it came about."

"So we heard."

"How's that?"

"This morning, the vicar."

"Wha, Borenius—?"

"He was asking round after the service. He'd gone to South-ampton yesterday, he told us, to see you off and give you a letter about getting confirmed overseas. He met your family there at the ship. They'd no idea where you might be, only that you'd gone on an errand that morning. He said your poor mam was quite rattled. He was inquiring if we servants knew anything."

Alec gulped more porter. "They're fine now, my folks— happy about me stayin', in fact." Simcox was enjoying having caught him off guard. "You see, I got an offer, last-minute, much to my liking."

"That so?"

"A new enterprise, involves game-keepin', with a bit of for-estry; pays better than I'd make overseas. Offices right here in town." Alec, eager to change the topic, nodded toward Mr. Sportive. "Friend of yours?"

"Known him for years."

"And that's his Alldays by the lamppost out front?"

"He was racing this morning."

"Nice bike."

"Ought to be, what he paid for it, and don't start him talking—he's fanatical about the damn thing."

So of course Alec started the fellow talking. They stepped outside to admire his motorcycle, and thus Alec managed to slip away without disclosing more of his business to Simcox.

Later, under the covers, the lovers exchanged accounts. Maurice's leave-taking had proved easier than anticipated. It seemed he'd grown less important in his household since his grandfather's death, thanks to the sheltering wings of the old man's money. Aside from bequests, Mr. Grace had divided his considerable capital (and its future income) between Mau-rice's Aunt Ida, the unmarried daughter who had cared for him, and his favorite grandchild, Maurice's youngest sister, Ada. Auntie had closed Grandfather's house to move in with her widowed sister, so Mrs. Hall now had a companion and confidante and relied less on her son. As for Ada, who was quite lovely, her inheritance had made her an even more attractive catch. She was engaged to Maurice's schoolmate William Chapman.

Ada, along with the older and much cleverer Kitty, had recently begun to betray a long-standing resentment of their big brother's quasi-paternal authority. Ada had yet to forgive him—she never would—for making her believe that her girlish attraction to Clive Durham had been one-sided, indeed off-putting, and that she had undermined the squire's friendship with Maurice. (In fact, Clive—along with his mother, after she learned of the girl's wealth—had encouraged her.) As for Kitty, she still carried a grudge for Maurice's refusal, a couple of years ago, of funds for tuition at the nearby school of domestic economy—no matter that he'd later reversed his decision and paid. More immediately, though, since Auntie had moved in (and since neither would consider the attic), the sisters were sharing a bedroom. With Maurice out of the house, they would appropriate his room, and each could reclaim her privacy. Kitty offered to pack his things.

"Mother protested politely," Maurice said, "and Auntie needed assurance that she could still call on me to speak with the servants . . ."

"Do let me take care of that for dear Auntie," said Alec.

"By all means. But the girls . . . they didn't even pretend to hide their delight at my leaving."

They laughed at Alec's story of meeting Simcox at the pub: "Picture him flyin' round London on the back of his fancyboy's motorbike—'Careful, dearest! Mah boutonniere!'" He also acknowledged uneasily that their hotel, like the pub, was someplace he'd heard the valet name at Penge.

Maurice winced: "Oh . . . wish you'd said. We might have found another."

"Yeah, sorry, stupid of me—never thought. That night—I only wanted to be with you, like we are now."

"Can't blame you. Me too. No matter, we'll go someplace else tomorrow. But you didn't mention my name to Simcox, did you?"

"Think I'm daft? Not a word more than needed to Nell Nosy. Blatherin' on about the vicar—he knew it would piss me off. Borenius, skulkin' after me, even down at the ship. Did you see him there yesterday?"

"Oh—didn't I say?"

"Would I be askin' now, bucko?"

"Well, yes, I saw him, even talked to him."

"Why didn't you tell me?"

"I don't know—with your family there, and my own insanity, I guess I didn't think him important at all, not to us, just more of a nuisance."

"Nuisance for certain."

"Oh, he's beyond the Dark Ages, you don't know, going on about how sex ought to be *illegal*—of course he didn't say sex, he said 'fornication.' Does anybody use that word anymore? Illegal! Is that the limit? Like the Inquisition! So the Church can reconquer England. He actually said that."

By now their limbs were entwined in that perfect way of theirs, hearts beating against each other. "Illegal, huh?" Alec murmured against his lover's moist neck; Maurice moaned with pleasure.

"For half a second I thought he was on to us."

"Borenius?" Alec pulled away a bit. "No."

"They're weird, those priests, I swear, like witches. But then"—Maurice drew Alec back closer—"then he confided in me he believes you 'Guilty of Sensuality—with Women.'"

"Remind me to thank him." Now serious kissing commenced. "Wait—Maurice?"

"Mmm?"

Alec pulled away again. "Why would he say that to you? About me? Don't they take an oath never to talk? Parsons? About the sins of their flock and such?"

"You mean the seal of confession?"

"That's it." Alec was peeved.

Maurice tried conciliation: "He said he was telling me because of my 'charitable interest' in you—since I'd come to see you off."

"Charity, indeed." Alec disentwined his arms. "Conspiracy of the rulin' classes against the workingman. That was wrong of him, sayin' such things about me to anybody."

"He seemed sincerely concerned."

"You sayin' he was right?"

"No; and I'm not saying I like him. I only believe he meant no harm." Considering the matter now settled, Maurice nose-dived for his lover's smooth navel. Alec fished him back up.

"Wha—?" Maurice said.

". . ."

"Oh all right. Reverend Sherlock somehow put it together that you'd spent last Tuesday night neither at Penge nor with your parents and deduced, God knows how, that you were in London, with A Woman . . ."

"He *said* that?" Alec was now in a full-blown snit. "And how did he suppose that might be any business of yours?"

"What's the harm? He already knew about you and those girls—you told me as much in your letter."

"That was betwixt him and me, not him and you."

"Well . . ."

"Well?"

"Well . . . ," Maurice said. "Maybe I'd nudged him in that direction a bit—without meaning to, of course—before, at Penge, when I mentioned I'd seen you with the Mildreds . . ."

Alec sat up abruptly. "That was *you*? That tattled on us to the vicar?"

"Alec—"

"*You*? My own True Love that I stood hours watchin' for, in the rain, like a lonesome puppy? Slanderin' me behind my back?"

"It wasn't slander, it was fact—"

In reply, Alec kicked him.

"Ouch!" They tussled. Maurice prevailed; he mounted Alec and pinned his arms to the bed: "That was before! I didn't know what I was doing. I didn't even know I was jealous. You'd made me so crazy in love with you, like a madman, really—"

Delighted by these protestations, Alec nonetheless made a show of meaning to get out of bed; Maurice, sensing his lover's delight, held him fast and continued whispering urgent promises never to offend again, all the while pressing his lips to that spot near Alec's ear that made him writhe. "When you followed the car that morning at Penge and I saw you there in the rain, I could have knelt in the mud at your feet, I could have cut out my heart and begged you, *Here, take it. It's already yours, it's no good to me without you*—"

With this speech (whose gallantry astounded the speaker no less than the hearer), Eros triumphed. Overwhelmed by the twin riptides of youth and ardor, the lovers ravished each other, panting and gasping like drowning men who would drag their rescuer with them under the waves. Thus the outlaws abandoned themselves yet again to their unspeakable crimes. And night smiled at the end of the first day of their new life together.

Next morning, on their way to find breakfast, they passed Simcox and friend, who'd also spent the night in the hotel, at the front desk, checking out. "Morning, Simcox," Maurice said, without breaking his stride toward the revolving door.

"Good morning, Mr. Hall," the astonished valet called after him.

Alec halted. "Mornin', Simcox."

"Morning, Scudder . . ."

"Good mornin'," said Alec to Sportive, then hustled off after Maurice.

13

In their hearts, Alec and Maurice had braced themselves to battle the world for the sake of their love. For the time being, however, they were busy enough with smaller skirmishes.

They needed a place to live. Maurice found furnished rooms in an ugly building with new plumbing on Bernard Street, not far from the British Museum. (They'd grown sentimentally attached to the neighborhood, which had the added advantage of being remote from the offices of Hill & Hall.) He told the landlord that Alec, a relation from the country, would be staying with him until they could make other arrangements.

And except for what Alec was wearing (plus a spare shirt and drawers), he had no clothes. Maurice addressed that problem by returning from his family's house with two suitcases and more on the way. The young men were about the same height; although Alec's frame was a bit smaller, the trousers and coats fit him passably. They made a game out of his trying things on, with Maurice as tailor standing close behind, calling him *sir*, reaching around to button the coat or adjust the trousers. (This skit always ended in sex.) They would share Maurice's clothes till Alec got more of his own. This made them feel even closer, as if they were daring the world to discover the clue to their crime in plain sight.

Alec needed work. His village upbringing condemned idleness; besides, he disliked accepting spending money from Maurice. Their big plan—i.e., to buy forestland and go off and be woodsmen together—was proving as elusive as any Happily Ever After. *Nottingham?* Sherwood Forest, they learned, was maintained nowadays mostly for tourists. It would take time to find any woods for sale in modern England, as it would take time for Maurice to extricate himself from the investment business his father had built. So on weekdays when Maurice was at the office, Alec hiked the city streets, always with an eye to help-wanted notices. One day on turning a corner in Knightsbridge, he caught sight of a domed building so grand he took it for a cathedral. It was Harrods. He gawked at the window displays, also the well-off clientele, plumed matrons with their tunic-frocked daughters, hardly a man in sight. Around in back, he found the delivery bays and a poster advertising for stock boys.

The supervisor did not know quite what to make of the applicant. Alec had been to a barber at last, Maurice's, a Milanese who rarely saw such a superb mane north of Lombardy and treated it as a work of art. The cut was perfect; it looked expensive (it wasn't), as did the clothes (they were). On the other hand, since his bowler had sailed to South America and Maurice's hats were too big, Alec was holding in hand an old tweed cap that had suffered not only the rains of Wiltshire but more than one tug-of-war with the dachshund. His workman's shoes were likewise at odds with the refined trousers, and the beautiful shirt was surely made-to-measure, but not for the fellow now wearing it. Nonetheless, the supervisor liked Alec's country manners and healthy kind-looking face. The lad appeared easily strong enough to do the lifting. He offered to try him out.

And there was that most basic matter of food. Since Alec would not have been welcome at Maurice's club, Maurice stopped eating there, and they both went equally hungry.

Their rented rooms had neither place nor means to prepare meals. Not that a kitchen would have done them any good: both Mrs. Scudder and Mrs. Hall had raised their sons willfully, even proudly, ignorant of the mysteries of cooking. Still, the lovers did survive—with takeaway, pubs, cafés, and now and then a restaurant. They were both too robust to last on a diet of Bohemian scrounging, so they ate heartily whenever they could, particularly, to their mothers' satisfaction, at Sunday dinners with their respective families. And Aderyn always sent Alec back to "that unholy city" with a sackful of homemade provisions from her pantry. Eventually, they bought a hot plate and taught themselves to make omelets.

But unlike Maurice's club, the settlement house where he volunteered as a football coach welcomed Alec with open arms. When they showed up together one Saturday afternoon, the youngsters jeered at Alec's accent, called him a bumpkin, a hayseed, a lout; said 'e was no gent like their fine Mr. 'All. Meanwhile, they clung to him like caterpillars. Two small ones each hugged a leg. Others jumped on his back or butted their heads into his gut, knocked him over, and threw themselves on him, pummeling him till Maurice blew his whistle. Alec absorbed their attack with laughter. (He knew what they really wanted, like all little kids, was to be lifted and tossed and caught in his arms, so he obliged.) He also out-mocked their mockery of his Dorset speech and was therefore a great success.

Saturday became the lovers' favorite day of the week. They both finished work at noon; then football with the kids at the mission (at which, unlike cricket, Maurice excelled and Alec did not). They'd come home and climb into the deep bathtub (their rooms' best feature), sometimes together, for a long soak. Afterward they'd dress in warm socks and Alec's big old homespun shirts—nothing else—and lie about spooning and playing or reading and dozing side by side for hours. It was their very highest happiness.

This was the young life they were building together. *A chance in a thousand we've met*, Maurice had said—generous odds, at that. Even less likely than meeting was overcoming their prejudices about each other's social class. But they did, thanks to the strength of their love. At twenty and twenty-four, they had achieved what nature demands at that age, but what Church, state, and family had forbidden them: union with another. When they gazed at each other, each disbelieved his good luck: to be loved by such a fellow! They wanted no more than they had. Their life was simple, but because it was theirs, it was always at risk of exposure, attack, destruction.

Meantime, they did find an ally. As soon as they were settled, Alec wrote to Morgan about his last-minute reversal of plans. When they met for a pint, Alec told the story about being offered a job. Morgan listened, less attending to the words (which sounded practiced) than observing the speaker. He discerned a change in Alec. It wasn't the smart haircut, borrowed clothes, and trendy address—in themselves they might have suggested a condition as crude and (given Alec's temperament) improbable as his being "kept." No. The change was deeper than appearance. Alec still spoke with his typical nervous vigor, but another characteristic, less attractive, was conspicuous by its absence. Last spring, when Morgan knew him as a student, an uncertainty seemed to hound him, about who he was or how he ought to be in the world. Morgan had interpreted this anxiety as having as much to do with Alec's character as with his sexual nature. He was too honest for the life of lying that England required of men of their kind. His self-respect, Morgan believed, had underlain the plan to emigrate: Alec imagined that somehow he might live not only more freely, but also with more integrity on the other side of the world. But now that former worry was gone. In its place, what? Confidence? Manhood? Morgan soon learned the answer.

". . . he's lookin' to buy forestland," Alec said, "for timber and game, which he wants me to manage . . ."

"Ah, I see, and when he finds this woodland, you'll work it together, you and he?"

"Yeah, that's the idea."

"And the two of you will leave London behind and live in the forest together?"

Alec lowered his eyes and blushed to the roots of his hair. Morgan reached across the tavern table; he covered Alec's hand with his own. "I'm so very happy for you."

"Thanks," Alec said quietly.

"He'd better be worthy of my student."

"Oh, Morgan, he's a champ," Alec said, getting teary. "Such a fine, fine man as I've no words to say . . ."

"Do you think he might care to meet me?"

So Morgan became their first visitor to Bernard Street, where they discovered that the Cambridge men had met five years before, when Maurice was an undergraduate and Morgan a visiting alumnus. Though they'd only shaken hands then, they remembered each other: Maurice because the older man was celebrated (therefore intimidating) as a writer and scholar; Morgan because the younger man looked, improbably, so like the model in the advertisements for Arrow shirts. They also discovered many mutual acquaintances. When they got to reminiscing about their teacher Harrison Grant, Alec jumped into their insiders' chitchat: "Haw, haw, mah good chappies. You know that *game*keeper fellow, what's-his-name—Stutter!—he too also studied poetry with old Granite-chin Grant, don't you know. The Working Men's College, haw, haw! It's the limit!" And then, with fey and dead-on varsity diction, he recited:

> *and the mountain shepherds came,*
> *Their garlands sere, their magic mantles rent;*
> *The Pilgrim of Eternity, whose fame*
> *Over his living head like Heaven is bent,*
> *An early but enduring monument,*
> *Came, veiling all the lightnings of his song*
> *In sorrow; from her wilds Ierne sent*
> *The sweetest lyrist of her saddest wrong,*
> *And Love taught Grief to fall like music from his tongue.*

Maurice and Morgan set down their whiskeys and applauded. Alec bowed, hand upon bosom.

"Name the poet," Alec charged, donnishly.

Morgan raised his hand. "Isn't it Shelley, sir?"

"I'll ask the questions. You name the poet."

"Shelley, sir."

"Good. Form of the stanza?"

"Spenserian."

"Good. Modeled on?"

"*The Faerie Queene.*"

"Of course. And you there," he said to Maurice, "you, trying to hide, what's your name?"

"Duncible, sir."

"Hmmph. Apt, no doubt. Tell us, *whoo* is the Pilgrim of Eternity?"

"Um . . . it must be Bunyan."

"Wrong pilgrim. Here's a hint: Childe Harold."

"Huh? Oh, I know, it's Chaucer—he wrote about pilgrims."

"Wrong again. Whatever *shall* we do with you?"

Maurice yanked Alec onto his lap and growled lustfully: "Sir, if you please, I'm sure I'd show great improvement if you'd detain me for a private lesson in your rooms."

Morgan laughed with them; he also understood how very rare was their happiness. He determined to be their friend and, much as he could, protector.

"I'd like you two to get to know a couple of old pals of mine," Morgan said, as he was getting ready to leave, "who manage to share a house, quite openly, in the country. They might help you find woodland for sale. Meantime, can you come to a concert with me next Friday?"

The concert with Morgan was the first public event the lovers attended together. Alec reveled in being out and about with his two favorite people on earth. He wedged himself between them and took each one's arm. He led them in a game of sidling along the streets to keep their link unbroken. The autumn dusk redeemed the city's ugliness, spangling the air with uncountable points of light: gaslight and incandescence, streetlamps, signs, windows, headlamps of cabs and trolleys. And the people! Here were thousands of young folks, away from their deadening jobs, as eager for fun as Alec, on their way to a meal or a dance or a show.

As for Maurice, nothing made him happier than seeing Alec happy. That was his nature as lover. He had been to this concert hall before, on a date with one of his sister's schoolmates, fairly recently (though before he knew Alec, so it seemed long in the past). He remembered he'd heard Tchaikovsky's *Pathétique Symphony*. The music was special to him because of Clive. The night they'd first met at Cambridge, Clive was looking for a piano version of the symphony in another student's rooms. When he found it, they went back to Clive's to listen to the second movement together. That marked the beginning of their friendship. The student who owned the music would also become important to Maurice's education: endlessly talkative, brashly queer Octavian Risley took delight in provoking those he believed had something to hide. Maurice, who at that time had lots to hide, found him both menacing and fascinating. He'd encountered Risley by chance when he was leaving the Tchaikovsky concert. Risley mentioned the name of a hypnotist. Maurice then sought the fellow out to "cure" his unspeakable condition.

But now there was Alec.

Tonight's program: Debussy and Beethoven. "Wise of them to offer the French delicacy first," Morgan said. "They hope the harrumphers will stay for the schnitzel."

Such highbrow music was new to Alec, whose experience was limited mostly to church and popular songs. Singing anthems and hymns (learned by ear) in the St. Osmund's choir had moved him as a child, especially when the boy-choristers would soar into descants above the adult voices. He'd try to separate the threads of the vocal parts, amazed how they merged into one, amazed also by the seraphic sound that came out of his own mouth, he knew not whence. But then his voice changed, and he was banished to the congregation, where in his boredom he'd study the notes in the hymnal and try to match them to the pitch of the choir. As for popular tunes, he liked them well enough for dancing, but they failed to intrigue him the way that church music had.

In tonight's first piece, *The Blessed Damozel*, singers would join the orchestra—a women's chorus and soloists. He took some comfort in that; maybe the voices would make it less strange to him. He read over the text in the program, an eerie

poem about a dead girl longing for her lover, who was still
alive. Alec was unprepared for what followed, for both the
sound and his response. He did not know that music could
shimmer like light or water; that it could stir him sexually,
cause him chills in a hot crowded hall; carry him off to a
heaven where the saints were ladies and knights, where the
Virgin held court among her maidens in a rose garden, where
paradise itself was incomplete without your earthly beloved,
because in this particular afterlife, love of flesh and love of
God were one.

Ecstasy—that was the word. Hadn't Professor Grant told
them that, for the Greeks, it meant a state of bliss—divine,
demonic—that took you outside yourself? In the dark, Alec
found Maurice's hand with his own, laced their fingers together, and held firmly. After the break, the *Pastoral Symphony* brought him back to earth, but such an earth where
his soul was happily drunk and dancing, even when fleeing
a musical thunderstorm. During the ovation, Alec grabbed
Morgan around the shoulders and yelled above the applause,
"That was—! What the hell *was* that?"

"So you liked it?"

"Yes!"

The three friends got separated in the crowd on their way
to the doors. Alec noticed a glamorous lady by the staircase
creating a nimbus around herself with the smoke drawn from
the cigarette at the end of a long ivory holder. It was his former employer, Mrs. Wentworth. He knew better than to greet
her: she would not recognize him or, if she did, would pretend
not to. But before he could look away, their eyes met. He expected her to cut him immediately, but instead she bestowed
a little smile, a tinier nod, and the very slightest wave of her
hand—or rather of her cigarette holder. In spite of himself, he

felt flattered to be acknowledged in public by such a person-
age, yet at the same time hated what he took to be her conde-
scension. Hadn't she once tried to pimp him? Did she think
she could still beckon him to wait on her? Then he decided it
would be ungallant for a man to ignore a woman's greeting,
so he approached and stopped at a respectful distance: "Good
evenin', ma'am. Did you wish to speak to me?"

"Tell me, darling, what did you think?"

"Of the music?"

"The Debussy."

"I thought it very beautiful."

"Oh good. That means I'm allowed to like it too. Your set
is miles ahead of me, and it's safer to ask before I venture an
opinion." She laughed and drew smoke. Alec smiled but did
not join in her laughter. He saw she was starting to fear she'd
made a mistake: "Help me, now—I'm such a forgetful biddy.
You're one of Tavy's sweet friends; do remind me where we
met."

"Scudder's the name, ma'am. I was once in your service in
Dorset, the gamekeeper's boy."

"Oh."

"It's all right, ma'am. Glad you enjoyed the concert. Good
night, now."

He found Maurice and Morgan in the lobby, talking with
a third man, tall and skinny, in evening clothes, whom he also
recognized. "Our young scholar," Morgan said to this third
one, introducing Alec, "who studied Italian cities with me at
the WMC."

Risley, squinting through his glasses, did not know him
at first, but when Alec stood close to Maurice, who then
rested his arm across the back of his waist with such chummy
nonchalance, the man's eyes widened with a double blast of

recognition: this radiant youth, with the perfect parted lips and brilliant eyes of a Regency portrait, was none other than the faun he'd once tried to rent in the woods, and Maurice Hall—unjustly handsome, fatally dull—had somehow tamed the Arcadian creature and was blessed with his affection! Risley, momentarily speechless, was preempted by Alec: "I'd the honor of servin' Mr. Risley once when I worked in Dorset—two years ago, was it, now? How d'you do, sir?"

"Oh, here you are, Tavy," Mrs. Wentworth said as she joined them and took Risley's arm. "Hello, Morgan."

"You look gorgeous as always, Cornelia," Morgan said to her. "Meet my friends Maurice Hall and Alexander Scudder. Mr. Hall was at King's with Risley."

The lady extended a gloved hand to Maurice. Alec watched him receive it lightly with a smile and a nod that somehow suggested a bow. When she extended her hand likewise to Alec, he imitated the example. She gave no sign of their prior acquaintance. To the group, she said, "Wasn't that lovely, especially the French piece?" and added, turning to Alec, "The experts are saying, 'Very beautiful.'"

14

At each place at the table, a booklet: menu and program printed together with the day's date, June 28, 1914. Within, a kind of manifesto:

> Our aims have the simplicity of need:
>
> —We want a place given up to gaiety, to a gaiety stimulating thought, rather than crushing it.
> —We want a gaiety that does not have to count with midnight.
> —We want surroundings, which after the reality of daily life, reveal the reality of the unreal.
> —We do not want to Continentalise, we only want to do away, to some degree, with the distinction that the word "Continental" implies, and with the necessity of crossing the Channel to laugh freely, and to sit up after nursery hours . . .

The design was jarring. The typeface suggested medieval monastic script, but the illustrations were up-to-the-minute—jagged figures, primitive, with masklike faces; men lunging at each other; women either running, naked and anguished, as if shrieking with grief, or chicly dressed at café tables with cocktails. The Cave of the Golden Calf. The club, set in the low-ceilinged basement of a textile warehouse, attracted a clientele that took pride in their self-selectivity: artists, socialites, intellectuals, expatriates, queers of both sexes (some of them artists, socialites, intellectuals, or expats). They supped till 2:00 a.m. and drank till dawn at tables arranged before a toy-box of a proscenium stage. Dancing commenced at midnight, after the show. FOR MEMBERS ONLY. Club status defended the Calf from censorship. Alec and Maurice were not members, but were guests tonight, along with Morgan, of the pair at whose table they sat: Octavian Risley and his friend the Baronne du Thoronet.

Alec had come around to tolerating, even liking Risley, at least in small doses. He was clever, funny, acerbic, never hesitant to speak his mind. After meeting the lovers at the concert last fall, he'd snorted at Morgan: "Maurice Hall, that tailor's dummy! And his Tess of the d'Urbervilles. 'I 'ad the honor of sarvin' Mr. Risley in Dorset . . .' I could have slapped her smug little face. Impossible. Men like those two never meet—it's not fair. Oh never mind. And the way they beam at each other! Unforgivable! An affront to the Misery of the Human Condition. But really, humping a servant . . ."

Morgan laughed. "You wanted to hump that one yourself."

"Of course I did, but not to marry him. It's just the limit. What can they possibly talk about?"

Morgan answered with a skeptical smile.

Risley, narrowing his eyes, hissed, "Mark my words, they won't last six more weeks."

Nonetheless, Morgan persevered. He argued that they were all, in the end, brothers-in-arms, so to speak; he also nursed his friend's bruised pride. He asserted that Alec's rejection of the proposition in Dorset had been in no way a judgment against Risley's charm; rather, the simple, honest youth had qualms, understandably, about accepting money for sex from such a well-spoken (and attractive) gentleman.

"Bollocks and balderdash."

"If only you'd wooed him with your famous wit instead of trying to bludgeon him with cash, you'd no doubt have won the lovely boy."

"Well, perhaps I may have been a bit too direct, but how could one know that a servant would prove so *sensitive*?"

"That's exactly why he's so charming."

Morgan prevailed. In due time, Risley became an ally, as did his friend the baroness (the former Mrs. Wentworth). Alec found his relationship with her even more odd than Risley's reluctant bonhomie. In a group, she would sometimes take him aside. "It's suffocating, Alec, darling," she once said to him privately, "marriage for a woman, and a paradox, because unless she subjects herself, she has no freedom at all. It's not even a matter of appearances, because everybody *knows*. It's about the lies we agree to accept. A widow is presumed virtuous, but a divorcée, dangerous. Yet a married woman may go months on end never seeing her husband and still remain somehow 'safe.' She's even better qualified to be someone's mistress." The baroness found her present arrangement quite satisfactory, its price a reasonable percentage of her windfall from the Anglo-Persian Oil Company and the sale of Michaelmount. In addition to the money, her new husband had gained an English passport, and she, a French title. ("Napoleonic," she confided, "but in London they're not fussy.")

Alec discerned that if she would speak thus to him, her onetime servant, the lady must be lonely. Maybe it was their inequality that put her at ease with him. She seemed at the same time to crave intimacy and to defend herself from those who came too close. So Alec, maintaining a respectful distance, was content to listen and learn about the world.

If his social life was expanding in ways once unimaginable

for him, Maurice's was shrinking. He routinely declined invitations. At first this withdrawal made him uneasy, because dining had always been a way to bring new business to his firm. But how could he leave Alec behind while he went out at night? Their love changed the way Maurice met life. In the light of its truth, he could name what was false. He knew that tonight was false, though less false than dinner with bankers, where he participated in the lies of others by his silence and allowed them to believe he was what he was not. Here with Morgan, Risley, and the baroness, the lovers were more than accepted for who they were, they were esteemed. But this modish place, smug and self-congratulatory, seemed untrue to them in its own way. He wondered if there would be anywhere they might ever feel at home, except in their own rooms. For now, though, Alec was flourishing in the city, its exuberance, its people—all new to him—and that made Maurice very happy.

He still winced with shame on recalling how he'd met Alec's bravery at Penge with abandonment, driving him to threaten blackmail. A foolhardy, even craven gesture on Alec's part, for certain, but how much better was his desperation than indifference would have been! Now Maurice marveled that anyone could feel as deeply as he did, to fear his own death less than any harm's befalling his beloved. Alec's passion had unlocked his own.

"I'm still trying to educate you," Risley said to Maurice, indicating their surroundings.

"You'll recall I'm terribly slow."

"Far less than I once believed."

Onstage, a goateed man with a rooster's comb of coarse brown hair stepped out in front of the curtain. Ezra Pound, the program said, who was reading from his new poems based on the work of the troubadours. He spoke with an exaggerated American twang, his diction like hammering typewriter keys, hitting the space bar twice between each word.

When the poet stepped off, Mrs. Strindberg, the club's owner, visited the table. She was the (second) ex-wife of the Swedish playwright, whom she'd left, the baroness later told them, to take up with another playwright, the German Frank Wedekind.

"It's terrible, of course, the violence, I mean, but, forgive me, in my opinion the archduke was a bit of a hound," Mrs. Strindberg said to the group, meaning Franz Ferdinand, shot to death that morning in Sarajevo. "Austria might be better off without him. Though who am I to say? Anyway, it's very sad about the wife."

She moved on to the next table as the houselights dimmed and the curtain rose on the little stage, set—cheaply, imaginatively—with crinkled cellophane, lit from within, and fake wisteria flowers. An unseen musician played a flute while the light changed color. "Syrinx," the program read, a new piece by Debussy. When Alec closed his eyes to listen, he saw the kingfisher, dancing in her flight above and under the water. When he opened his eyes, here was Maurice beside him, as he had been last summer when he'd opened his eyes in the boathouse. *We shan't be parted no more . . .*

15

In that passage from sleep to waking, Alec would realize, to his delight, that the sunlight coaxing his eyes open had not fought its way past chimneys and sooty bricks, but was flooding freely through fields. His many months in the city had been so crammed with excitement that he'd no time to miss his contemplative countryside. Now he marveled he'd put up with London for so long. Here, amid these woods and pastures, tension had drained from his shoulders. And had his pulse slowed too? Not that he felt at all sluggish, only peaceful.

At the offices of Hill & Hall, on June 30, 1914, succession had at last been effected. Maurice was now a client of the investment firm where he'd once been partner. For his part, Alec had gladly given notice at Harrods. He'd come to dread his days there, shuffling boxes in the stockrooms' sunless dungeons.

Morgan, true to his word, had introduced the lovers to his old friends—old in both the sense of long-standing acquaintance and of age. Ted was soon to turn seventy; George was forty-eight. When Alec rolled out of bed in their guest room, opened the curtains (sewn by his hosts' own hands), and squinted into the July sun of early morning, he saw them, as was usual this time of day, naked in the backyard, Ted reading, George gardening. Rare birds, those two. Ted believed that "air baths" enhanced both mental and physical well-being. To judge from appearance, there might be truth to the notion. On the verge of his eighth decade, he was trim and spry. The younger, stockier George carried himself with the swagger of a well-set man in his prime.

They'd been together for thirteen years now; for the last six, they'd lived openly as a couple in Ted's house near the village of Millthorpe in Derbyshire. (To Alec, it looked like the heart of England on a map.) Morgan had brought his young friends to them for advice about buying land, though his deeper purpose was pedagogical. These elders had much to teach them, chiefly about how to live with honor as men who loved each other.

Like Alec and Maurice, they'd contended with a difference of class. Ted came from a rich, well-connected, strictly religious family. After Cambridge, he'd even been ordained in the Established Church and had served briefly as a curate. He later renounced his ordination over a matter of conscience. He rejected the teaching that his sexual nature was unnatural and sinful. Rather, he discerned that the desire for "homogenic" love was innate to certain persons, therefore part of creation's order, and therefore good. He had come to distinguish himself in his long career as a writer and speaker on topics ranging from international politics to Hinduism, and as an activist for prison reform and the rights of coal miners.

In contrast, George had grown up in the slums of Sheffield, one of nine children of an alcoholic father and a good-natured mother who learned to make do with her lot. George inherited her resourceful temperament, along with her talent for joking and cursing. At thirteen, he'd taken a job at Sheffield's public baths, where he frisked around in no more than a towel all day and became a great favorite—particularly of the constables who lounged there after their shifts, or sometimes during. He showed his young guests a provocative photo, taken outdoors when he was eighteen, of himself in no more than a scant pair of trunks—handsome and grinning, smooth and shapely—standing next to a fully uniformed bobby, the man's arm draped over his shoulders and a look on his face saying, *How lucky am I!* Later, George had worked in pubs, tending bar, serving tables. Since he came from a home where Victorian values were turned upside down and the kids took care of the parents, he learned not to be ruled by the expectations of others, much less by their mores. And the amorous bathhouse constables had exposed to him the law's hypocrisy against his kind.

On the day they met, he knew little of Ted's credentials. Rather, the handsome older gentleman with whom he'd locked eyes on a train was the object of his desire, and so he pursued him. When Ted detrained at Millthorpe with his cohort of feminists and socialists, George followed, although it was not his stop. He lagged some distance behind the group walking to their host's house. Very much aware of the jaunty stranger's attention, Ted fell back, thus tacitly inviting him to catch up. George did so and said, "I seen you about in Sheffield, but missed you last winter. Where were you?" Before Ted could answer, he went on, "Never mind. Let the others go now. Come back to my place. Come with me. Now. You want to. You know you do."

By all means Ted did want to. He found this bold fellow very attractive indeed. And so their life together began.

In the guest room on this summer morning, Maurice opened a drowsy eye. He humped the mattress lewdly and said, "Whar's Licky?"

Alec, standing naked at the window, turned to show him his outsized good-morning erection. Maurice ducked under the covers. Alec hopped onto the bed and yanked them aside.

Millthorpe was proving to be an Eden for the young lovers as well as a school, as Morgan had hoped. Here nothing was more natural than their hosts' love for each other, and therefore their own. The older pair had created a gracious home, where they welcomed and cared for their guests. If queer life in the city was a thing apart, rarefied, nocturnal, always furtive, here it was plain life, lived in the sunlight and unburdened by what Ted disparaged as "civilization."

George's lessons were, not surprisingly, down-to-earth, chiefly about food and sex. Ignoring such contemptuous categorizations as "women's work," he'd turned himself into an excellent cook, who liked to amaze guests with dinners of three courses, featuring food raised on the farm. By eating (heartily, gratefully) and by observing, by slicing, chopping, and cleaning up in the kitchen, the younger ones learned that their manhood would not of itself condemn them to a life of bad meals in the home they planned to make for themselves. Their hosts also encouraged them to spend their time outdoors nude (but please to stay out of sight of the road). George liked nothing better than to join the naked lads on a stroll, an arm around each. "We're in heaven here, ain't we?" he'd say and draw them into a three-way embrace.

Ted spoke to their minds. He'd spent a lifetime reading and talking, and thinking, traveling, writing, and trying to align his actions with his conscience. The bourgeois culture he was born into condemned him. To conform to its values would have meant a life of self-hatred. Instead he'd developed a unique, expansive vision of justice, wherein the rights of women and workers and same-sex lovers were coequal causes in a world in need of reform. Some younger thinkers had come to regard him as a relic in their new age of progress. But in fact, as Risley (also a fan and frequent guest) liked to point out, they forgot that it was Ted who'd initiated the progress that now made them regard him as quaint.

The lovers had come for their stay at Millthorpe at a fortuitous time. About a week after their arrival, Ted traveled to London to attend the inaugural meeting of the British Society for the Study of Sex Psychology, where he was to be honored for his efforts to free same-sex love from bigotry, ignorance, and that particular kind of hatred that liked to call itself biblical. He framed the issue with questions of science and law; he did so by the authority of his education, his talent, and his humanity.

He returned from the city happy, "but completely talked out," he said. "Hoarse, stupefied! Writers, professors, lawyers, you can't shut them up. If I could just bring them here to see Alec and Maurice together, there'd be no need to say another word."

To the lovers, Ted was a figure to be cherished, mild, grandfatherly, yet youthful. He'd seen India; he'd traveled to the States—choosing steerage class once, living below deck with the emigrants. He'd visited Walt Whitman in Camden and promoted the poet's work in England.

Sometimes, though, his socialism rankled Maurice. "This life that he lives," he had said to Alec quietly once in their room, "his education, this house, it's all from the money his family left him."

"He's earned some for himself."

"Yes, but inherited more . . ."

"Like anybody else we know?"

"But *I'm* thankful—for my advantages, I mean. He wants to turn all England upside down."

"What's it now, right side up? England wants you in prison,

me too, and Teddy himself and George and all our like. And what about our poor footballers at the settlement house in the city? Skinny as sticks, stunted from lack of decent food, while there's plenty to eat all round them. *A disgrace to the crown*, as Aderyn Prothero might say, *and a crime against Christ's very cross!* We've no need for Marx here in Britain. We've got the slums of Sheffield."

"I only meant . . . Oh, I don't know what I meant."

Alec caressed him. "One thing for you to put down your pride and take tea with the Butcher and Wife of Osmington . . ."

"They're all right, your folks—"

"Chocolate-box villagers, eh, 'picturesque'?"

"Alec—"

"But quite somethin' else, now, with these others we're gettin' to know, in town and out here—fruitcakes and frumps and bluestockings. Poets. Fuckin' philosophers! Even when they're well-off an' well-bred as yourself, you're not truly comfy amongst them."

"Conventional, am I?"

"More of a snob, I'd say . . ."

"Fair enough."

"Though, to be fair, much less now than before," Alec said.

"All right, so maybe I'd rather play tennis—"

"With Archie London?"

"With anybody. Even with you."

Alec pounced and caught him in a hammerlock. Maurice struggled: "That's right—I'd rather play tennis—even with you!—than listen to Dame Risley—your great admirer!—rhapsodize about—take your pick—"

"Algernon Charles Swinburne." Alec tightened the hold.

"Aaaack! Worse!"

"Eleonora Duse!" he said, triumphantly trilling the *r.*

Maurice jabbed with both elbows at once, broke the hold, pinned Alec onto their bed, and declaimed in stage-Russian, "Nikolay Rimsky-Korsakov!"

Alec narrowed his eyes and hissed at him, Risley-like: "Sigismondo Malatesta."

"*Now* you've slain me . . ." Maurice rolled over and died. Then he opened his eyes and asked sweetly, "And how about you? How comfy is Alec with all this?"

"Oh, I get a kick out of our oddballs, bein' one such myself. I'm queerer by far than any of them."

"Surely not queerer than George."

"Just give me time, darlin' boy."

"All right . . . but meanwhile, may I suck your extremely lovely cock . . . ?"

"Kiss first."

Maurice obliged.

"More."

Maurice obliged again—throat, chest, mouth. When his lover moaned, he commenced on his original mission.

A warm breeze stirred the curtains. Alec said, "Was there ever a summer so balmy?"

One afternoon late in July, after sawing back an overgrown yew, Alec carted the larger branches and trunks to chop for firewood. He found Maurice splitting logs by the shed, attired appropriately for work at Millthorpe (as was Alec), in a pair of Ted's homemade sandals and nothing else. Alec had grown accustomed to Maurice's beauty, but now, at a distance, it struck him anew. His lover's skin had browned during their weeks in the sun, making his eyes seem greener. When he raised the ax, the muscles of his torso, shoulders, arms, and legs tensed; when he brought it down, he released the strength of his whole body to split the wood, and his glossy hair fell forward over his brow. To anyone, he would have appeared heroic; to Alec, he was the paragon of young manhood. "Practicin' to build us our place in the woods?"

They unloaded the logs from the wheelbarrow. Maurice spread an old blanket on the ground among the fragrant wood chips. Their desire for each other had increased during their time together, as their lovemaking had grown more skillful. They'd learned to come together, or if one should come first, they might be so lost in each other at the moment that neither could quite tell who. Today, before that moment arrived, Maurice murmured, "I want you to enter me."

Alec knew the longing Maurice now gave voice to, a desire at once sensual and mystical and at last impossible: to incorporate the other into himself. Despite their passion, they'd not yet tried penetration, held back by a fear of giving pain. "Won't it hurt?" he said.

"I don't care. George told me how. He gave me an ointment." Maurice applied the salve and guided Alec from behind. At first he winced. "Wait!" Alec stopped. Then Maurice relaxed and said, "Yes, all right, now, go ahead, easy." Alec slid inside and held still in the perfection of this intense new pleasure. Maurice turned his head to offer his mouth to kiss. Alec imitated with his tongue the thrust of his prick. Hardly moving, Alec came. When the spasms ebbed, then ceased, he withdrew. They held each other. Tears, not from sadness or pain, mixed with their sweat.

Alec said, "Now you inside me, just the same."

"We don't have to."

"Please, Maurice, yeah, I want to."

IV

THE PLAINS OF ILIUM

16

In London, on that night in August 1914, crowds gathered along the Mall by the palace. At 11:00 (midnight in Berlin), the ultimatum expired without a satisfactory response from Germany concerning the neutrality of Belgium.

No one could say whether the tolling of Big Ben cued the throngs to sing "God Save the King" or the singing started first and the bell seemed to join in. But the scale of the sound, and its might and solemnity, anticipated the events to follow.

Twenty minutes later the War Telegram was dispatched across the empire: WAR, GERMANY, ACT.

Their hosts at Millthorpe tried to talk them out of enlisting. George argued from practicality: "You've just found your parcel of woodland—you could sign for it next week. Somebody will snatch it up while you're gone."

Teddy, ever altruistic, preached the pacifism of Gandhi and Bertrand Russell. He'd quoted, fervently, from *The Kingdom of God Is Within You*. He excoriated the Established Church for its hypocrisy—no, heresy!—in condoning, even promoting, this immoral war.

The baroness and Risley traveled to Millthorpe to join the cause of dissuasion. "For God's sake, don't!" she urged.

"What you possess is too precious to risk. Listen to me: I've seen it before, and how often? It's useless, all of it, except to the damned gunmakers."

Morgan also visited, but he seemed resigned to his young friends' enlisting, as he was to the war. (He was already planning to volunteer with the Red Cross.) When the others got loud, he stayed quiet. When the others groaned as the boys disclosed their scheme to stay together by joining the Welsh Fusiliers, Morgan's silence grew even deeper.

For the lovers, volunteering had hardly been a matter of discussion, much less of dispute. Neither could bear that the other might think him a coward. (At Mr. Abrahams's school, fifteen-year-old Maurice had received his only student prize for composing a short theme in Greek on the virtue of bravery in battle.) Since other men of their age and good health were volunteering, they must too. To be sure, though, the declaration of war, when it actually came, surprised them. Not because they were unaware of the crises playing out on the Continent, but because it all seemed so far from Millthorpe, where their summer was passing in a paradise of working outdoors and reading and making love.

"Together?" the examining doctor asked them at the recruiting station in Cardiff.

"Yes sir," they both answered at once. They stood naked in line with scores of others. Maurice, ever protective of Alec, kept as close as he dared. But this was not Millthorpe: their nakedness was clinical, not glorious. Like the others they shivered even though it was August, more from jitters than the breeze. The medic seemed weary. Poor fellow, Alec thought, thumping ribs, being coughed on and who knew what else all day. When he leaned his head against Alec's chest to listen, the recruit was sure he felt something wet. The doctor turned on his swivel stool to mark the clipboard on the table behind him. When he turned back to Alec, he saw tears in the man's eyes. "Perfectly sound," he said. Alec started to step away to be weighed. The doctor stopped him: "You may wait for your friend."

The two of them had called on the Scudders in Osmington to say goodbye. They made their case to Aderyn for the Welsh tradition of valor. (In truth, enlisting in Wales was more about their getting away from South East England than honoring Alec's maternal forebears. Maurice knew too many people around London who might ask why the two were so close. Anonymous in Wales, they imagined they could stay together.) But the mother cared nothing for valor, only for her son: "Now I wish you'd gone on that ship with your brother," she said to him.

Maurice tried to reassure her: "We'll look out for each other, ma'am."

"He'd be safe overseas but for you, Mr. Hall," she answered tartly, "and your enterprise."

Maurice visited his family alone. The ladies of the Hall-Grace household took it as a matter of course that their scion would enlist, noblesse oblige. When he told them he'd picked the Welsh Fusiliers for their fine reputation, Mrs. Hall did not question her son's choice: men knew about such things. She protested that she faltered in her words and sniffled only because he'd made her so proud with his courage. Ada and Aunt Ida betrayed a less tender emotion. For months the two had been planning a September wedding. They had persuaded the groom to defer enlisting till October, but would Maurice be able to get leave so soon after signing on? If not, who would escort the bride? Kitty, embarrassed by their pettiness, said she intended to volunteer as a nurse and boycott their loathsome social event.

But the lovers' scheme of serving together was undone within days of enlisting: Maurice received orders to report to London for officers' training. It was unthinkable, his superiors informed him, that a man of his class should serve with the other ranks. What could he and Alec do? They'd signed on for the duration. Received opinion claimed that it would be a matter of months, involving "some cavalry charges, followed by infantry skirmishes," and so they hoped. Alec remained in Wales; Maurice left for the city.

17

The Fusiliers seemed the right fit for Alec. Fusiliers are rifle-men, and the gamekeeper knew how to shoot. He was issued a Lee-Enfield Mark III (nicknamed Smellie), at heart a hunting rifle, an excellent gun, accurate despite having its barrel short-ened to make it easier to carry, fitted with a magazine that held two rounds of five bullets each. The men were assured this would be a great advantage over their foes, whose best rifles held only one round of five and so would need reloading twice as often. A well-trained British infantryman could fire fifteen shots a minute. (Their instructor fired thirty-eight.) With practice, Alec was soon averaging about twenty.

Marksmanship, however, played a small part in his soldier's life. Most of the time was spent learning rules, or marching for hours under the weight of his gear. He wondered how they'd have any strength left for battle once they got to the front. And the bayonet practice! Lunge, thrust, rip, pull it out, finish him off, and then step over the body, cursing your foe the whole time. The instructors always yelled, because in battle there would be no polite conversations. "Scream at him! Cut his balls off! He'd do it to you, fucking Jerry would!"

After six months of training in Wales, in February 1915 Private D. Alexander Scudder was deployed to France. Disembarking from the troop transport, he slipped on a bit of ice on the gangplank. The plank's skewed angle plus the weight of his gear brought him down. Then the hefty Scot next behind, tumbling over and crushing him, added calamity to what might have otherwise been a slapstick pratfall. His left thighbone snapped under his comrade's bulk. Fuck almighty, the pain! Yet the medics told him he was lucky. The skin was untorn, so the break was simple. They could take care of it on the base in France, no need to ship him home. They pulled the bone straight to set it. Then splints and plaster to keep it rigid. Because they were saving the morphine for battle casualties, they let him drink whatever was on hand, cheap beer, cider, and brandy so rough it turned his face red. For the next three weeks on his back he was never quite fully sober, a good thing, since whenever they slid the bedpan under him, he felt like they were breaking his thighbone anew. Then more weeks of limping around on crutches. But he was young, so when they finally removed the cast, they found the break had indeed mended neatly.

During the time Alec was unfit for battle, the British Expeditionary Force had found him other work: canine duty. In light of his gamekeeper's experience, he was put in charge of the base's kennels, maintaining the war dogs at ready. Not a bad job as army jobs go, except for the daily shoveling of buckets of dog shit—which he found less distasteful than scrubbing the human latrines, as his Jewish brothers-in-arms were made to do on Sundays while the Christians attended C of E services or were marched off to Catholic mass.

Blanche Richardson and her husband, Lieutenant Colonel Edwin Richardson, had made a science of training dogs for war. They'd begun in Scotland with collies and shepherds, but settled on Airedales as the ideal breed for service because of

their size, speed, and stamina. Then they expanded the program to all sorts of dogs, finding suitable work for each. To
Alec, the results were nearly miraculous. Beautiful animals,
many of them, so patient they even let him fit their canine gas
masks over their snouts, a sight at once bizarre, comic, and
heartrending.

There were no ranks among the dogs, but very clear divisions of labor. The sentries had to be cloistered because of
their upside-down schedules. They were fed in the morning
and rested all day, their kennels quiet and darkened, to keep
them alert for the night, when they'd be on patrol on the front.
They also had to be kept apart from the men, since too much
human contact would dull their sharp sense of the Stranger.
The messenger-dogs were more ragtag, recruited from Bat-
tersea Dogs Home, from strays sent by police stations around
the kingdom, even from pets volunteered by their families—
mutts and show dogs together. They too were trained, fed, ex-
ercised. Alec knew that his leg was fully healed when he could
jog along the roads with the pack on their daily workout.

One day some ratters arrived from England—three terri-
ers and a dachshund. The dachshund grew crazy-excited as
Alec approached the transport cages. When he knelt down
to spring the door, the little guy's tail was wagging so hard
that it shook his long body with it. Once released, the dog
stuffed his nose into Alec's crotch and would not relent in his
whimpering.

"Affectionate, aren't they, those little hounds?" said a
woman in uniform with a black mourning armband, who had
traveled with the new dogs across the Channel. "Or perhaps
it's the burrowing instinct." Alec stood at attention. "Affectionate and madly brave," she continued. "The French take
them boar hunting. Imagine—small as they are. This one's

from Wiltshire. A gamekeeper sent it with a note saying the villagers were pelting it with stones, because he's a 'German.' He'll make a good mascot, won't he, and pity the rodent that crosses that schnozzle." The dachshund, on his hind legs, was now scratching at Alec's trousers and whining for notice. "Bruno, sit!" she commanded. Bruno sat. Alec's eyes widened.

"Ma'am, odd as it seems, I believe I'm acquainted with this very scamp from Wiltshire."

"Indeed!"

"But I can't say if I'm more astonished to be seein' him here in the army or seein' him do as he's told. You'd never sit still for me back at Penge, would you, now, Bruno?" When Alec spoke his name, the dog rolled over and pawed at the air.

The lady in uniform was Mrs. Richardson herself, inspecting the kennels of BEF bases in France. She was pleased enough with Alec's care of the dogs to ask if he'd consider becoming a trainer at their school. Without saying why, Alec declined.

"As you wish, Private, I understand," she said. "My son also said no to staying in England." She touched her black armband.

"My condolences, ma'am."

"Thank you. At Loos, last month. He was eighteen."

In the autumn of 1915, after Alec had dispatched the third cohort of his charges to their canine missions on the Western Front, he himself was likewise dispatched.

18

30 July 15

Sometimes (often) I feel I'm the dimmest man at mess.
For example: did you know that turquoise, the word, has to
do with geography? I thought it just meant a certain hue or
a pretty stone. But no, it's about Turks! Turkey, Turk-woyse.
Sunny Turkish blue. It's the color of the world here, below and
above, the sea and the sky. Along the Greek coast and islands,
we pass whitewashed villages. The whitest ever, because the
blue all around them is deep and bright at once. Turquoise.

Back to my ignorance. So we're sailing east, getting closer
to the straits, and my fellow juniors fall to swooning about
Troy and Achilles and how we've a ship in the water called the
Agamemnon and if the fighting should move just a tad down
the coast, we actually might do battle on the Plains of Ilium!
(At this point I'm still following the references, but can't say
I'm feeling any Homeric tingles.)

Then Brewster leaves me in the dust when he holds
forth on how Xerxes the tragic Persian emperor whipped
the Hellespont to punish it. That's right, the water! Because
he wanted to invade Greece and the oracle said he would
win (so he thought), but he couldn't get his army across the
straits. So the ninny had his goons spank the water! Naughty
Hellespont! Lunatic. Crazier than Kaiser Wilhelmina. Xerxes
the Harebrained.

Anyway, Xerxes loses his shirt, or whatever underthings

ancient Persians wore, because what the oracle had <u>actually</u> said was 'an empire would fall' if he invaded Greece. Turns out she meant his own.

You probably know about Xerxes, maybe you even know about turquoise. Unlike my mess-mates, who may have paid better attention in school, you're truly cleverer than I. Not much of a compliment, I'll grant. You also have an amazing talent to soak up learning, which is but one of your many amazing talents, some of which I'd better stop thinking about.

When we get through it all, I'll give you this little book to read by our cozy fire and you'll know how close I've been holding you every day.

5 August 1915

Today nobody's talking about Homer. Oh there's some hail-fellow-well-met bragging about our edge over the Turks, those craven yapping gutless goat-eating rug-peddlers, and how they might have got lucky last spring with the Anzac outpost and Helles but now a large dose of British manhood at Suvla will set them to rout. Blather, blather.

Of course what we're <u>not</u> saying is what we all know, i.e., that <u>none</u> of us, not a single one of us junior officers nor the NCOs nor any of our men has ever seen battle. The <u>most</u> experienced have been in training for less than a year, others for just a few months. Many (most?) never even held a gun before signing on. And here we are, the first of Kitchener's New Army, all volunteers, to actually <u>fight</u>! Egad!

Tomorrow we disembark after dark. Less than 24 hours. Between you and me, I can hear my pulse pounding in my ears. And <u>how</u> do I qualify as a leader of men into war?

Because I read economics at Cambridge and played varsity tennis?

17 Aug

We set off from Imbros right after sunset on the 6th aboard ten destroyers each towing a beetle that would shuttle us to shore. Silence, blackout, not even cigarettes. Flotilla on the dark sea a grand sight, eerie because soundless, then dividing for diverse destinations. Destroyers <u>Beagle</u>, <u>Bulldog</u>, and <u>Grampus</u> bring us toward our landing site on Suvla Bay.

What looked smooth in planning proves a madhouse. The beetle, a blunt-nosed barge with an engine tacked on, hard to get free from the destroyer and still harder to steer. Except for the engine throbbing, all's quiet in the approach.

We run aground on a shoal farther out in the water than planned, maybe a hundred yards. Yet Captain orders the gangplank lowered. Soon as he speaks, rapid shots burst on us from the shore. Our first time under fire.

The men don't know what to do for cover and try flattening on deck. I hoarse-whisper some rot: "He can't see us; he's just taking potshots. Let's get off this damned tub while it's still dark. We're here now!"

And—to my amazement—they stand, God love them, ready to follow <u>me</u>!

Water well over our heads, each of us with sixty pounds, more, on his back, and many can't swim. One naval skipper strips down and dives in with the end of the towrope from the destroyer tied round him and swims to shore and secures it to a rock so we might have something to hang on to. Bullets pock the water around him the whole time.

We want to cheer him but stick to orders and keep our
mouths shut. His show of backbone bucks the men up, as I
think does seeing us officers go over first and with the help of
the lifeline make our way, noses just above water.

Halfway to shore at last we touch bottom. We stagger
onto the beach, gear and uniforms soaked, weight doubled.
Facing battle at last: wet, already worn dead, shivering,
ordered not to shoot. (Can't shoot anyway—rifles clogged
with water and sand.) Bayonets in place. We're to charge
with blades only. Except us officers, who have no rifles, just
gentlemanly pistols.

In the dark, the Turks keep firing at the empty landing
boats. We get to thirty yards of their trench on the hill before
they realize. Fewer of them than I thought, 40 or so. Still they
take some of us down.

That's when I see my first man killed: a Turk, bayoneted
in the gut, side, and back, left to bleed on the sandy ground.
Several more quickly thereafter.

Then I hear others approaching. I'm useless, with my pistol
and forbidden to fire. A good thing too. Those charging us
are some of our own, East Yorks of the 32nd, landed farther
south. We took them for the enemy.

Turns out that they belonged there, not us. We'd landed
too far south, near the 32nd's objective, Lala Baba fort. Captain
determines to set things right. He orders us to make our way up
to Hill 10: mission to take it.

Big problem now thirst. Out of water. But even if we'd
triple rations, still not enough: we'd swallowed whole quarts
of salt sea getting ashore from the boats and squandered fresh
water trying to clean the sand from our guns (before we find

our piss more efficient). Many men even offer the little left of their drinking water to cool our one machine gun enough to keep firing.

Meantime the Turks never ease up their sniping. How good they are! Lost hours mean we're exposed in daylight. Chilly night air gives way to hot hot sun and thirst gets truly maddening. Where are our reserves?

Out in the bay we see destroyers and transports teeming with men that seem never to move. Meantime we keep up our assault on Hill 10, many going down under fire. Hours later, reserves arrive and we fall back toward the beach. We take roll. Two hundred and more wounded or killed!

17 Aug later

So that's how we landed ten days ago.

One can no longer say that one has never seen battle. One has seen, smelled, touched, tasted, swallowed, and shit it out, explosively.

Back in school, when they were rubbing our noses in Homer, it seemed to me the bard spent most of his time describing somebody hacking off somebody else's arms, legs, or head. Enough! You see one act of Iron Age savagery, you've seen 'em all. On the other hand, he got the ferocity right. How did he manage that? Wasn't he blind?

Does Homer ever write about <u>boredom</u>? Doesn't he skip the ten years the Greeks spent camped out on the Trojan beach playing cards swatting flies waiting for their damn generals to make up their minds?

When I dream, I dream about water. Not that I dream

much—too thirsty to sleep. A dream faucet. Turn the tap and
water flows without end. Madness to think about, but here
on the shore, every drop brought hundreds of miles in a ship
when there's plenty just over the hill. But that's <u>their</u> water.
<u>Ours</u> gets pumped from the ships onto barges, then piped into
troughs on the shore, whence we fill our bottles.

Rationed one pint per day. Thirst makes animals of us all.
A brother junior manages thus: takes a mouthful and spits it
back into his mug. Then again, later, sips the same water he
spit out. That's discipline.

Not so our men. When the barge arrives, they're so
desperate they cut the pipes with their knives and suck them.
Those trenched farther inland must carry their company's
bottles back over three miles of sand and rocks, like two-
legged mules getting shot at most of the way. Yet, <u>yet</u> they beg
for the duty—because the carriers get to drink their fill at the
barge. Warm brown dirty water.

18 August

Medics the real heroes—in harm's way with no means
to fight back. Sick and wounded lined up on the shore.
Bandaging and tagging those not fatal for transport out to the
Red Cross ship offshore. Quiet the dying with a bit of dope,
bear the wounded through trenches too shallow for full cover,
jostled in agony, the bearers sick themselves, potshots never
letting up all the while.

Medics are villains too because after dispensing juju drops
to the sick, they send them back to the trenches where nobody
gets better but worse. Higher-ups holding guns to their
Hippocratic heads to send the sick back into the fight.

19 Aug

Major ordered me treated for dysentery. Spent hours
waiting on the beach fanning flies from those who could
not. Black flies, our hell their heaven—heat, blood, shit
everywhere, maggots in wounds, God help us.

Still we keep losing people, more and more, wounded,
killed, sick. What's the plan, the purpose? Nobody knows.
Staff remains at HQ, a yacht called the Jonquil anchored safe
distance offshore.

21 Aug

Today the earth caught fire. Anzacs here since April tell
us this land was green once upon a time. Hard to picture, all
barbed wire and ruts now, scrub bushes and thorns, all tinder-
dry. The brush caught fire from sparks during the attack—
spread instantly.

We were already out when the fire broke, had to run
through the flames, gunned by the Turks all the while. The
ones who died fast from a bullet were lucky, because the
wounded burned alive where they fell, fire torching their own
ammo. Hearing them moan & die.

Turk grenades have longer fuses than ours—so tempting
to pick up & toss back before they go off. Saw a fellow with
good pitching arm doing so. Luck failed and one went off in
his right hand. He kept it up with his left. Yes, I saw him
do it! Died later.

We mill round, always under fire, getting sick from

our own filth—diarrhea, dysentery, wiping our bums with newspaper scraps till they ran out, then letters from home, then leaves, when the leaves were gone nothing.

No water to spare for washing and the Turks watching the waves should we try to rinse off in the sea. We spent our time scratching shallow trenches with shovels smaller than toys in ground needing hammer and chisel. Yesterday we got orders to take the W Hills. So today we tried, as above, and, made God's earth catch fire.

19

29 Sept 1915

Hopeless. There I've said it, albeit silently and only to you. (Which is like saying it to myself because we're one.) I dare not say it to anybody else, or even think it too loudly, because we're all thinking the same and we're bound to overhear one another's thoughts, jammed close as we are together, and that might lower the already impossibly low spirits of our men, especially the sick ones—who are about half of <u>all</u> the men up and down the shore. Officers fare no better, self included.

To one another we say: Complete Trust in the High Command. We mean the opposite.

If we needed any proof of our hopelessness, we got it some days ago when the French pulled two divisions out of Gallipoli. To dispatch them for better use on the Western Front. <u>Au revoir! Merde</u> . . .

<u>What are we doing here?</u> Rumor says take the Sea of Marmara. Hah! We can't climb the hill twenty yards in front of us. Then what? Rumor says seize Constantinople. And how the <u>hell</u> would that get the Germans out of Belgium?! Which is what we're fighting for—remember? Never mind. This tantrum is dragging me lower and lower.

If I weren't sick and depressed to death, maybe I'd be equal to the misery, or if I weren't in a state of constant high anxiety over the safety of my men. Or if I weren't so very, very

afraid for you, which means that I'm afraid for me, since I
have no life except with you.

Glad you can't see these words now—or me in this rotten
state of self-pity.

18 Oct 15

We juniors, at our level of insignificance, are not shown
the photos from above. Word does get around, though. Seems
the Turks (who daily prove more determined and skillful)
have an overwhelming advantage of supply lines and terrain.
(It takes aerial reconnaissance to see <u>that</u>?) As the photos
also show, the Turks have a fleet at ready in the water by
Constantinople. So much for the Sea of Marmara.

Yesterday General Hamilton departed his HQ at Imbros—
involuntarily, permanently, and none too happy. Canned. (Word
does get round.) He'd been absolutely certain of victory in the
Dardanelles. Monro's taking over for him—much less keen
than Hamilton on this whole Gallipoli crusade, so one hears.

And now we've another enemy at work against us: the
weather. When the winds blow from the south, they're deadly
hot, full of the North African deserts. They stir the sea to
crashing, pounding the supply docks, soaking whatever we've
stashed on shore, making havoc with the tents, and scaring
the bejeezus out of us all.

9 Nov

Your birthday. 22 years old today. Put me in such a
wretched mood this morning to remember. Because we're

apart, as we were last year. Also because time moves in but
one direction and won't give back these days taken from us.

I'm doing better now this p.m. Guess why? Because
I'm remembering 9 November 1913! Such waywardness on
Bernard Street! We'd barely known each other ten weeks—is
it possible?—and yet it seemed forever! Because my life <u>began</u>
when we met.

Love hoodwinked time, at least for a little while then.

11 Nov 15

At first these November winds, blowing mostly cool from
the northeast—the Caucasus?—seemed a blessing, sending
the flies back to hell. Spirits even rose a bit among us. Still
always thirsty, but less mad than in the heat. (Also, cold stink
from the latrines less sickening than hot.)

But as the north winds keep persisting, they've gone from
cool to cold, damp to raw, and hint at worse to come—we've
only summer uniforms.

Monro quietly took off for Alexandria about a week ago,
so one hears. To confab with his fellow bigwigs—about
'something.' (Everybody hopes evacuation, though no one
says.)

While the mighty dither, debating pros and cons, men are
dying every day from sniping and sickness.

18 Nov

Fickle, crazy, demon winds! Three days past now they
shifted south again, and dry, blowing a groundswell against

the shore. We could land no supplies—the barges and pontoon docks smithereened by the waves. No bread! Water, already scarce, <u>half-rationed</u>.

Then the sky goes deadly black, lightning bolts over the Aegean, search beams from the big ships sweeping through the midday darkness over the sides of the cliffs, the ships themselves rolling and tugging their anchor chains. Hellish nightmare!

Still silence from the High Command.

2 Dec

On the evening of 26 Nov it began to rain, soaking through our tents and summer uniforms. After three hours of this downpour, when you'd swear there was no water left to fall in all the heavens, the rain came even harder, trenches filling to three feet. Waist-deep.

Then the real flood.

On the hillcrests, the Turkish trenches had likewise filled. When the water's weight reached the tipping point, the trenches burst and sent everything rushing down from above us in torrents.

The water sought sea level. It cared nothing for our puny efforts to hold it off, rushed through our encampments right into the Aegean, taking lots of our stuff along, but fortunately none of our men.

There's more. It's worse.

The temperature falls, fast and steadily, throughout the next day. Anything wet from the rain froze & everything was wet.

On 28 Nov, not long after midnight, it starts to <u>snow</u>.

Gently first, big wet flakes, then the wind picks up, and the snow becomes a blizzard, blinding and endless.

HQ sends supplies. But our men got turned around in the storm & failed to meet the delivery. So HQ left it for us to pick up later. We sent a second party, who failed to return. I led another group to search. We found them lying in the snow.

Seems the Quartermaster had sent us plenty of rum for the cold. They'd drunk the rations meant for dozens of men. One was dead, frozen. The rest we slapped to keep them moving and alive.

Can't say I blame them for wanting to sleep forever in the snow.

9 Dec

Yesterday came the orders we've been waiting for: to evacuate. We've about a week to prepare. Some men actually disappointed with our 'failing.' They're better soldiers than I.

Most disheartening to me the orders to kill our horses, about two hundred all together, at night, out of sight of the Turks, with silencers on the pistols.

All preparations take place in silence.

V

SUMMER SOLSTICE

20

Along the line of march, at regular intervals: foot inspection. Llewellyn quipped: "Jesus Washes the Feet of the Disciples." Llewellyn saw the Bible everywhere—except where he saw Arthurian legend or Druidic myth. Sometimes all traditions converged, as he claimed they did in that tiny church near Carnoy—ancient, empty, blasted, scorched, its portal no longer shaded by a dead dogwood. The Chapel Perilous, he called it. Who was its stone saint, they wondered, slender and veiled, in that frenzied, dancing pose? Llewellyn insisted that the inscription, in runelike letters with subscripts, did not say Brigitte but Brigantia, ancient goddess of summer, who (he explained), on raising her veil, revealed the glory of the season's fullness—which was, somehow, herself. "Long before there was any Sainte Brigitte or Notre Dame or Bon Jesu around here, this place belonged to her."

Alec groaned. "And you were her chief warlock, Lulu?"

"Can't help myself, Scuppy. My heart's the dolly shop of Christendom."

The gospel story about the foot-washing had struck Alec as funny when he was a schoolboy. The other men of his section, Brooks, Swavely, Talbot, were grinning now too, despite (Second) Lieutenant Hampton's efforts to impress them with the inspection's importance. Blisters or even a small cut could lead to trench foot. A limping soldier could disrupt the line of march and become a dangerous obstacle to his brothers, especially at night. Like his men, though, Hampton was aware of the intimate ritual's humor.

Strangely pale, even delicate-looking, their feet were, in contrast to the grimy brown uniforms, faces, and hands. The woolen socks kept them so. They wore them no matter the season. In June the wool kept their feet moist, therefore cool, from sweat, even as last February the same wool had kept their feet from freezing outright in the icy bilge, which inspired Alec with new gratitude for sheep. Their lieutenant insisted they take the socks off at least once a day to dry them, best they could, by a fire. No trench foot among Hampton's lads. They knew he was proud of that.

How beautiful are the feet of them that preach the gospel of peace and bring tidings of good things . . . Was it Llewellyn who'd quoted that verse? Maybe not. Maybe Alec remembered it himself. From a hymn, an anthem? *Peace, tidings of good things* . . . If Llewellyn's heart was Christendom's dolly shop, his own must be its junkyard. They were by no means messengers of peace.

Ah, the wizardry of language: Alec and his brother Tommies weren't lice-ridden bumblers; no, they were intrepid warriors defending liberty from tyranny, empire from barbarism, fair Albion from the Powers of Hell, saintly Belgian nuns and their orphans from the rapacious Hun. To Alec, the truth was simpler and had to do with families: Wilhelm, Victoria's oldest grandson, had pitched a tantrum, kicking and pounding his wee pudgy fists (one of them misshapen from birth) because his uncle, Edward VII, had not taken him seriously as a ruler and because Edward's wife, deaf Queen Alexandra, openly despised him. Hadn't Alec witnessed her contempt himself? At the king's funeral pageant, when Wilhelm leapt from his horse to push her footman aside and open her carriage door himself, hadn't his auntie, the royal-imperial widow, scowled? Moreover, Edward had been hailed as a hero in Paris, where Wilhelm was unwelcome and newspapers mocked him. France and England, England and France, why was the world infatuated with those two? Paris had draped her streets in black when Edward died, as if that gluttonous whoremonger were her own king! If the French wanted a king, Wilhelm would show them one. He'd teach their newspapers not to laugh at him. He'd take back Alsace and force the English to show their spinelessness. Welcome in Paris? He'd trample the place under thick Prussian boots.

"Check the head of the hobnail inside near your right heel," Hampton said to Swavely. "I'm feeling a dent in the callus."

"Rub the boo-boo, please, sir," Swavely said.

The young lieutenant winked in reply. His hair, parted on the left, fell forward over his right eyebrow when he inclined his head to examine. Maurice's hair fell just so, Alec recalled. How often had Maurice caressed Alec's foot, or Alec, his? Cherished, kissed, pressed cheek or prick against it . . .

The soldiers were fighting for love. They were trained to believe they fought for no cause or nation, but to protect or avenge their brothers. Ergo, the men fought for love. Alec's military education led him to this conclusion. He wondered if Second Lieutenant Maurice C. Hall II, wherever he was, also conducted such inspections, and if his men loved him as they loved Hampton. Of course they did.

Lieutenant Hampton checked Alec's soles and toes with a light touch. When he looked up, he let himself smile. He squeezed Alec's calf and said, "Back to the ball, Cinderella."

Hampton's touch, the sight of his hair and his smile, made Alec hard. His mind ran to nakedness and lips and the sweet friction of youthful stubble in tender places, lying side by side with Maurice, an arm about each other, tongues lightly touching, a leisurely wank by the brook, on a July afternoon at Millthorpe. But "Licky" wanted his way even here, in this land of wasted mud, where the trees themselves were unreal, props from the camouflage factory of Amiens; even now when his own body, once love's sweet vessel, disgusted him with lice and dirt. At night, the warmth rising to his face from under the blanket reminded him of coasting between slumber and waking in Maurice's arms—only briefly, though, because, always worn out, he'd soon sleep, in spite of gunfire and snoring. Hadn't he even slept once standing up? Yes, he was certain, when they stopped because of the pit in the road. On the night march that had brought them here, to journey's end. This would be Alec's first battle.

They heard the distant rumble and shriek. "Taranis bestrides the heavens," Llewellyn said.

"Whazzat?" Swavely said.

"Celtic thunder god."

They looked up at the bright sky of late June. Swavely said, "Not a storm cloud in sight, not even a cotton ball . . ." Then the shot exploded. "I'd say ol' Taranis was cuttin' a fart, not fuckin' treadin' the heavens."

Much later, after night had fallen, Alec, Llewellyn, and Swavely lay side by side under their laced-together groundsheets, sucking butterscotch candies that the corporal had tossed their way. Hundreds of other bundles lay likewise on the hillside with them. The meager light of the moon, waned to its palest quarter, could not have kept them awake; nonetheless, no one slept. Too many comings and goings, too much asking and guessing, too much fear. The guns insisted on fear. Heavy battery, howitzers, nine-inchers—no, nine-point-twos—out of sight beyond the ridge, blasted at intervals of minutes now, causing the earth to tremble under their tarps. But he, Jerry, kept the tempo slightly irregular so they could not prepare to hear the next round, always fired just seconds before they braced themselves or after they'd relaxed. The sound had three parts. First the thud of the firing: BOOM, basso profundo, its blowback so strong they imagined it knocked down the gunners themselves. Then the shell's traveling, in reality somewhat like water dripping into a metallic bucket, but to those who heard, it was the flight of a banshee on a vendetta, because it climaxed in disaster, the third part, the explosion that brought home the wallop. Any part of this threefold sound, heard anywhere only once, would have set infants wailing, dogs barking, horses a-panic, cows beshitting themselves. But tonight the guns delivered their doses of terror by the score, without end, a countdown to End-time. The men were camped beyond their reach. Fear was the guns' only mission tonight.

Side by side under their groundsheets, Alec, Llewellyn, and Swavely shook, like the earth, with each new round of fire. They said nothing of their terror. In the distance, from under the ridge, where by day they'd seen chalky striations of gouged earth and bramble masking barbed wire, nine tongues of flame now rose precisely in sync again and again. "Quite a show," Swavely said, as if he were watching the fireworks of a royal birthday over the Houses of Parliament with his girl by the Thames, not shuddering in fear of death near the banks of the Somme. But at last, because they were lying down, because they were weary, because they were close together and thus somehow protecting each other, one by one they slept.

21

Bivouacked together on the hillside, they slept through the short summer night, as did their thousand comrades destined to march into battle. The drivers, however, did not lie down; they spent the night walking beside their supply wagons (to lighten the loads on the final gradient); nor did the gunners, sweating over graph paper to map the counterbattery; nor the signalers, plotting their wires. At dawn, Swavely was summoned to headquarters, where they wanted him for another runner. His two mates tried to talk him out of taking his groundsheet with him, thus wrecking their makeshift shelter.

"You won't need it. Likely they're hoarding whole stashes at HQ," Llewellyn said to him. But Swavely insisted he must show up right and proper with all his equipment or lose the job and get jailed. His mates called him a mouse. They grudgingly unlaced their sheets.

Then a day of waiting. Alec and Llewellyn expected to be moved to the line, but instead there was tea and mess, and the usual cleaning of rifles (kept cleaner than they could keep themselves). They even found that rarest of hours to sit on the grass and talk, about their people at home, about the duration, about Welshmen and Cockneys, the virtues and vices of the French, about Lloyd George and Churchill, the poems of Rupert Brooke (who'd died on the way to Gallipoli, where, Alec had last heard, Maurice had been deployed). They talked about the stories of Stevenson that they'd read as boys; they planned how they might meet up in London, after. But while they spoke, each friend's eyes were drawn away from the other's face to the farther picture, where the road switched back tightly near the top of the hill and the mules, forelegs splayed for the incline, wobbled in fear under their loads. Or opposite, where puffs of smoke grew smaller and smaller, receding, signposting a withdrawal of German guns—or a ruse. And each wondered if his friend was as wretched as himself, nervous and crushed and wobbly as those mules on the road. But then it was time for god-awful tea again, and for mess, for the gentle and long summer sunset.

They watched the shadow of the hill of their encampment climb by grades up the opposite slope, where light still shone. In the distance, shrapnel burst and blazed and fizzled. Alec saw an owl take flight on her nocturnal hunt. Other cawing birds circled about. Some men had already settled down, even slept. Alec was anticipating another night of fear, but then the platoon commanders came, and sergeants, corporals, runners, all with one message: "All bivouacs come down." He and Llewellyn untied their groundsheets. Then each withdrew into himself, packed his own things, minded his own troubles, and made room for the two extra grenades they'd just been required to carry.

When the numerals on Alec's standard-issue wristwatch glowed 9:39, the great movement began: all four companies, fifty yards between platoons, with guns rolling on both sides of them down the hillside. How loud it was! A thousand men marching, plus the battery, the wagons, the animals—and over it all, the pounding of enemy cannonade. Alec didn't speak, no one did. If he'd wanted to say something to Llewellyn, who was marching beside him, he would have needed to yell into his ear.

The clear sky, at the cusp of evening transparence and night-time infinity, went suddenly flat. Rain soaked them, doubling the weight of clothing and gear. They were stalled, and no one could say where. They sat. Some tried to dig foxholes; others just lay down on the ground and risked the exposure. Hour by hour, the mortar fire grew more massive, oppressive, enervating. When the morning broke into full light, they were ordered to withdraw across open terrain. "He'll pick us off like quail flushed out of the bushes," Alec said to Llewellyn. But he did not attack.

So they advanced. They stepped into a world of his ingenuity, recently abandoned. When the rain stopped and the noon sun struck fully, the chalky walls of the German trenches sweated and stank. But the earthwork itself! Everything nicely finished, with regular electric lights and switches. And utensils and tools and widgets and gizmos left behind, all up-to-date, manufactured and stamped by his hands. Comfort, convenience, efficiency. Nothing like the scruffy lives the British Expeditionary Force had been living. The sergeant said, "Careful the place ain't booby-trapped. He'd do that, ya know, lure us down here and fuckin' blow us to blazes."

Llewellyn said to Alec, "Who's his god, do you think? A vengeful one who'll punish us for trespassing among the dwellings of the chosen race?"

Then they went deeper into the swath of land he'd withdrawn from: the hilltop village, ruined, its church and graveyard exploded, granite monuments toppled, shallow new graves hastily marked with white-painted slats of wood lettered in black.

The mules died, many at once. It was as if on reaching the line, their destination, the animals chose death rather than be forced to go farther. They dropped where they stood. When the men were unpacking their carcasses, some wept to see how the straps of their burdens had flayed the beasts' hides. The best they could do for them was to shove them to the side of the road.

Another night in bivouac. Alec asked Llewellyn, lying next to him, "What does it mean, 'D.E.R.'? Today, in the church-yard, the new graves, with just the wood crosses, I seen it writ upon several."

"I'd guess *Dona Eis Requiem.*"

"Ah, that must be it. 'Grant them peace . . .'"

"Yeah. Seeing that church today in the village, I thought about other churches just like it—before it was smithereened, I mean—in Bavaria, where mamas and aunties and sweethearts and sisters are praying their rosaries night and day on their knees, so holy Mary will turn our own weapons back against us and bring home safe their dear young Hans. They never let up, those women at prayer, pounding heaven with their novenas as regular as this fucking battery fire."

"We don't stand much chance against that, do we, now?"

"Who knows? Maybe God will send an angel to stop the slaughter."

"Whose god? His?"

"Anybody's will do. And the angel will say unto Commander Abraham, 'Put down thy knife, thou crazy old coot! Kill not thy son! Why would God want some lad's bloody corpse?'"

Next day in the afternoon rain, Alec saw from where he stood on a hill divisions of BEF infantry move forward to the assault.

That night, there was no bivouac at all. During the darkness, he and his comrades were guided into battle positions: by four in the morning, they were in place, spread wide in a single line across the slope. They reclined there till light should reveal him to them, and them, of course, to him. Despite the salvos of the big guns—throbbing, monstrous—Alec could hear the chatter of birds, waking above, busy with more important matters than war. Meanwhile, some of the men lay on the ground, seeming at peace; others tossed like prisoners on the eve of execution. All were silent, except Cohen, who lay to Alec's right, calling softly for Rachel, the bride he'd married on leave. Behind Alec's head, two senior officers met, exchanging hearty greetings and reminiscences about Mrs. Stewart-Ryder's Indian cooking. Then a salvo of guns. Someone screamed in panic. The officers shut their mouths and left separately.

Alec looked at his watch. Seven minutes to go. He wished he could turn off the pain in his gut. He'd emptied his bowels twice during the night. He hoped that was enough, that he wouldn't need to shit again when they moved forward, which would be shameful. He sat up. He held his head in his hands. Please would somebody shut off this dripping faucet of terror inside? His hearing had grown sharper in the darkness; he could hear voices within the artillery din, but could not make out the words. Sometimes his mind went to reverie, like to that day of the footrace at Brenford, and the joy of running freely as a colt, of music and dancing and food and kids in their paper wings zigzagging like dragonflies. Then the guns would insist that such a peaceable world had never been, that life was always a terror.

Now came the order to align with the next company lower down on the slope, still closer to where his machine-gun fire was blasting white powder from the chalky terrain. The men of this lower-down company were already covered with dust, like an army of ghosts so leprous that even their clothes were diseased. When Alec stood to advance, he found his limbs had suddenly grown heavy. And his rifle—why did it weigh five times more now? How would he be able to shoot it?

The corporal shouted into his ear: "Two minutes to go." Two minutes left to run away. Too late to run now, the screw of fear had been overtightened, the gauge itself burst. Rays of the rising sun struck the top of a thousand saucer-shaped helmets. In the brightening light, his aim grew sharper. Alec saw the first hit: Williams's messtin was stung by a fierce metal wasp that burrowed and drove through the tunic into his skin. Yet he hardly paused, keeping his face down and helmet correctly angled. Had Alec not seen the strike, he would not have guessed it. Not so with Hammersmith. Shot in the leg, he jumped, yelled he was dead, and fell down, relieved, to wait for the bearers. All the while the guns drummed louder, faster, sounding the coming apocalypse: "Divisional synchronization," the corporal called. Zero hour.

Alec marched face down, helmet tipped against the enemy, in line with the others, rifle in the high-port position, diagonally across the chest. The sunlight played tricks with the gun smoke: sometimes the cloud was dense, hiding the way forward, sometimes translucent, like morning mist. He felt he was walking above the world, not on solid ground. Then he glanced right and left and saw no one. He panicked. Had he strayed from his section? Lieutenant Hampton, as if sensing Alec's terror, called softly a few yards away, "I'm here, Scudder." In reply, five shots savaged the air. Hampton sank down first on one knee, then the other before he fell. The firing betrayed the gunner's place among the trees. Alec threw himself on the ground and fired ten shots back. No more from the gunner. He crawled to Hampton. The buckle of the young officer's helmet strap was caught under his chin, and the top was jammed over his face, blocking whatever last breath he might have tried to draw. Alec loosened the strap and removed the helmet. As he did so, that silky hair spilled downward. He was about to smooth it back when a corporal materialized from the mist. "Leave him for the bearers," he ordered. "No time for a funeral. Advance now, at the double." Alec obeyed.

Jerry had hidden barbed wire along the ridges, woven it through the bushes. Alec got caught at the knees. He feared a bayonet blade in his back while he tried to get free. Instead he heard Carlisle shouting the prescribed curses as he stomped down and cut away the wire. Then a single file of a half dozen German prisoners marched toward them, their arms held Y-style over their heads. Alec noticed a very young one, his greatcoat as smartly belted as any toy soldier's, his correct martial bearing at odds with his face's exhaustion and despair. Alec thought he had never seen a salute so gallant as the one that this boy presented to his captors' officer.

By noon the dead were being laid out in rows, officers side by side with the other ranks. ("When the game's done," Llewellyn had said, "pawn and king both get tossed into the one box.") Father Phelan was talking to the corpses and tracing crosses with his thumb on their foreheads. Among the living casualties, the bearers first carried off those whose viscera were ripped open. They would be overdosed with morphine.

Smoke and sunlight streaming together through the leaves were confusing Alec's eye now, no telling tree trunks from shadows. That was why he first doubted what he saw there in the glade: a man, no longer a man, a dead body, a thing, who'd been caught in the hidden barbed wire, like a ram he'd once seen tangled in thorny brambles in Dorset, so that the bleating animal would shred its own flesh when it struggled to get free. Half the soldier's uniform was torn away by the barbs; his right leg was naked; his sex, small and boyish, bared. Unlike Alec, he'd not been freed from the snare of barbed wire: instead a bayonet had pierced him in the middle and then the blade had been ripped up through his gut as far as his heart, exposed now, framed by rags and bones. No angel had stopped the knife. Alec heard the clink of a tripod behind him. He found his last grenade, pulled the pin, and lobbed it with a cricketer's skill just when the machine gun started to fire. The grenade exploded even as the bullet struck him.

Then the noise of the guns became drumming, a music not fearsome but dancelike, and the wind in the leaves, women's voices heralding. From where he lay, Alec saw her enter the clearing: Brigantia, queen of the woods, robed in streaming-down sunlight, veiled in diaphanous smoke. She cradled Llewellyn's torn body, claiming him, dead, for her own. She graced his head with a circle of flowers and ivy, the way the child had crowned Alec once in Dorset on a midsummer night.

VI

A SENSE OF PRESENCE

22

"Put it down on paper," Sister said to the group of them. "Don't worry about grammar or commas or spelling—least of all, penmanship. It's a chance to get it out; it's hiding there, festering. Like all evil things, it fears the light of day. Write for your own sakes, not mine. You need never show anyone. But if you should ask me to read it, I shall, or to keep it for you unread, I shall, or, if you like, even burn it."

How old might she be? Thirty? Hardly older than her patients. Kind and wise. War accelerates aging. At twenty-two, he was already an old-timer in the ranks. Was he any wiser . . . ? She was so very thin, careworn, and amazingly clean. How did she do it? Those white cuffs and that elaborate kerchief—what did you call the thing? Something medieval . . . Llewellyn would have known the word. *Wimple!* And always that fresh smell about her, of soap and starch. How did she stay so crisp in this knackery of wounds and seeping stumps, of coughing and spitting up? Brooms, mops, hot water, soapsuds, day and night wielded by angels of hygiene battling the demons of grime. "Your worst memory," she said, "the worst sight you saw. It's only a thought now, it can't harm you anymore. Write it down and cast it off."

Mental hygiene! Ah-HA! Expose the sick memory and scrub it away. But now why (given all the human wretchedness he'd witnessed), why did he first think of animals? A horse made to drag the carcass of another horse into a ditch.

(Had the two once pulled one wagon together?) Or then think not of battle, but here, just outside, yesterday, the legless master sergeant in his wheelchair. He was smiling for a camera. Why? What girl would ever have him to bed? How long would the man live, and always on charity? Or in Kensington Gardens, the model "trenches." Or Trafalgar Square, the "ruined village," bombed and burned. Stage sets so civilians might get a clean look at the war and toss money into the empty artillery barrels to keep it going . . .

Alec wrote nothing. He closed his eyes. She approached. "Try not to dwell on it," she said quietly to him. "It's better to write it out quickly."

"I'm all right, Sister," he said. When he shifted in his chair, a sudden sharp pain made him squeeze his eyes shut, pressing hot tears out from under the lids. It would pass, it would pass; don't hold your breath, that prolonged it . . .

The bullet had not been a dumdum, like those the Austrians were using against the Serbs. Those shattered on impact, blasted shrapnel inside you; that meant cutting off the stricken limb—or death if it hit the torso. Alec's bullet had been conventional. It pierced his side under the arm. Two ribs had cracked with the force but stopped the bullet just short of his lung, which, though not penetrated, had collapsed from the pressure of the air entering his chest through the hole in the skin. Good bullet! Did its job, its only job—i.e., to kill or to maim and thereby remove a pawn from the board. He heard someone say that about a third of those with a collapsed lung die of it. Odds working in his favor, he survived. Still he wondered: If one simple slug cost him so many hours of agony, and the medics and nurses so much labor, what was the price of those millions of rounds fired at the Somme in one day? What price was the other fellow paying, the one he'd shot, who'd killed Lieutenant Hampton? He wrote nothing.

The Scudders came to visit in the afternoon, as they'd been doing regularly. Their visits were easier now. Weeks ago, at first sight of their wounded son, Elwood held stoic, but Aderyn could not contain her anguish.

"Please, Ma, you're makin' it worse," Alec said, "like you need this bed more than I do."

She wept. "Don't you know how gladly I'd lie there in your stead if the Lord God might take your pain and give it to me?"

With time, she'd come around; she'd even found a way to make Alec chuckle, along with others within earshot, by threatening to go to the trenches herself and teach those brutes not to attack such fine boys. Today she was bubbling with good news: Jane had given birth to their first grandchild. "Six pounds twelve! A big healthy baby! They're christening her Rita because it's the same in Spanish and will go easy in school. Lovely, isn't it, Rita? Jane's mother says she's going soon as she can and stay six months. 'However will you get to the Argentine with this hateful war?' I asked her. She says, 'I'll row my own boat if I have to.'"

Alec smiled, though the news saddened him, he couldn't say why. Maybe because he felt no part of a world where couples had children and grandparents doted?

"Folks ask for you often," Elwood said, as they were about to go.

"Do they, Da?"

"Yes, son, they care about you."

As they were departing, the Scudders passed an elegant woman by the doors who seemed out of place in this ward for other ranks. She waited till the villagers were gone. Then she went to their son's bedside, attracting the attention, as she always did when she visited him, of patients and staff.

"Sweet Alexander," the baroness said, smoothing his hair, kissing both cheeks, then dabbing away the red smudges. "Sorry . . ."

"Might as well leave it, the way you set tongues awaggin'. They're all wantin' to know, 'Oo's she?' When I tell them the truth, my former employer, there's such winkin' and hootin': 'Send milady's footman young Scudder to attend her bath.'"

She laughed. "I've heard so much worse. Now tell me, are you feeling better at all?"

"Yeah, I think so. The throbbin's calmed down. That means I'm on the mend."

"Good."

"Don't suppose there's any news—?"

She sighed. "I do wish there were . . ."

"Thought not. You'd have said right away . . ."

Indeed, she would have. For nearly two years now, this lady's friendship had been crucial to the love of Alec and Maurice. It was impossible for them to write each other: correspondence between officers and other ranks was suspect, forbidden by custom if not rule. Of course they couldn't communicate through their families. Teddy and George had offered to receive letters from one and pass the news on to the other in some coded way, but that scheme got ruled out because the older men were being watched for their public opposition to the war. The baroness stepped in. Aware of the censors, Private Scudder wrote to "Mrs. Wentworth," housekeeper, care of her employer's house on Bedford Square, with updates on his health and army life and always a message of love to "Mary." Second Lieutenant Hall wrote to the same house, but to its owner, Mme la Baronne du Thoronet, with assurances of his

good health and tender words for "Alice." The lady responded
to each with news and affection from the other. At first it had
almost been fun, when the lovers were writing frequently about
training and longing for Mary or Alice. But after deployment,
the notes got radically shortened. She could sense her young
friends' fear in the way they'd try to sound lighthearted.
Sometimes, when there was hardly any news to send, she'd
been tempted to make things up for the sake of their morale,
but she did not. Instead she managed for these nearly two
years to convey to each that the other was alive and devoted.

Because of the censorship, information about whereabouts
was always sketchy, hardly more than Alec's being at the
Western Front and Maurice in the Mediterranean. Then the
handwritten notes stopped, and she'd receive only those pre-
printed field service postcards, maddeningly vague and eva-
sive, headed with this message:

> NOTHING is to be written on this side except the
> date and signature of the sender. Sentences not re-
> quired may be erased. If anything else is added the
> postcard will be destroyed.

In July, "Mrs. Wentworth" had received one such card from
Paris with checkmarks next to three phrases, **I have been ad-
mitted into hospital**, and **Wounded**, and **Hope to be discharged soon**. Others crossed out. So she'd learned of Alec's
injury. As for Maurice, there'd been no word for months.

"I search the lists every day," she said. "We must believe it's
a good sign, Alec, really. Let's trust that he's well and things
just aren't getting through."

"They're still countin' the dead from Gallipoli," Alec said,
then choked up. She held him while he sobbed.

Someone approached and called out, "Licky!"

Alec sniffled and said, "Ma—?"

Aderyn rushed to the bed. "What's wrong? Where's the nurse?"

"I believe he's all right, Mrs. Scudder," said the baroness. "Just having a sad recollection . . ."

"Is that so?" said Aderyn, shocked and suspicious.

"Ma, the lady's—"

"Cornelia Wentworth," the lady interjected.

The mother fixed her eyes on her, who felt obliged to speak: "Your son worked for us in Dorset a few years ago . . ." She garnished the facts to spare Alec the need to explain: "I came here today for a governors' meeting. I recognized his name on the patients' list and thought I should greet Private Scudder. How proud you must be—"

"Of course we are. Didn't we see you earlier, waiting?"

"I didn't like to intrude. You were enjoying a family visit."

"Most thoughtful of you."

"Ma, I'm fine. Just a bad recollection, like Mrs. Wentworth was sayin'."

"What could so trouble you?"

"It's nothin'."

"Tell me!"

"Why drag it up?"

"I knew it. I *knew* you were keeping things from us. Didn't I say as much to your father?"

"What brought you back? You're gone but twenty minutes."

"My glove—there 'tis—from my good Sunday pair. And don't the Lord work in mysterious ways? As if he were calling me here to find you in such a state." She turned to the lady. "A mother always senses. Thank you for your solicitude. I'll stay with him now."

"But where's Da?"

"Where I left him, I suppose, at the tram platform."

"He'll be worried—"

"Then let him come find me."

"'Don't dwell on it,' she says. What's it matter if I dwell or not? They're only fixin' me up to send me back for more."

"Might you please tug the sheet on your side?"

Alec did so, awkwardly, from his chair; on her side of the bed, the nurse snapped the hem taut, made a triangular fold, and tucked it under the mattress for a sharp corner. She was his favorite: from the Voluntary Aid Detachment, like many who worked here at Slough. He liked her round-rimmed glasses, the way they magnified her greenish eyes, the short cheeky cut of her very dark hair. Of her haircut she said, "Good riddance to Victorian froufrou! You men can't conceive the upkeep. Hours of washing and drying and combing, and then twenty minutes at least, never less, to pin it in place—each time! My week's gained an entire day since I snipped off the tresses, though my aunt still groans at the sight." She laughed: "And of course that's another advantage."

He wished he might know her name, but it was forbidden. But he noticed that the professional medics treated her more respectfully than they did the other VADs, who, being women of middle or upper class, were unused to menial work and seemed offended when given orders. She came from privilege, that was clear, but she betrayed neither disgust nor resentment at what she was told to do. "There," she said, satisfied with the clean bed. She stuffed the used sheets into the pillowcase and tossed the bundle into the laundry cart. "Ready to climb back in?"

"Might I walk a bit instead? A turn round the ward? Have you time?"

She consulted the watch fastened to her apron bodice, the one with the upside-down face. "Five minutes and a half. Shall we ambulate?"

"If that's what you've got to call it."

She offered to help him up from the chair. He declined, gripped its arm with his one hand, and pushed himself up to standing.

"Excellent!" she said. "You'll see, in a week you'll be steady again." She extended her arm to him, making a fist to keep it level and strong.

Alec accepted her support. He said, "Steady and ready and right back to hell." She made no response. "Sorry . . . I know you're not allowed to say things against the war."

"Well, you can't know for certain they'll send you back."

"I know they're desperate. This latest conscription's only the start. Already kids and granddads servin' side by side, people they'd never have took two years ago, each bunch shorter by four inches and thinner by two stone than the last. There's no end in sight. You'll see, next they'll be draftin' alley cats. Meow, meow, sir."

She chuckled.

"Glad you find me funny."

"Well, you are. I've got a year almost till I'm twenty-three, and so of course I hope it will all be over by then, but if it's still on, with my training, they'll take me to serve abroad, closer to battle—back in hell, as you say."

Alec stopped their progress. "Why would you go? You've no idea, this hospital's a garden in springtime to what's waitin' for you over there."

"That's why. I can't abide it that you, all of these fellows, suffer horribly while most of us go on about our lives. On the street I see girls old enough to know better trying to pin chicken feathers on any man not in uniform. The nasty twits, I hate them! Why don't they go to battle themselves? I'm sure I sound naïve to you, ridiculous."

"No. You sound like a very good-hearted person."

She tried to lighten his mood: "And you sound like a kindly gray-bearded gent, when you're a boy no older than I. You ask why I'd want to serve. Why did *you* enlist? A gallant gesture to dazzle someone special?" They'd reached the foot of his bed. Alec did not answer. When she saw how sad he'd grown, she said, "Oh . . . I'm so very sorry. Pay me no mind. Really, I could just *kick* myself!"

23

Today the river looked like sludge, brown, dismal, scabbed with oil and tar, like bilge in the trenches, rat-slime. But in Flanders or France, you could raise your eyes from the ditch and in those few feet of open space see such a brilliant blue sky—*The splendorous firmament!* Llewellyn might say . . . No splendor in London today, only flat gray cloud cover. City, city. London Bridge definitely not falling down.

Private D. Alexander Scudder had been released from the hospital in the third week of August 1916 and ordered back to combat. In light of his extraordinary service (i.e., getting shot, not killed), he'd been granted a week's extended leave. He'd spent most of those days with his parents in Osmington, where all his old friends were long gone, boys to battle, girls to jobs making weapons. Just Alec and the elders in the village, along with the kids too young to fight or work in munitions factories. At first it felt good to be like a kid again himself, Ma and Da keeping him snug and fed. But he soon got fidgety. His mood made no sense: he both dreaded returning to the front and longed to be nowhere else. He'd pass the time walking aimlessly, once even as far as Lulworth Cove, to the sight of the Durdle Door, that stone archway over the water. Weird work of nature, awesome, even sublime. The sight caused him to realize that he was truly alone for the first time since enlisting, therefore truly himself, not playing a role for family or comrades or visitors in the hospital. (Only with Maurice could he be with another and still truly himself.) The sunlight struck the sea at such an angle that it seemed to pour through the Door, as if laying a path on the water to wherever Maurice might be.

Or might not be. If he learned Maurice was dead, Alec decided he would die as well. He immediately laughed at his own bombast, silly as the Mildreds pledging to throw themselves into the ocean after his ship. Or maybe not. Where he was going, wasn't it easier to die than live? Wasn't death the purpose of the soldier's life? His own death, or somebody else's? Somebody else who was also a lover, brother, son, father . . . Oh, why the fuck even be born?

He'd set aside the two last days of his leave for visits to London and Paris. Of course, he hadn't told the parents that he would be seeing "Mrs. Wentworth" in town. Aderyn had formed an opinion of the lady after one meeting: "Going painted and perfumed among our poor suffering boys." So now he found himself skulking around the city once more in his clandestine other life. No "illicit" sex involved this time, just supper at the lady's house on Bedford Square, where he would spend the night as her guest before returning to France tomorrow. Then tomorrow to Paris for a day and a night with Swavely, also on leave, then the two of them back to the front.

He wasn't looking forward to the evening's socializing. At Maurice's side, he'd gotten along in that crowd as half of a young couple deemed fashionable. But on his own? He guessed he'd be all right. Anyway, he couldn't refuse the lady's invitation; she'd been so kind.

He thought of how silently his father had embraced him before he boarded the train in the village, how forlorn Aderyn had looked. She turned away from the train; Da waved till he was out of sight. Should he have stayed another day

with them? He tried to put it out of his mind. There was no
winning in this upside-down time when the old were burying
their young.

At the blue hour, with evening descending on the city, Alec
found himself back in Bloomsbury. The cloud cover had
broken: the mugginess escaped, drier air breezed in, and he
could see the sunset sky. He'd taken a little detour on his way
to the baroness's. He knew that walking on Bernard Street
would make him sad, but he couldn't help himself. He paused
before the building where he and Maurice had lived for ten
months, third floor rear. What a time that had been: all day
in the stockrooms at Harrods, he'd be eager for their nights
together—reading to each other, or screwball political argu-
ments, always food and laughing and sex and hours of rest in
each other's arms in perfect trust. How often had they walked
down this street side by side?

   An uncanny feeling stopped him in his steps, of someone
close behind him. He gasped and turned his head and started
to say, "Maurice," but there was no one. He paused till his
heart stopped racing, then walked on.

24

About to enter the salon, Alec heard the piano and the singing:

> *Everybody loves a baby, that's why I'm in love with you,*
> *Pretty baby, pretty baby . . .*

He hesitated. He knew the tune and the words. Everyone did. But could he make himself sing along?

> *And I'd like to be your sister, brother, dad and mother too,*
> *Pretty baby, pretty baby . . .*

The room was dazzling. Seven-branched candelabras burned on stands before tall mirrors. Knots of people were talking, laughing, drinking, among them several men in uniform: staff officers all. One of them noticed the arrival of a member of the other ranks. Unsure of what to do, Alec saluted sloppily; the gesture was acknowledged with a raised eyebrow and a nod. Those around the piano kept singing:

> *Won't you come and let me rock you in my cradle of love?*
> *And we'll cuddle all the time . . .*

He found himself mouthing the words near the end of the chorus:

Oh I want a lovin' baby and it might as well be you,
Pretty baby of mine . . .

His hostess approached. "Welcome, darling. Let's find you a drink." She took his hand and led him to a credenza, where she poured whiskey into a faceted tumbler; it scintillated when she gave it to him, like her jewels, like the room. "There. Knock it back, have another, and then the noise won't seem so dreadful. I'm just loitering in the quiet corner." She steered him around islands of guests and furniture to a table where a plump older woman in a fringed shawl seemed to be playing Patience. Others were paying rapt attention. No, she wasn't playing cards but reading them, a Tarot pack. She sneezed.

"*Santé*," someone said.

"*Merci*," the lady answered. She dabbed her nose. "I do not find the Hanged Man."

"Well, that sounds lucky," said the subject of the reading, with a nervous titter.

"Oh, he's not a bad card. He chooses the higher good over his own pleasure . . ." She sorted through the deck till she found and revealed him. "See? *Le Pendu*, he hangs not by the neck but by his right ankle, quite daintily, like an acrobat. His red tights signify pleasure, but his blue jacket, closer to his heart, wisdom."

She turned to her hostess. "I'm afraid I'm not feeling well at all, Cornelia, dear. I do regret I can't stay for supper. I should have stopped at home." She stifled another sneeze. "Might someone please hail me a cab?" She gathered her cards. When she got up, she saw Alec standing near her chair. She said to him, "This face inspires strong passions—love, envy . . ."

"Believe me, ma'am, there's nothin' to envy."

"Some might think otherwise. Do beware them." Then, "May I meet your companion?"

"Ma'am?"

"The one who was with you when you came in. Whenever I looked up, I saw someone beside you . . ."

"I'm by myself tonight."

"But surely—" About to contradict him, she glanced around the room, then closed her eyes for a moment. She opened her eyes and shook her head: "This cold, such a nuisance in the summer, I should go right to bed." Other guests closed around her, recommending a hot toddy and rest, and she was gone before Alec could ask about the one she said she had seen.

After supper, the baroness introduced a soprano from Prague, who would sing a piece from an opera not yet staged in London. The pianist quieted the room with an introduction that suggested the plucking and glissandi of a harp. And then the perfect sound of the singer's voice. Its strength and beauty gave him chills. He couldn't understand the words, but did understand the emotion: her whole being vibrated with passion, womanhood, loveliness, and with a longing akin to grief. To Alec, it seemed she was singing about the war. As if for every death on the battlefield, she mourned the death of love itself. She wanted life, life for the young soldiers, for herself, and for all women whose love the war would kill. She ended on a high phrase that blossomed as she sustained it, then floated into the room's deepened silence. He realized he had been holding his breath to listen.

Later, after most others had departed, Alec and the baroness sat together on a couch by the unlit fireplace. The young

woman at the piano played "Clair de Lune." Risley stood by
her and recited:

> *And your eyes have caught the light*
> *Of a moon-enchanted dream . . .*

He looked over to the pair on the couch and winked.

> *And your arms glide round about me,*
> *And I fade into a dream.*

He stepped away from the piano to join his friends. "Sy-
mons's translation of Verlaine, who was likely writing about
that exasperating boy, Rimbaud." Dissonant chords crashed
at the piano, sudden and loud. Eyes widened; heads turned.
Risley called out, "Good God, Doris, what's that?"

"Stravinsky. *Le Sacre du printemps.* I got hold of the re-
hearsal score for the ballet. Isn't it marvelous? Like I'm
pounding drums on the keys—"

"No wonder it caused a riot in Paris!"

"A sign of things to come." She struck a final chord. She
swung around on the bench. "Cornelia, thanks a million for
a wonderful evening, really. We all needed a break from the
endless doomsday of this war." The men stood as she crossed
to the couch. "Good night, Tavy, darling." She turned to Alec
and took both his hands in her own. "Dear, lovely Private
Scudder, please, please come back to us safely," she said with
deep sincerity. When she started to wipe away a tear with her
hand, she realized she was still holding Alec's. She laughed at
herself: "Forgive me, I'm a mess." She squeezed his hands in
farewell. The women left the room together.

"Well, laddie," Risley said, decanter in hand, "had enough of this devilish poison?"

Alec extended his glass for a refill.

"That's the spirit." Risley poured for them both. "Drink up. Cheers. Better, I'm sure, than what they're serving at the front."

"Cheers."

"Scudder, I do wish . . . I wish none of this were happening. I, I—oh, never mind, what's to say?" He sighed.

They sipped their whiskey in silence. Alec asked, "Any news of Morgan?"

"No, and I don't know why. He'd been writing regularly, then nothing. We do know he's alive, at least—and not injured. His mother receives one of those damned postcards with the checkmarks once a month from Alexandria, but his signature's forged. She's prostrate with worry, poor old thing; I'm baffled." He took a lumpy parcel from a table. "Here, this is for you."

". . . ?"

"Something to make you laugh, I promise."

Alec unwrapped it and found a drab muffler the color of his uniform, misshapen and homemade. "What's this?"

Risley looked up at the ceiling.

"Did you—?"

"Yes. Granny has taken up knitting woolens for her troops." Their laughter started as a chuckle and got louder. "George taught me how to knit—"

"Aunt Georgie—!"

"Now I'm cranking these things out by the dozen! You should see the socks!"

Alec and his hostess lingered together in the quiet after Risley had gone home. At last she said, "You know your room?"

He nodded. "Took my bag up earlier. But if you don't mind, I'll sit up a bit yet."

"Of course. Just let me—" She struck a match and lit the kindling in the hearth. "This house can be damp at night, even in summer." She watched the tinder start to blaze.

Alec sensed her reluctance to leave him alone. He said, "Your friend who sang—that was beautiful."

"I'll tell her you said so. She was in good voice tonight."

"It seemed to me about the war."

"Ah, but I heard it before the war—in Vienna. The story's a fairy tale, in Czech; *Rusalka*, it's called. She's a water sprite in love with a mortal boy. She's praying to the moon in that song, who sees everything, to watch over him and make him think of her and bring him back. So, yes, it could be about the war . . ." She stared into the flames. The flickering highlighted and shadowed her face.

"Baroness?"

"Yes, dear?"

"The fortune-teller, who was she?"

The question made the lady smile. "I'm sure her devotees would prefer you call her a *clairvoyante*. A famous one, at that." She watched the logs catch fire. "Mardash is her name. Armenian, I believe."

". . . She said somethin' to me I can't get out of my head."

"Oh?"

"She said she saw somebody beside me when I came into the room tonight; she said whenever she looked up she saw someone beside me, but when she was talkin' to me, the one she saw was gone."

The lady, still gazing at the fire, said, "The room was crowded."

"Earlier, though, before I came to your house, I'd walked down Bernard Street where me and Maurice used to live, and I felt someone near me. I'm tellin' you I could *feel* someone there close behind me, the way you can feel somebody next to you. I even turned round to look. But there was nobody. Have you ever heard of such a thing?"

Still focused on the fire, she paused, then said, "I have."

"Truly?"

"Yes. It's called a sense of presence."

"Sense of—?"

"Presence." She turned to face him now. "Alec, there's something I wish to tell you."

"Ma'am?"

"I knew Maurice's father," she said.

"You did?"

"Years ago, twenty, more—shortly after I married Wentworth. He was a guest at our dreadful business dinners. I had always struggled to hold up among Wentworth's friends, even more among their wives, but with Maurice Hall, the father, I found it easy to talk. At first I thought perhaps because he'd always come to these occasions on his own. His wife had recently given birth and didn't like to be away from the nursery at night. But it was more. There was a kind of playfulness in our conversation, you see, a relief in each other, as if we were both outsiders in a foreign city.

"Alec, listen, the father was like his son, and like you."

Alec blinked. "What's that? You don't mean—?"

"Yes."

"But no—he had kids—"

She said nothing.

"Oh . . ."

She continued, "I was planning to tell Maurice in due time, privately of course. But the war took you both away from us so abruptly—I hadn't the chance. And now . . . it's nothing I can write to him, not with censors reading every word, and besides, it's better said face-to-face."

"For certain . . ."

"By right the knowledge belongs to Maurice. That's why I hesitated to tell you. I have every confidence that he'd tell you himself, but it's not for me to presume. Now, though, if I ever doubted that the two of you are united always, the doubt's gone." Again they fell silent watching the fire.

Then Alec said, "Why do you tell me just now? Do he think he's dead?"

"No—"

"Do you think that fortune-teller sees the dead? That she saw his ghost with me tonight—'present'?"

"Alec, stop, please. I believe Maurice is alive, as I believe that you'll come home safely from the war—to those who love you, to Maurice above all." She sat beside him on the couch and continued, "But no one can *know*, certainly not Madame Mardash and her pack of cards.

"Please listen to me: the father died for lack of what the son possesses—what Maurice possesses in you, what you two have together. Yes, it sounds far-fetched, but honestly, I mean it. The man didn't kill himself, I'm certainly not saying that, but anxiety may have brought him down, and loneliness. He'd been made to believe he was corrupt and evil. If he'd been less fine a person, perhaps he'd have been able to live with such judgment, but instead his pain worsened over time. He feared he might lose everything—through some misstep or betrayal—that he'd disgrace himself, that his wife and children would come to hate him.

"One day, at the top of a flight of steps he'd climbed too quickly, he fell. They said it was heart and brain at once, a spasm and a seizure. He survived a couple of days. He was forty-five. The first time I saw young Maurice was at the funeral, a little boy in mourning clothes. For the father's sake especially, I cherish my friendship with you two."

After she went upstairs, Alec kept vigil alone before the fireplace, pondering the story of Maurice's father and the tender image of his beloved as a grieving child. He watched till the flames burned down. He gazed at the moon through the window. The singer had asked the moon to guard her love, to make him think of her, to bring him to her. Her longing, like his, was too deep for words; only music could give it voice. He had no music of his own, so her song comforted him.

At last, too sleepy either to stay awake or to go to bed, he dozed on the couch till dawn when he trudged upstairs to his room.

VII

ELEVENTH DAY, MONTH, HOUR

25

Paris had determined to be gay. It wasn't quite false gaiety. Rather more of a duty? Yes, that was it, the citizens' duty to carry on blithely in defiance of the war. Musicians played in the streets; children in the parks. Painters painted in the open air. Elders browsed for books and pictures in the stalls along the Seine and stopped to argue the day's news with much gesticulation. Young women, filling in for men as trolley drivers, metro workers, mail-porters, wore their service caps with the panache of the latest millinery and managed to tuck and pin their drab uniforms fetchingly. Meanwhile, shopwindows featured frocks "in the Egyptian style," which somehow related the wearer to the battles of the Mediterranean and therefore expressed her patriotism. *Oo–la–la.* As civic virtues go, Alec found gaiety far more appealing than, say, piety. Today he'd been grateful for the city's hubbub, squeeze-boxes and mandolins and kids yelling back and forth.

He and Swavely, two Tommies, were now standing in a room of suffocating opulence, agape at a pair of strange objects enshrined there. One was a bronze bathtub in the form of a fantastic beast. It had a woman's head, the hindquarters of a lioness, and wings along the sides. It was attached to no plumbing because it was meant to be filled by hand, with Champagne. The other was an odd kind of chair, upholstered in brocade and designed to allow a man comfortable access to the private parts of two women at once. The young soldiers were trying to figure out how the thing might function in terms of anatomy. Did he—? And she—? And then the other girl—? The room was dedicated to the memory of Edward VII; the arcane objects had been made for him.

"No wonder they loved the old king here in Paris," Alec said. "Sure he donated half the Exchequer to this place alone."

"Our fuckin' taxes at work, the ruttin' warthog," Swavely muttered.

The Parisians carried on with life as if victory were certain. Hadn't they already beaten back the invaders? Yes, two years ago, when the Germans had advanced to within twenty miles of the towers of Notre-Dame herself! The citizens readied for a siege: they removed masterpieces from the Louvre and sent the government out of town; they stockpiled foodstuffs, even herded cattle in the parks. They reduced the population by offering free train tickets to outlying suburbs. Then the taxi drivers were called to shuttle troops from the squares to the front. And so they did, in their shiny Renaults and Peugeots, five soldiers at a time in each cab, six thousand men in a matter of hours. General Gallieni had even instructed the drivers to keep their meters running and paid them all for their transport service, market rate. Thus the City of Light had dispatched her defenders and drove back the Hun. When Paris deemed the enemy once again at safe remove, she rehung her paintings and brought home her regime. But that was two years ago, and still the war kept on. Nowadays, gaiety required determination.

Swavely had arrived the night before Alec. He boasted that he'd wasted no time at all. He'd found his way around, made connections, and so learned about the hospitality of certain brothels (the swank ones) that opened their doors, usually barred to common soldiers, to them on special nights once or twice a month (provided the doorman approved your looks). The doorman gave the nod to Alec, who pulled Swavely in behind him. Thus the two had gained entrance to the Chabanais, the celebrated high-class whorehouse lately and extravagantly patronized by King Edward the Peacemaker, rest his soul.

Their admission, gratis, although offered as a gesture of goodwill, was also very good for business, and the proprietress knew it. The trim figures of young warriors in uniform brightened her stage picture. (Sailors in whites were for that reason most warmly welcomed.) Alec and Swavely soon discerned that not all the women in the crowd were employed there. Some were tourists with their naughty beaux, but many were clients themselves, out to enjoy the night. They found the show of virility stimulating—otherwise deprived, as they were, of the sight of healthy young men by the war. And while it was understood that the ladies would not need to pay a tariff to the management for any pleasures incidentally provided by the visiting men-at-arms, it was likewise understood that they would treat the boys to drinks and, should a tryst result, pay to rent one of the rooms available on the premises.

There were other female clients who did not seek the company of men, but of one another and of certain demoiselles of the Chabanais. The proprietress catered to them likewise. And of course many of her patrons were men who sought men, whom she also served with tact. She could rely on this special category of customers to turn out in large numbers on her open military nights. She prided herself on attention to details: her ability, for example, to call upon those few youths in the city—no more than could be counted on the jeweled fingers of her hands—who would agree to be photographed in certain ways together, suggestively but tastefully. (Cabinet cards were for sale at her desk.) In addition, she knew a larger group of fellows willing to perform in shows and to make themselves available to customers, with a percentage of their fees going to the house.

For his part, Swavely had been assured by "reliable sources" that Frenchwomen found an English uniform irresistible. Should one—or two!—of these Parisian *femmes* take a shine to him, he'd give them such a time. Wishing to minimize his competition, he suggested that he and Alec separate. They agreed to rendezvous after midnight in the foyer; if one of them should fail to appear, that meant he was amorously occupied. Alec, without disclosing why, was also glad to split up. Before going off on his own, he watched Swavely stake out a spot across from the open doorway to a dining room where he could observe groups of clients of both sexes being served at little tables by waitresses wearing only high-heeled shoes and stockings and black ribbons around their necks. Swavely, bug-eyed at the naked girls, tried to appear bored. He smoked his cigarette carelessly, even scornfully, hoping a show of insouciance would prove seductive.

Alec wandered the corridors. His pal's enthusiasm had sufficed to bring him here tonight, but he'd no expectations for himself. He thought he might view the scene for an hour or so, then go back to their grubby hotel to wait for stories of Swavely's adventures. Meantime, other prowlers often caught his eye along the corridors and stairways—women made themselves smile, men tried to appear stern and stalwart. As the night grew later and the crowd drunker, the lust turned more overt and the come-hithers more explicit. The scene was becoming grotesque, like the drawings in the program of the Golden Calf, where brutality and madness mixed together with the city's high life. He'd heard that part of the front was only seventy miles from London's nightclubs. How much closer must it be to Paris? Tonight at the Chabanais everybody wanted to dance and drink and kiss and fuck, the war's desperation driving the frenzy.

At last he found his way to where his kind belonged, a dark hallway on an upper floor with doors left ajar to invite watching or joining in. Through one he saw an old fellow—an aristocrat, to judge by the top hat on the floor—begging a thug to thrash him harder. Alec shuddered. From another room he heard a honky-tonk piano playing *Scheherazade.* A pantomime was in progress there, more to his taste. He joined about a dozen others watching two "Moroccan" lads, dressed in the mode of *Arabian Nights,* acting out an amorous scene with overblown gestures of desire and hesitation, which led, of course, to canoodling and the removal of their sheer Persian trousers. Then a strapping fellow, turbaned, with an earring, entered the scene. He menaced the lovers with his stage scimitar. At first it seemed he wanted to punish them for their unspeakable transgression against natural law, and so the audience booed, but soon it became clear that he wanted to transgress himself, and the booing turned to cheering. He coerced one of the lads to embrace him. He was so rapt with the pleasure of holding the comely youth in his arms that the other was able to seize the scimitar and turn the tables. In order to punish Mr. Turban, they prepared to rob him. They made him undress. He shyly stripped to the tune of a snake dance on the piano and, to no one's surprise, revealed a heavenly physique, shaved and glistening. When the only bit of clothing left on him was a tiny sex pouch bursting with its contents, the lads peeked inside. Pleased with what they saw, the lovers forgave their assailant, tossed away the sword, and made a merry threesome.

Silly as it was, the show had taken hold of Alec, seizing his mind by way of his cock and accomplishing its commercial objective. He wanted what he saw; he might even pay for it. Suddenly a man embraced him from behind. Alec was about to break the hold with a kick when a familiar voice murmured into his ear, "We two might give them a far bigger eyeful, now, couldn't we, darlin'?"

Staff Corporal Ivanhoe Blunt had mastered the art of Wearing the Uniform. His tunic, detailed in red, was meant for headquarters, not battle, and had been tailored to ensure that it glorified the fine figure it covered. He was a regular at the Chabanais, also a favorite. His allure was so good for business that the proprietress often welcomed him herself. He now guided Alec to a couple of chairs in a quiet anteroom where they could drink and talk.

Van had put off enlisting for service as long as possible. "I'd the farm to run," he said, "and my own poppet Phyllis to dandle, still toddlin' and ploppin' down on her sweet behind. Why should I abandon the land that my people took generations to gain? To fight the family feuds of our Johnny-come-lately overlords, the Saxe-Coburgs, and their fuckin' German kindred?" Only when Van could see no way to dodge the impending draft did he sign on, grudgingly. "Oh, I fumed for days. Leave me alone, is all I was askin', to guard my own house from the Hun, not to die like a rat in some Belgian ditch."

When he did volunteer, he did so with one intention paramount: to survive the war by any means and survive it intact. "I've a child and a home to live for. And Mabel, the best

woman in the world, she's too young to be makin' her way in
the world as a widow with a fatherless babe, or, should I be
maimed, to spend her life luggin' a useless cripple of a husband back and forth to the toilet."

In the army, he soon learned to make the most of his assets.
It was an open secret that some officers liked to keep the best-
looking Tommies at hand. Not a week into training, a major
approached Van to serve as his orderly. He had no scruples
about accepting. "Only it pained me that I'd never been servant to any man before, and now I'm tidying up his quarters
day and night, and him gaping at my buttocks the whole time
with his tongue hangin' down. But I put my life before my
pride." He went on, "We both knew what he wanted. When I
helped him dress, his prick would stand stiff as a flagpole on
parade. But I'm tellin' you, they're all bollixed, these Harrow
types. If the man had only once said to me, *Blunt! Let's go at
it*, for sure I'd have told him, *Yessir!* I even fancied the fellow
a bit. But he couldn't admit his own wants and I wasn't about
to make it easy on him."

After some months in the major's service, Van caught the
eye of a staff colonel, who poached him away from the lower-
ranked officer and had Private Blunt promoted to corporal.
"So ended my stint as a chambermaid, praise the Lord God
Almighty!" The colonel brought Van to Paris, where he was
now permanently stationed. "The old fellow's a bit more relaxed than the major, with an arm about me now and again
and feelin' the muscles. But Alec, I promise you, I'm not
blatherin' on in this manner to brag—"

"It's a good story, I'm glad for you."

"Hear me now: I know how to get you on staff—"

"What's that?"

"I'm sayin' if you'll give me the word, I'll get started on

things tomorrow. I'll drop a few hints and shuffle some papers, and once the officers get a look at you, they'll want to keep you near. Within a week, I'm quite certain, you'll be out of harm's way and stationed at headquarters."

Alec couldn't take in this proposal or even think straight, not with tonight's distractions: the sex show, and Van's nuzzling and groping, and this brandy they now were sipping. They could strip down and have at it right there: others would watch and cheer.

He shook his head to clear it and looked into his friend's eyes. More than sex, he wanted Van to hold him, caress him, comfort him, tell him that Maurice was on his way home. He stammered, "I, I'm—"

Van pulled his chair closer. "It's about your gentleman, ain't it?"

"How'd ya know?"

"Osmington, darlin'; news gets about. Mabel heard from your folks, or maybe from someone who'd heard from them, that you'd visited home to say goodbye on your way to enlist in Cardiff, you and your gent, Mr. Hall. They say he's most courteous, no airs about him at all, and handsome as he can be."

Alec lowered his eyes.

"Aw my sweet Jesus, Alec—not killed, is he?"

"There's been no word for a while now."

Van took his hand. "Listen. Will you do that, please? And look at me." Alec did so. "How sad would it be for him to come back from the war and learn you'd died in battle? Do as I say. Stay with me here for his sake. We'll watch out for each other."

26

In the autumn of 1918, everybody was blue, even the die-hard jingoists. This reversal of mood had been abrupt. Only weeks before, during the summer, morale was skyrocketing, when the Yanks were arriving in France by the hundreds of thousands. Some said there were two million! How fresh they looked, fit and chipper with their spanking-new uniforms and broad-brimmed hats. To hear them talk, you'd think they planned to win the war on their own and rescue the feeble Old World from its own folly. They were earnest, if unseasoned; they fought hard if naïvely. With a bit more know-how, surely fewer would have died.

By no means did they win the war on their own, but they did make the crucial difference. The Kaiser's General Luden-dorff had tried his best to crush the Allies last March—before the additional muscle had time to arrive from the States. To that end he unleashed his new weapon, the storm trooper, a human machine fueled by pep pills, geared for surprise attack with a flamethrower and light machine gun. At first this in-novation proved effective. The storm troopers were returning the pace of the war to its beginning, with Germans claiming miles of territory at a thrust instead of paltry yardage. Once again they seized the places near Paris they'd been forced to give up in 1914—like the forest of Crépy, whence their artil-lery could fire on the capital. A million Parisians fled.

The storm troopers were efficient at taking territory, but

they couldn't hold it. Their speed worked against them, because they advanced farther and faster than supplies could reach. They took to looting for food: that slowed them down, and their deep penetration into France exposed them to the enemy on three sides. So finally these elite fighters proved as mortal as ordinary soldiers. But, trained at great length and staggering expense, they could not be replaced. Germany was running out of men. When the Americans, fresh and well-fed, joined the Allies, the German-led Central Powers found themselves outnumbered. Thus they were once more beaten back from Paris, from Reims and Amiens as well, pursued by the French innovation, tanks, produced by the hundreds in their auto factories. The tanks pushed the Germans back to their last edge of defense, the Hindenburg Line. At last, refreshed by the Americans, the Allies broke through.

Germany was hungry. War had devoured the nation's food as well as the flesh of its men. Berlin kept trying to feed her soldiers, but the city itself was starving, and what reached the battlefront was stretched, adulterated, unhealthy. Hunger weakened the army's resistance to sickness: it was said their medics were treating a half million cases of influenza. Their spirit was starving as well. This Great War was no longer a showdown of national character: Teutonic knighthood versus Gallic hypocrisy; German idealism versus English greed. No, it was no longer even a contest. In their hopelessness, they sometimes surrendered rather than die. One of them, laying down his rifle, approached his enemies with his hands above his head and called out in English, "Don't you know? The war is over!"

Hearing this German soldier speak English confused Alec. Was the man telling the truth? Did he truly know something being withheld from his foes? The British troops had long since stopped trusting their commanders. Turkey had surrendered, they heard, the Austrians were suing for peace, and wasn't Ludendorff himself asking for an armistice? What were the bigwigs holding out for, Lloyd George and Poincaré and now fucking Woodrow Wilson, playing God with his Fourteen Points and his League of Nations? Useless old men, too weak even to end a war that was already over. Let them take the bullets themselves! So the soldiers were waiting every day for news that didn't come. Meanwhile, as they had been for years, they were rotated from their second and third lines to the front for yet another week in the trenches. How wretched it would be to die now, or to be maimed, when the end must be near. Why keep fighting? But they were offered no choice except to dodge bullets or take one in the head for treason.

Alec had been offered a better choice once, but that was two years ago now, when Van asked him to stay in Paris. He'd chosen not to remain in safety while his beloved might still be in harm's way. So on the day after their night at the Chabanais (where a generous demoiselle had rewarded Swavely's defense of her homeland with an hour he would always remember), the two Royal Welsh Fusiliers reported for transport to the front.

A most frigid winter ensued. "Bleedin' fuckin' Ice Age," Swavely called it. Alec survived the cold with Risley's scarf tied around his face. The ugly thing did keep his lips from freezing. Unfortunately, it also made him laugh, thinking of Risley squinting to count stitches, and the laughter hurt: the rush of icy air would burn his nose and throat. When he'd try to stop, he was like a kid not wanting to giggle in church, so he'd laugh all the more, his thoughts running off to the "fuckin' Ice Age" of woolly mammoths and dancing mastodons. He couldn't help himself. The cold made him crazy.

When relief came at last, it was unwelcome. In February 1917, Private Scudder was granted five days' leave to attend his father's funeral. As mother and son followed the coffin from their cottage to St. Osmund's church, Alec's heart lurched between grief and rage. "Da! Couldn't you've waited?" he thought. "Just till after the war? There's too much dyin'! With me gone and Fred too, how will Ma endure?" Aderyn leaned heavily against him as they walked arm in arm along barren lanes. She was getting old and before long would likely need care.

Fred arrived from Argentina on the last day of Alec's leave. Even though their time together was short, the brothers found an hour to bicker behind the closed door of their old bedroom. Fred blamed Alec: "If you'd sailed with me as you'd promised, instead of chasin' after your grand Mr. Hall, you'd be livin' safe overseas, likely married and settled. Ma and Da would have followed you and we could all take care of her now."

"Great prognosticator, ain't you, Freddy?"

"It's true! Didn't she tell me as much? They'd have followed me and Jane but for you stayin' here. And once you'd enlisted, that was that. On no, they wouldn't leave you behind. It was frettin' for you that hastened his death, and seein' how she fretted too."

"Did I ask for this fuckin' war? What do you think I'm fightin' for? I'll tell you what for: it's so's you insurance purveyors can enjoy your easy life in the colonies."

"One's got nothin' to do with the other."

"You're blind if ya can't see it, and ya haven't the brains to imagine a battle. You just don't know."

"We can't leave her here by herself."

Aderyn opened the door without knocking. "Enough of

this, both of you. I shall go nowhere. Who'd tend your father's grave?"

Fred threw up his hands: "Tuh . . ."

Several weeks later Alec got a letter from Fred, who'd spent the rest of his time in Osmington trying to persuade their mother to come back with him to Argentina, to no avail. He wrote, "I'm not proud of doing it, but it had to be done." At the dock, Fred invited her onboard to his cabin for a last goodbye and to see one more picture of her granddaughter. He asked a steward to bring them tea, and while she was cooing over the photo, Fred slipped something into her cup. She woke six hours later, far out to sea. Fred had booked her passage without telling her and procured a powder from the village druggist "to help our grieving mother sleep."

> You can just picture the seen, or maybe you can't.
> Suffice it to say she spoke hardly another word for me
> during the <u>entyre</u> crossing, only that she woud not
> even set foot on shore in Buenos Ayres. But wily Jane
> met us at the dock with little Rita and <u>that</u> proved
> too much to resist. Ma agrees to stay for six months.
> She makes me swear to send her back then. O she still
> skowls and snits at me with such lady-like disdain!

Now, more than a year later, Aderyn remained in Argentina, to Alec's relief. Fred was using the threat of German submarines to postpone the promised return.

Meanwhile, rebellion had broken out throughout the nations, it seemed. In Ireland, the English rulers squelched it quickly with the full brutality of war; then in Russia, where the citizens forced the czar from his throne. Their army claimed

they couldn't win the war against the Kaiser under a Roma-
nov monarch with German forebears (and therefore treason-
ous sympathies), so they mutinied. Alec remembered Ted's
lessons about Russia: at Millthorpe he'd told his young guests
that some of their thinkers took Christianity at its word and
believed that the enemy was no foreigner, but rather the "beast
within." After a second revolt in 1917, Russia withdrew from
the international scene and sued Germany for peace. Were
the Russians looking within, Alec wondered, searching their
national soul, or was the beast merely practicing some sleight
of hand?

Then the French army also mutinied. Their government
had been trying to hide the number of fatalities, but honest arithmetic showed that nearly a million French soldiers
had already died at the Western Front. Yet their generals
kept ordering men forward, disregarding their exhaustion,
their families' hardship, and the pricelessness of their lives.
The mutineers protested that they were neither cowards nor
weaklings; rather, they wanted to be treated as fellow citizens by their leaders, all brothers in the republic. They were
heard. Deployments to the front line were shortened, leaves
lengthened. Thirty-four hundred soldiers were nonetheless
court-martialed for treason; five hundred of those tried were
sentenced to die, though finally all but forty-three of the condemned were spared.

No mutiny among English soldiers. ("Too downtrodden
from the cradle," Swavely griped.) But on the home front defiance was growing. Women united the cause of peace with
that of suffrage. Writers spoke out in papers and pamphlets.
Bertrand Russell was fined and fired from teaching at Trinity College, Cambridge, for voicing opposition. In Alec's own
Welsh Fusiliers, a young officer named Sassoon publicly ques-

tioned his nation's motives for prolonging the war, asserting that soldiers were being made to suffer and die for "political errors and insincerities." Since this declaration came from a man wounded in battle and decorated for valor, he could not be labeled a coward. To avoid the scandal of trying a hero for treason, the government quietly committed him to a psychiatric hospital.

Despite the protests, things worsened for the military. England was now dispatching underage boys into battle, kids from the slums so needy they would lie about their birth dates for the sake of a meal and some clothes. And the army pretended to believe them. One of them approached Alec: "Mr. Scudda?"

"No need for 'Mister,' I'm a soldier just like you." The boy accepted the cigarette Alec offered.

"But that's 'ow we knew ya back then. We always called ya Mr. Scudda, and the gent was Mr. 'All."

"Whazzat—?"

"Foo'ball, sir, of a Saturday afternoon, in the city, a' the mission 'ouse."

Alec searched the boy's features. "Not Billy Wrenn?"

He grinned. His teeth had green streaks; still, the smile lighted his face. "Ya remember, then? Good fun, wa'n't it? Yer a fuckin' disaster a' foo'ball."

Alec laughed. "True enough! But Billy, how could it be? That was but five years ago—the lot of you seemed no more than tykes to me then. You can't be old enough—"

He winked and said, "Sshh!"

Alec judged him sixteen at most, likely younger. He smoked and spat and blustered and swore and gulped his tot of rum, but he had no need to shave, and he struggled under the weight of rifle and gear. Alec wondered how he would ever manage to wield a bayonet, should it come to hand-to-hand fighting. He tried to watch out for the boy.

One chilly night in October they found themselves neighbors in the trench, positioned a few yards apart. Alec was wrapped in his blanket on his sleep-shelf, about three feet above the duckboards, just wide enough to lie down on. He was neither fully awake nor asleep, which was how nights passed in the trenches. At the sound of boots on the boards, he sat up suddenly, rifle aimed.

Billy Wrenn jumped back: "It's me, Mr. Scudda."

"Jeezus! What's wrong?"

"Nothin'. Had to piss."

"Sshh. Get back to your post."

"Just movin' my legs. Fuckin' cold, ain't it?"

"You'll catch hell from the corporal."

"But I'm all stiff."

"Wrap up in your blanket—that'll help. Lie down."

"Wha' for? Can't sleep."

"Just lie down and rest while you can."

"Awright." He hesitated. "Got a smoke?"

"Ya know we can't smoke, he'd see the light."

"Yah, right. Bloody idjit, that's me."

Alec was sure he heard the boy's teeth chattering. He made room on his shelf. Billy Wrenn sat next to him. Alec covered both their shoulders with his blanket. He kept shivering. Alec put an arm around him to warm him, and the boy was asleep immediately. Rather than wake him, Alec managed to lie back down on the shelf on his side with his back to the damp wall and to spoon Billy Wrenn beside him, both under the one blanket. He held the sleeping boy close to keep him from slipping off.

How very small he felt. Alec realized the baggy uniform

made the boy's figure appear bigger than it was, because he felt like a child. He kept watch for them both. The gunfire had been diminishing for a week; orders were to return shot for shot, but not to initiate. Who knew how long the relative quiet would last? The sky was clear tonight, hence the frost. The harvest moon on the wane cast highlights and shadows along the length of the trench as far as Alec could see.

He recalled the forest at Penge, before the war, when hunters would shoot by the light of October's full moon, and November's, and he would guide them. How lovely the woods had been then, the crisp smell and showering leaves in the otherworldly light. The frost would set his skin atingle . . . The youngster beside him stirred in his sleep and was still again.

Alec had lived for more than two years now with no word of Maurice. At HQ, he would read the lists of the dead, wounded, and missing, always with heart pounding and panic in his gut. Then he would put himself through the ordeal of reading again, lest in his desire to find no news, he had willfully overlooked it. But there was nothing.

When the moon set, he tried to wake Billy Wrenn, but the boy clung to the safety of his sleep in Alec's embrace. So he carried Billy in his arms a few yards to his own sleep-shelf, lay him there, and covered him.

27

The maps kept tantalizing him with how close they were to England, to safety. They were stationed near the town of Romeries in the Nord, only about a hundred miles from Calais, thence just a short jump across the Channel to Dover. Swavely said he would hike it in one stretch, if they'd let him go. They wondered if poor Jackson had such a hike in mind when he'd bolted. He pleaded at the court-martial that there was madness in his family, but this was the second time he'd been caught running away. Alec feared they might not be able to find six volunteers for the firing squad and he'd be made to join, but six did volunteer and so he was spared being forced to shoot a comrade for doing what they all had thought of doing.

That was November 7, 1918. On the same day, word got around that a German delegation under a white flag had formally requested a cease-fire, but that Foch sent them away empty-handed. Egged on by the American generals, recently arrived, eager for glory, he said he wanted the enemy on their knees. Meantime, men kept dying.

On the morning of November 10, a dozen Welsh Fusiliers were dispatched from Romeries to the town of Escarmain for what was called a cleanup operation. Germans had been caught there, most captured or killed. But a few were left, said the report, and these stragglers were to be overtaken. On entering the town, the Brits found a German soldier lying blood-spattered on the roadside. He did not resist capture. He told them that he was the last alive of his company and that they would find the bodies of the rest by the church nearby. He pointed toward its shattered square tower. When they approached the church, two machine guns opened fire on them from behind a low wall, each discharging three hundred shots per minute. All died on both sides in the ambush.

That evening, bearers brought the bodies of the Fusiliers back to Romeries for burial. When Alec saw how the sprays of dumdum bullets had slashed and torn the childlike body of Billy Wrenn, he collapsed to his knees and doubled over, forehead to the ground. Swavely tried to lift him. Alec would not be raised; rather, he keened from such a depth of grief that those who witnessed shook their heads. When two others then tried to lift him, he shut in on himself more tightly and sobbed till he had no more breath. Finally he rolled over onto his side in the dirt, his face a silent openmouthed mask of anguish.

Next morning Swavely tried to cheer him: "'E's in a better place, Scuppy."

"Uh-huh . . ."

"Listen, I know it: 'e's 'appy now—told me so 'imself. I seen 'im last night."

"Had a dream about him, did ya?"

"Not a dream, no, I seen 'im, swear I did—"

"Get out—"

"It's true. Seen 'is face in the sky."

"Yer daft."

"Entirely. I felt 'im beside me too, like you here with me now. 'Appens to me sometimes, get it from me mam. She claimed 'twas a fairy gift for seein' the dead."

"Wha—?"

"She called it 'er sense of presence."

At that moment, rumor interrupted their talk: It Was Fin-ished. Foch had signed the cease-fire agreement before dawn. Men cheered, then shut their mouths when they heard that they were to keep fighting till 11:00. Eleventh day, eleventh month, eleventh hour, that's when it would end, not before. They were ordered to advance. Swavely shouted: "What's this shit, now? 'Eleventh Day, Eleventh Hour'? It's no bloody fuckin' mellerdrama, it's the life and death of us men! Why not just stay put till eleven?" A noncom grabbed him, and he pushed back: "Fuck off, Sarge—"

"Obey the goddamn order, ya lowlife cunt, or I'll shove your own bayonet up your arse."

They obeyed the order, advancing over the top of the re-inforcement trench toward the first line. At 9:00, at 10:00, the firing kept up; at 10:30 it intensified, as if both sides wanted to enjoy the fun before their legal killing would become murder. Alec's speed with his rifle had improved with years of prac-tice: today he was firing twenty-five shots per minute toward the unseen enemy firing at him. It was reflexive action because his mind had been numbed by Swavely's words. *Sense of pres-ence.* A gift for seeing the dead. Had that fortune-teller seen Maurice beside him in London, the way Swavely had seen Billy Wrenn? And that day on Bernard Street, had Alec felt Maurice beside him, as Swavely had Billy? Maurice . . . dead for more than two years?

At 11:00 the gunfire ceased. Soldiers on both sides peeked above the trench wall. The sight of their helmets provoked more fire, now illegal, by their enemies. Then both sides started tossing hand grenades, unaimed, for no reason it seemed but to have less to carry away. One of these exploded near Swavely. His legs shattered below both knees, exposing splintered bones and torn sinews. He wept and screamed,

"Ain't it over? They said it was fuckin' over!" Alec used his own belt for a tourniquet, which he pulled so tightly around the stumps that the strap tore into the flesh. Did he think he could thus contain his friend's life? In his panic Swavely panted and pleaded, "Get me home!"

"We'll get ya home, I promise."

Alec braced him under the arms and tried to lift him, but the movement made the man wail in agony. Alec waved and shouted; when the stretcher arrived, Swavely was dead. The bearers left him to seek after wounded survivors. Alec sat in the blood-streaked mud by the corpse. He squinted up at the sun approaching its zenith in the glorious autumn sky.

Among Swavely's belongings, Alec found an English version of Marx's pamphlet, which did not surprise him, and a copy of *Pilgrim's Progress*, which did. Then he remembered that Llewellyn had given it to his friend. He packed the things to be returned to Swavely's family, who would receive an official letter to the effect that their son and brother had died honorably in battle of a single bullet wound, quickly and without suffering. Alec's final order before dismissal was to widen the mass grave where Billy Wrenn was buried to make room for those who died on November 11.

That was when he stopped eating, or rather started forgetting to eat. He didn't feel hungry. He did feel sleepy all the time, though, and cold. He joined the transport to Paris. Thence he could have gone to Calais and home to England with everyone else. Instead he lingered in Paris. His father was dead, and his mother and his brother were living in Argentina. Why was he going to England? Confused by the question, he'd stop in midstep, unsure of where to go. Others, who knew where they were going and wanted to get there fast, would brush past or shoulder him aside. Then he'd remember that Maurice was why he was going to England. But the fortune-teller had seen Maurice among the dead. Those who glanced at him at that moment would see his face contorted, silent but openmouthed, into a mask of anguish, like when he had mourned Billy Wrenn. They would turn their faces and hurry on.

For a couple of days he wandered Paris. He spent what he had on cigarettes; smoking kept him awake, also seemed to warm him. Then he'd sleep wherever he happened to sit down, sometimes so very deeply that he'd fall over to his side on a bench and the police would wake him. The weather was raw, drizzly; he stayed close to train terminals because they afforded some shelter. That's when he had the idea that he should take a train to the port of Marseille, where he might make the passage to Buenos Aires. It would be springtime there, and warm; he would find his brother and his mother. He thought he must be thinking clearly again because he remembered the seasons were opposite in Argentina.

Late on the rainy afternoon of November 15, 1918, he boarded an express at the Gare de Lyon, bound south-southeast to the Gare Saint-Charles in Marseille. In the overheated second-class compartment, in the darkness, he felt safe. He was going somewhere: that gave him a reprieve from needing to think about what he would do when he got there.

Hours later, when the train was approaching his destination, he felt the familiar overwhelming need to sleep, so when he surrendered his ticket to the conductor, he asked the man in broken French and with gestures to be sure to wake him in Marseille. And then he did fall asleep, deeply, beyond care or memory or knowledge of time or place.

VIII

THE WHITE ROCKS

28

At the Gare Saint-Charles, the train changed crew as well as direction. In the hubbub the conductor forgot to wake Alec. What woke him was the whistle and jolt of the train pulling out of the station, now eastbound, now local, just as the new conductor came along to punch tickets. Alec had none, having surrendered his to the first. The new conductor might have relished chiding such an English imbecile, but since he was still in uniform (his only clothes) and looked thinner and more haggard than anyone so young ought to look, he treated him kindly, this soldier who'd fought a war he himself had been too old to join. He managed, in broken English and with gestures, to make Alec understand that he would do best to get off at the next stop, a little town not many miles down the track. If he'd wait there till morning, he could catch the westbound local back to Marseille, a very short trip. He issued a return ticket, no charge. That's how Alec came to be lying awake on a bench, his head on his old canvas bag, on the platform that served as the station of the town of Cassis on the Mediterranean coast of France, shortly after a midnight in mid-November 1918.

Ain't it over? They said it was fuckin' over! At the very moment when Alec's tears were salting Swavely's blood, people were cheering, dancing, drinking in Piccadilly, Times Square, on the Champs-Élysées. He hated them. There were only two

kinds now, those who had fought and those who had not, and
he hated those who had not.

Memories like Swavely's agony, the most recent in a scrap-
book of four years' making, kept him awake at night and
weary all day: Billy Wrenn's body savaged by machine guns;
Llewellyn's heart, pierced by the bayonet's blade; the dead un-
buried; the maimed hopeless; men's severed limbs mixed with
mud; carcasses of pack animals and horses, their stench min-
gled with the smell of bacon frying in the mornings. These
memories could sicken him in no figurative way, because if he
dwelled on them, he would heave up whatever was in his guts.

Still, his invisible wound hurt worse than any memory; its
pain would strike so deeply that at the same time he'd sweat
and shiver, gasp for breath and pant like a runner, burn as if
stung with shrapnel. It caused him to cry out aloud on the
empty platform, startling the birds into silence: "Maurice . . ."
He keened, rocking and sobbing, the heels of his palms
pressed into his eye sockets. When at last he was quiet again,
the birds resumed their predawn songs.

He struck a match to read the schedules on the kiosk:
hours yet till the next local would stop here. Though he didn't
feel hungry—these days he never felt hungry—he figured
he ought to eat something because he couldn't recall the last
time he'd done so. The light was just beginning to show the
road, an alley of packed earth between rows of trees, and he
followed it.

The road became a cobblestoned street that sloped down toward the town's little harbor. Fishing boats were already sailing out past a lighthouse to open water. At a café facing the

docks, he asked for coffee and bread. The barmaid helped him count his French coins and giggled at his accent, but when he tried to say sorry for manhandling her language, she grew solemn with courtesy, protesting that she found it charming, truly, when a stranger made the effort. He closed his eyes to savor the warmth of the coffee. This pleased the girl; she spooned some fresh butter onto a saucer and offered it for his bread. He thanked her and left without eating.

The last of the fishermen were sailing out. The sky was growing sunny, the morning warm, nothing like gloomy Novembers back home. Rather than return to the station to wait three more hours for the train, he walked along the humble esplanade that skirted the harbor and led up to a road hugging the shore.

The air seemed fresher than any he'd breathed in years, scented with—what? Herbs? Even the weeds in the cracks of the pavement were fragrant. He passed a hotel on the right, advertising rooms (in English and French) with saltwater baths; then farther, on the left, an empty beach. When he reached what seemed the crest of the hill, he noticed a path leading down from the road. He couldn't see where it went because of the pines and shrubs, but knew it must go toward the sea. He was getting drowsy again, so, hoping to rest by the water, he followed it. The footing was tricky, all stones and roots and brambles; when he pulled aside branches, they'd whip his back as soon as he let go. But when he parted the last of them, he gasped at what he saw: a kind of plateau of enormous rocks, their flat white surfaces sloping right to the edge of the water adazzle with the sunrise; and there, across the sea, a headland—astonishing in its mass—guarding the cultivated hillsides at its base. Smoke rose from the hills, like the wings of an enormous ghostly bird. Its motion somehow made the scene's stillness visible. The smoke smelled savory, autumnal, like chaff or fallen leaves set fire at home. The farmers were burning the pruned-away branches of grapevines, their harvest having been claimed. He sat on the warm smooth rocks and gazed.

All of a sudden for no reason he panicked because something unseen wanted to break through the surface of the sea from below, bloodthirsty, monstrous, and more real than the peaceful vision before him. When the terror passed, he lay back in exhaustion. Soon he slept as he had on the train, deeply, unreachably.

He woke in terror—he could see only darkness. It was the wool of his sleeve. He'd covered his eyes with his arm in sleep. He sat up too fast; that made him feel dizzy, sickish. The smoke from the vineyards was gone. How long had he slept? Hours, to judge by the sun. Midafternoon now, and he'd missed the train back to Marseille. He'd have to wait at the station again. About to start on his way toward town, he heard splashing and noticed someone else's belongings at the edge of the rocks.

A tall boy climbed out of the sea—sixteen or seventeen, naked and handsome, with dark hair and wide shoulders, his skin ruddy brown from last summer's swimming. He dried himself with his shirt and called out to another. A second boy stumbled onto the rocks from the water, likewise naked, but shorter and slight, with curly hair and a mischievous grin. He dried himself with the first one's shirttails—no reason both their shirts should get wet. The taller one swatted at him and lay down.

Schoolboys. Copybooks among their dark clothes. *Lads*: that's how officers spoke of their men. Too young by just a year, he guessed, to have been conscripted for even the end of the war. How he envied them, their limbs lithe and smooth, braving the threat of a chill to be naked together in the sun on this fine fall day.

The taller one wanted his friend to lie with him. The shorter had put on his glasses, noticed that Alec was awake, and warned the other with a glance. The tall one half raised himself up to look. He sized up the soldier and decided he was harmless: he smiled, waved, called out, "*Salut, Tommy!*" Alec returned the wave. Then the tall boy removed his friend's glasses and drew him close. They tussled and laughed. They embraced; they kissed, playfully at first, then ardently. The sight of their love began to probe Alec's wound.

He got up and walked back the way he had come, downhill now, past the beach, toward the hotel with the sign in French and English. He sat on a bench across the road from it. His head ached. That meant he should eat, even though he felt no hunger. Except for the coffee at dawn, he'd had nothing today. Maybe he could stay the night in this place and have a meal. Tomorrow he'd catch the train.

On entering the lobby, he saw a bald man of sixty in shirt-sleeves taking books from the bookcases, dusting, sorting, and replacing them. He greeted Alec: "*Bonsoir, monsieur.*"

Although his tone was perfectly cordial, *monsieur* stung Alec with unintended irony: his uniform of the other ranks, crushed, shapeless even when new, announced that he was no gentleman. Moreover, this place was posher than he'd taken it for, with lots of buffed woodwork and brass lamps. "*Bonsoir, monsieur,*" he replied. He cleared his throat and continued with the sentence he'd rehearsed in his head, "*J'ai besoin d'une chambre pour la nuit.*"

"It's okay, sir, you may speak English," the man said. His accent was American. Putting on his coat, he went to the front desk and showed Alec a list of accommodations with prices in francs and pounds. "Here we are. Most everything's available, off-season rates."

Even the smallest room would have emptied Alec's wallet. "Might I find a place cheaper down by the harbor?"

"Yes, I can help you with that." He paused, folded his hands on the ledger, and looked Alec in the eye: "Do you have time to rest a bit first? I'm about ready for tea. Will you drink a cup with me?"

"I'd like that. All right, sir."

A maid brought the tray. "Years ago," the man said while he poured, "when I first came here, the local folks claimed tea was poison. Now it's a big fad. Anyway, lots of our guests are English; most, even. Tell me, what brings you to our little town?"

He told the man about missing his stop in Marseille, about serving in France, and deciding that he ought to join his brother, who'd emigrated before the war, in Argentina. In a big port like Marseille he figured he could find work on a steamer and so make the passage to South America.

"That's quite a trip you're planning," he said. "You won't go home to England and get your bearings before you start?"

"There's nothing for me there."

"Ah, no family, no girl?"

Alec's hands were shaking. This caused the footed, dainty teacup to rattle in the saucer. The noise embarrassed him. His host pretended not to notice. He sliced the apple tart and of-fered it. Alec accepted a piece and set it aside.

"My dad's dead; the rest, overseas with my brother. Any-way, England's all changed, everything; there's nothing there for me now." He noticed the cigarette box on the table. "May I have a smoke?"

"Of course, by all means." He passed Alec the matches.

The maid lit a fire. He was glad for it: the autumn air, warm earlier, chilled quickly with the coming of evening. This room felt full of solace: lamps and a fire, quiet talk, a comfortable chair; cleanliness, order, calm—things he'd once taken for granted. He wished he might rest in this chair forever, but it was time to go. "I thank you for the tea. Maybe now you'd point me to where I might find a room in the town."

The hotel manager sighed, as if duty required him to say something unpleasant. "Forgive me, son," he began, "but you don't look well to me, quite ill in fact. You're all done-in. Darkness comes quickly, this time of year. I don't like sending you away."

He knew the man must be right about his looks. And he was surprised by how deeply this stranger's concern touched him. He felt tears rising, as he often did these days, for no reason. He smothered them with a little laugh and said, "Oh, a wash and a shave, I won't seem such a tramp."

"Listen. We own the building across the way. There's a pleasant room, empty, a caretaker's place. I believe you'd be quite snug there tonight, if you don't mind the sound of the sea. I could send over some supper. What do you say? Rest there tonight. Then in the morning we'll see what's what."

He felt obliged to refuse the charity: "I don't know . . ." But he was too exhausted to keep up a show of manners. "Only if no one's put out."

The manager was pleased. "No one's put out, I promise. Come on, then, let's get you settled."

He unlocked a wooden gate in the wall across the road. When they stepped through, Alec beheld the panorama that the guests enjoyed from their pricey rooms above: the harbor, the lighthouse aglow in the fading daylight, the sea, and that sublime cliff he'd seen earlier across the water; and to their left, in the distant northeast, another gigantic outcropping of white stone. The manager said, "They call that the Crown of Charlemagne."

The outbuilding appeared to be two stories high in front. But as they walked toward the sea, they descended steps to its lower levels, built into the rocks. The manager opened the door to the lowest. They entered a dusky room. When he parted the long shutters of the big window, he revealed a balcony no wider than an army cot, perched over the Mediterranean. The flood of soft evening light transformed the dim interior into a place of welcome, a refuge. Together the two of them unrolled the mattress and made up the bed. The manager lit a lamp, said he'd send supper at seven. He wished Alec a good rest and left.

Alec was sure the man knew he would feel more at home in this humble room, with its two rough chairs and gingham curtains for cupboard doors, than he would in the ritzy hotel. He closed his eyes and listened. The sound of the sea, though calm, was loud and close, breaking against the rocks below. Its rhythm took charge of the room, of his thoughts, silenced their anxious nagging, and for that he was grateful. He stepped onto the balcony. Such peacefulness. The lighthouse's beam pierced the twilight, kept watch over the harbor, where the fishermen's boats, sails furled and bound, were rocking at their docks. There was nothing between him and the water below. Too weary to stay on his feet, he knelt, gripped the rail, leaned his forehead against it.

"Come," he whispered.

The maid was practiced at balancing a tray while knocking. No answer. The sea breeze was chilly—she'd left her shawl in the kitchen—so rather than wait to knock again, she chinked the door open and called, *"Monsieur?"* No answer. She stepped into the room, as cold inside as out. The English soldier had left the balcony doors wide-open—typical careless foreigner. When she set down the tray to close them, she smelled something foul. Then she saw Alec, lying where he'd sunk down on the balcony, limbs akimbo, a bit of vomit by his mouth, eyes open and glazed. He had soiled himself a bit too, front and back. Taking him for dead, she gasped, *"Mère de Dieu!"* She crossed herself and ran back to the main building for help.

She returned with the manager, who knelt next to him. Alec was whispering nonsense now, terrified, rapid-fire. The manager tried to soothe him, "You're safe, no one can harm you," but the words failed to get through, and he raved in a crazy undertone, opened his horrified eyes, and blacked out again. They undressed him, shaking their heads at his bony chest and bruised skin, the bullet scar on the ribs under the right arm; they washed him and put him to bed. Since none of the town's physicians were yet home from the war, they sent for the animal doctor who'd been too old to serve and who, with simple wisdom, diagnosed acute thirst and hunger; or, in medical terms, dehydration and starvation: likely self-inflicted, he conjectured, but likely unintentionally, resulting perhaps from melancholy or despair or prolonged fear in the trenches, what the English were calling shell shock, or, in medical language, neurasthenia.

They would need to address the thirst before the hunger. But the patient would not wake to swallow water. The veterinarian called for a clean handkerchief. He soaked it in water and twisted it and worked one end gently into Alec's mouth, between his left cheek and gums, away from his tongue. Thus liquid might be absorbed from the cloth in minute amounts into the patient's system. He had used the technique successfully with sick livestock.

He instructed the others to keep the handkerchief wet through the night in the hope the young man might come around. If and when that should happen, then they were to withdraw it slowly and give him water by the spoonful until he could drink.

A corpse in an officer's uniform, missing a third of his skull, called the steps: waltz, foxtrot, cakewalk! Who were these dancers, these musicians, all goggle-masked? What was this place? Indoors or out? Was the ceiling so high it was out of sight, or was that the sky overhead, lightless and hard as the gigantic stone walls? Were they bats with baby faces flying above, or babies with bat wings? Why the scaffold, why the noose?

The officer-corpse led a prisoner aloft to the gallows. The prisoner was Alec. Alec watched himself being led. A hangman covered his head with a hood, yet somehow the blackness within was visible. He felt the noose being slipped over the hood and tightened around his neck. He heard the hangman cock the lever that governed the gear that would release the platform underfoot. He knew that unless he woke up, he would die when the platform dropped, and not just in this dream. He tried to yell, but the hood, having gotten stuffed into his mouth, gagged him. At last a choking noise came out of his throat—

A child whispered from somewhere beyond the stone walls, "*Maman, le soldat se réveille . . .*"

Then an unseen hand pulled the part of the hood that was gagging him out of his mouth, up over his nostrils as far as the bridge of his nose. He still couldn't see, but at least he could breathe now, and the hanging was stopped. Then he felt a trickle of water on his lips, as welcome to taste as the air was to breathe. He opened his mouth to taste more. He felt metal, a spoon, press against his lower lip and pour its little measure of water into his mouth, more delicious than he'd ever drunk. He swallowed; he felt it go down and cut through the parchedness in his throat; then the spoon again, the measure of water, and he swallowed.

"Happy," she called the cat. She breathed heavily on the *H*, because (she instructed both Happy and the soldier) that is how it must, *must* be pronounced in English. Hortense, seated near his head on the pillow, also received the lesson, but the doll's *H*, unlike Happy's, was not to be so roughly breathed because then (Mama said) it sounded like a very rude word in English.

She was content to dawdle in his room, which they kept warm and was bright all day and lively with the sounds of the harbor. She was content to have such a compliant grown-up

among her playthings, someone not always correcting her behavior and speech. Like the cat and Hortense, he didn't talk
back; no, he didn't talk at all.

Today she decided that Hortense should marry the English
soldier. She tried to get Happy to sit still for the wedding,
but the cat wanted to jump on the table or stalk birds outside. Then she changed her mind and decided that she would
marry him herself, with Hortense as the judge, and that he,
the bridegroom, must be a fisherman with a blue boat. Then
she changed her mind again: he must be a schoolteacher from
Marseille. No, he must be the patron of the manor with the
pink walls on Cap Canaille. No, the patron was too old; he
must be his son. His name must be Henri.

At last he found voice enough to speak. *"Mais non, made-
moiselle . . ."* The child's eyes widened at the gravelly sound. He
cleared his throat and continued: *"Je m'appelle Alec."*

She ran off yelling, *"Maman, le soldat peut parler!"*

29

When he tried to stand, he felt dizzy and nauseated and immediately sat. The child's mother found him thus on the edge of the bed and helped him to lie back down; she lifted his ankles and pulled the covers up. The cat jumped onto his chest to snooze. She shooed it; Alec was soon asleep again.

He slept mostly till Christmas. Daytime dreams were pleasant, not that he could recall details, only that they occurred in sleep so deep that he woke knowing neither time nor place and befuddled by the light rippling above him. Was he underwater? In the pond at the boathouse? Then he'd remember where he was and recognize the movement of the sea reflected on the ceiling. He felt safe. Not at night, though, when panic might wake him up yelling. He was glad the sound of the waves muffled the noise so that he didn't scare the child and her mother, who lived upstairs.

During those weeks, the horse doctor looked in on him every third day. Alec wondered how this man's hand was able to feel both warm and cool at once. It was a welcome touch. He would press his ear against Alec's ribs to listen; he would sit Alec up, thump his back, and listen. Another man, younger, maybe forty years old, visited regularly too. He'd served as a medic on a Red Cross ship but was not a doctor. A big fellow, he helped Alec wash and could easily lift him out of bed onto a chair. Alec felt himself light in his arms; he'd lost much weight.

By New Year's he was walking again and by mid-January
doing chores to reduce the debt he wished to assume for his
care. His mind was clear enough to find his brother's address
in his knapsack. He wrote to his mother there:

> I was under the wether a bit shortly after the peace,
> nothing serious. <u>Dont You Worry.</u> I'm fine now and
> found work in France for the time being, even putting
> some by. Soon I shall make my way to see you.

The reply came from Fred, who wrote "with the very greatest sadness" that Aderyn and her granddaughter, Rita, were
buried together in the Protestant cemetery in Buenos Aires,
"both carried off November last by the Influenza. The child
took sick and Ma would not be kept away from her, Jane is
brought low in her spirits."

At the foot of Alec's bed was a rocking chair, turned to face
the sea, where he sat with the letter in his hands on his lap. The
lighthouse lantern shone through the dusk. Tonight was the eve
of Candlemas, he recalled, though he couldn't say why. In Osmington, they blessed candles in church. Ma deemed it a harmless custom and lit the candle given to her choirboy son by the
vicar's wife. Of course, Llewellyn knew all about it, Joseph and
Mary presenting their firstborn in the temple, old Simeon the
priest recognizing that the infant was divine: "A light to lighten
the Gentiles and the glory of Thy people Israel." God had assured Simeon that he wouldn't die till he'd seen the Promised
One. "Now may your servant go in peace," he prayed. He fore-
told to the young mother, "A sword will pierce your soul . . ."

Llewellyn claimed Candlemas was a Celtic ghost in Christian dress, a feast to mark the sun's returning strength in mid-

winter. When did he say that? When they were gearing up to march somewhere, stop somewhere, march again . . . yes, to the Somme . . .

From the rocker he watched nightfall. Clouds gathered and hid the moon and stars; then the lighthouse was the only light, plus lamps in the windows of houses and bars around the harbor. They winked out one by one. Then only the lighthouse. He wondered, could a grown man be an orphan? He got under the covers with a puzzling pain in his gut. What was it? Then he remembered: the first stab of grief, same as he'd felt when his father died. The sharpness would dull in a month or so. Meantime, it helped to be able to name it.

By mid-February, he was noticing signs of spring: crocuses sprouting; rosemary and lemon thyme budding on last year's dried-out stalks. Also the sunlight's angle changed. Charlie Cavale, the hotel manager, allowed Alec to work pruning shrubs and painting shutters, but ordered him to rest in the afternoons. Michel, the former Red Cross medic who'd helped with his care, a Corsican, was Charlie's boyfriend, lover—by law his adopted son. That's how certain couples established legal households in France, Charlie said, and therefore inheritance rights. Alec was glad he could speak frankly with his boss.

"Why did you move to France from the States?" he asked Charlie once.

"To study in Avignon, at first," he said. "But I stayed because it's easier here. Stateside, with my family and everything else, it was just too much. In France people may despise me for being who I am, but they can't put me in prison, thanks to the laws of the Little Corporal, whose right-hand man was one of us. The adoption custom lets everybody save face. If

people care for me and Michel, they can pretend they believe
the legal fiction—childless older man, adopted heir. And if
we care for them, we can pretend we believe they believe it.
I've bought us a little house in Marseille. When I die, it's his."

Since the armistice, Alec had been living, mind and heart, in
a cold quiet place. The winter's chill comforted him, numbing his grief for family and friends; numbing the horror of
certain memories (Swavely's corpse, Billy Wrenn's, Llewellyn's), maimings that no one's body was ever meant to suffer,
obscenities no one should ever be made to see. But spring was
coming now, and the west wind grew warmer and the sun
stronger, day by lengthening day. Unlike the caressing spring
sun in England, this Mediterranean sun reached into the es-
sence of things. Its brilliance, its heat, its unyielding evocation
of life penetrated the layers of Alec's sadness and shattered the
ice that had crusted over its source, his grief for Maurice. The
spring undammed his sorrow.

He did not rage. Instead he walked—one day away from
the hotel west along the shore road. He walked beyond the
path to the White Rocks and kept walking with determination but no destination. Miles later, he saw signs for Les
Calanques. The signs guided him to the edge of those eerie
fjord-like inlets chiseled into the seaside cliffs by glaciers, ages
beyond ages ago, and where now the boats bobbing on tethers
in the waters a hundred feet below seemed like toys. He made
his way down to a shelf about ten feet under the top of the
ridge, just wide enough for him to squat down on, sliding his
back against the stone that scratched through his clothes.

In battle it would have been easy to die. No, he corrected

himself, it would not have been easy to die—it would have been easy to get yourself killed, never to die.

But now? He need only lift his heels and lean forward to tumble. He flexed the balls of his feet to try what it might feel like.

30

Dear Lady Baroness,

I hope this letter finds you in good health. Please
accept my apalogy for not writing sooner (as I am
truely grateful for your many kindnesses thru the
years) but I took ill after the armistice and recieved
news from overseas that my mother passed away, also
my brother's little girl from the Influenza. That set
me back. Its only these days I have come to my senses
enough to remember my friends. Rest asure that I am
well now. I have found work in France in a town called
Cassis not far from Marseille the big port.

I will thank you for any news, not that I harber
false hopes. The address of the hotel that imploys me
is as printed at the top of this paper. Also if you might
tell Teddy and George I am allright, as I am not sure
when I shall be abel to write them. Also please tell
Mr Risley I still have the muffler which he made which
kept me warm many a night and jolly to think about
him nitting with George.

Your friend,
A. Scudder

Should he write about the horses? Yes, she would understand. He added:

PS. Yesterday I saw a sight so very odd and lovely it made me remember my dear friends and that I must write. There are cliffs nearby this town on the sea. I went walking there to have a think and not in the best spirits. I sat down on the rocks and closed my eyes because of the sun, then opened them and I could not believe what I saw, a horse standing atop the cliff across the inlet. It was small I could tell even at the distance, white with a tawny mane and tale. Such a creature, I could not believe my eyes! Then another joined the first! Also white and tawny. Seeing these sturdy little fellows pawing the earth and winnying in the sun on the top of the cliff got me out of my fog.

Only after he had posted the letter did he realize that he'd addressed the envelope not to "Mrs. Wentworth," as he had during the war, but to the baroness herself. Was that a mistake? No. No need for games anymore, no censors to outwit, no war. He was glad he'd written her about the horses. He'd wanted to tell everybody about them, but didn't know the right words in French. He did tell Charlie, though. Charlie said they're wild, or semiwild, since they could be mounted by a rider with the right skill, a point of pride for the local cowboys. He was amazed that Alec had seen them so far east, because their homeland, called the Camargue, was west, on the other side of Marseille. So his sighting was indeed a marvel.

He'd run after them when he had seen them, to get closer, to be sure they were real. He wanted to catch up, to stroke their heads and necks, to talk to them, to feel the sensual pleasure of a horse's nuzzling. But they'd galloped off and left him gazing after their swooshing tails and tossing manes.

Though he'd told the baroness he held no false hopes, writing to her had made him hopeful. To ask for news meant there might be some to give. Word of Maurice's death would not be news. Reason told him Maurice must be dead. So the only real news *must* be good news. He thought about others he might write to, like Morgan. But suppose Morgan hadn't returned from the war. Then wouldn't it pain his mother to receive a letter addressed to him? He even thought of writing to Mrs. Hall, whom he'd never met and who likely had never heard his name. He would say he'd worked for her son before the war and esteemed him and wished to inquire . . . No, he couldn't do that either. He was stalled.

He was anxious all the time and couldn't shake it off. It felt like wartime jitters, but at the front there'd been a reason, and the pain would ease up when he was out of the noise of the guns. Now there was no respite, and having nothing to pin it on made it worse, so he got anxious about feeling anxious.

Sometimes, when the church on the square was empty, he'd sit in a pew and try to be still. The mural behind the altar showed Joan of Arc and her soldiers, the girl in silvery armor, her banner white, with fleurs-de-lis. He could lose himself for a few minutes there. But then he'd remember the reality of battle, so unlike the pretty scene, and the anguish would return, and he'd need to get moving. Today he walked to the White Rocks.

And who should he see there but those two schoolboys, the lovers he'd seen on his first day in Cassis. They were taking food from their knapsacks. Would they remember him as he did them? Not likely. He'd been in uniform then. They'd called him Tommy. Still, the curly-topped one caught his eye and held up an apple, offering it. Alec smiled to say thanks and shook his head to decline. He kept walking till he was out of their sight. He needed to piss.

At the edge of the rocks, where the water was just a couple of feet below, swimmers usually stepped down into the sea. But in other places the rocks stood upright over deeper water. One day earlier in the spring, when it was still chilly, Alec saw a man, fit and strong, stand naked on one of those taller rocks, legs apart, hands on his hips. Without touching himself, he pissed and watched the stream arc down three yards or so into the water. Then he stretched backward to face the sky, righted himself, and dived in.

Alec climbed the same rock. He breathed in the freshness. He unbuttoned his shirt; unlaced his shoes; stripped off his clothes. He stood naked with his hands on his hips. He watched his piss stream into the sea. Then he stretched back to face the sky. He noticed someone on the coastal road turn down the path toward the rocks through the scrubby pines. At first he thought he must dress again quickly or be shamed. But Charlie had told him that folks took the sun and swam nude at the rocks, even families with children. The particular section where he was standing now was, by tradition, the spot for "single men." That's why the schoolboys felt safe to dally here. So Alec did not scramble to cover himself before the approaching stranger. He held his good long stretch with his arms over his head and fingers laced together.

When he straightened up, the man was no longer on the path. He was climbing up toward him. He could see only the top of his head, hatless because the breeze had knocked off his boater and he had left it where it fell. His lustrous black hair was threaded with gray. When he reached Alec, they did not speak—indeed, they could not.

They faced each other. The spring sun, exultant, just past its midday zenith, dazzled them both—Alec stood with the coast and rocks behind him; behind the other man was the sea. To Alec, it seemed that his greenish eyes had taken on the color of the water, its light and spirit as well, as if he were part of it, had emerged from it. To the other, Alec seemed one with the massive stones he stood on; that the earth had quarried and carved his form—naked, war-hardened yet tenderly young—and then blessed him with its breath.

They faced each other. They did not speak. The moment, like the sun, dazzled them. Restored to each other. Returned from—where? They thought nothing of how this may have come about, nor of the future. Nor could they know that this moment would sustain their love for a lifetime. Its memory would overcome anger and exasperation with each other; boredom; malaise; journeys together and separations; temptations and sins against each other; illness, age. This timelessness of sea, sunlight, and stone would always call them back to their true selves.

Without speaking, Maurice touched Alec; he kissed the battle scar on his right side and then his mouth.

IX

"JERUSALEM"

31

Alec read:

6 Jan 1917

I'd always found writing a chore. But not to you.
Because when I'm writing to you you're here with me,
the two of us together, alone with each other. I made
that discovery when I started writing you on the ship
sailing to you-know-where. Even though there was
no chance of privacy at all, when I wrote to you I was
alone with you.

Maybe that's why after all the misery, madness,
drugs, being tied up and talked down to, or talked
over as if I neither heard nor understood nor was even
in the room, it actually made me feel <u>happy</u> to get this
journal back, which they'd kept with the belongings of
the other MIAs.

I'd forgot what happiness felt like. So when I felt it,
I wept and laughed at once. That was dandy with the
medics because it confirmed their erudite diagnosis
that I was crazy. Which I was.

But they didn't know that getting back my battered
copybook with the torn cover and script so smudged
and crabbed that only I (and you) could read it was like
being <u>with</u> you again!

He looked up from the notebook. Maurice was sleeping, spread-eagled across their bed. For a couple of days they'd hardly gone out, making love again and again. They were staying not in the hotel but in Alec's room, right over the water. The same sea, he thought, that had nearly drowned Maurice now soothed his sleep with its gentle lapping. He went back to reading:

> 7 Jan 17
>
> When they finally ID-ed me, they danced a jig, I'm told, because then it was official: the evacuation had been effected with no loss of life! Believe me, I was glad to contribute to <u>that</u> statistic.
>
> I had dropped everything on the beach, I remember, in order to give a push to a lifeboat overloaded with too many men—being transported out to the ships for the evacuation. Their weight snagged the boat in the shallows, so I waded in to shove it.
>
> At first the water was up to my knees, then to my waist, and then one more step and I could not feel bottom.

Alec closed his eyes. He was reading slowly, pausing often to try to picture the events. He read on:

> I heard commotion when I went under, but couldn't tell which way was shore—blackout, no light but stars thru clouds—and the lifeboat was already being towed by a barge.
>
> It was cold! The sea in December! My wet clothes were pulling me down, so I wiggled them off and

tried to keep my limbs moving—I kept picturing that frozen corpse in the snow. Then that's it. Then I don't remember.

"It was the Anzacs who fished me out of the sea, they said, and I went unconscious soon as they lay me on deck. I was naked, in shock, going blue with the cold. My tags snapped off while they were hauling me up—name, rank, nationality went down in the Aegean."

Maurice was telling Alec other parts of his story, things he didn't write about, or couldn't:

"They decided I was French. Maybe because of the black hair or maybe because the nearest Red Cross ship was French, and they wanted to get rid of me.

"On the ship, they said they pegged me for an officer, but after I came round to consciousness and still didn't speak, they had their doubts about the rank, because pretending to be mute was no game for officers. Too common, too easily faked. They said the English would not coddle me, no: the English would use electric shock on an enlisted man who played dumb. But among the French, Equality and Fraternity prevailed, so they let me be. They gave up trying to barber me, though. I was too prone to sudden movements.

"After three months onboard and still not a word out of me, they'd had enough. Plus their ship was being dispatched to the Atlantic. The English hospital at Malta agreed to receive me as a casualty of Gallipoli.

"They isolated me—seems my appearance demoralized other patients, as did my silence. Also I provoked ridicule.

'Joe Bloggs,' they called me, Name Unknown. Most of the time they kept me restrained, wrists and ankles tied to the bed frame or arms of the chair. Nights, they drugged me.

"Medical wisdom held that a soothing voice had a palliative effect on maniacs, even on those deemed unreachable, as I was, so they assigned a volunteer to read to me.

"He told me later that when he came into the room I seemed asleep in the armchair where they'd restrained me. He said, 'Hello, my friend, I'm here to visit awhile.'

"No response.

"Then he said, 'I'd like to read to you, a poem. If you're English, you may know it. But I've also got Victor Hugo with me—in case you might be French. Anyway, let's start with English. This one's called '"To Autumn."'

"No response.

"He placed a chair opposite me and read:

> *Season of mists and mellow fruitfulness,*
> *Close bosom-friend of the maturing sun;*
> *Conspiring with him how to load and bless . . .*

"He told me I made fists and pulled against the wrist bindings, but still didn't lift my head, so he spoke more softly:

> *. . . and bless*
> *With fruit the vines that round the thatch-eaves run;*
> *To bend with apples the moss'd cottage-trees*
> *And fill all fruit with ripeness to the core . . .*

"Then, he told me, I stopped struggling. I swayed my head from side to side. He thought maybe I was listening. He kept reading:

To swell the gourd, and plump the hazel shells
With a sweet kernel: to set budding more,
And still more, later flowers for the bees,
Until they think warm days will never cease . . .

"That's when I raised my head and opened my eyes, he told me. I stared out the window. I moved my mouth, but there was no sound. He moved closer, to hear if I might be whispering. I did say something, he told me, but he couldn't understand it . . ."

Maurice, whose gaze would wander or turn introspective while he was telling his story, now looked Alec steadily in the eye. "That's when I started to remember things again," he said. "I remember what I said, what he couldn't understand. I said, 'Alec.'"

Knucklehead, Alec was calling himself. If he'd but looked at a map weeks ago!—he might have shortened their anguish for each other by that much time. He would have seen on a map that Le Thoronet was a real place in France, not (as he'd supposed) a fairy-tale hamlet in Neverland. He'd also have seen that it was nearby. Even so, he could not have known that the baroness, seeking a break from the latest political hullabaloo in London, was staying there. Nor could he have known that, after months of searching for him in England, Maurice had learned nothing more than (1) Alec had gone missing and (2) the last time anyone saw him was in Paris just after the armistice. So he came to France to find him.

When Maurice wrote the baroness of his plan, she urged him to visit her at Le Thoronet. (She pitied and feared for her young friend, imagined him scouring the backstreets and morgues of Paris in desperation.) And while Maurice was there with her, she received Alec's letter at last, after it had crossed the Channel twice, forwarded back to Provence from Bedford Square.

He left immediately for Cassis and soon reached the hotel. Charlie Cavale told him that Alec liked to walk to the White Rocks.

Today was the third since his arrival. They had again walked to the rocks, whose surface was warmer than the air, but with a nippy April breeze blowing down from the northwest, they did not undress. They huddled side by side. Maurice continued his story:

"My silence all those many months?" he said. "Yes . . . I talked about it with the doctors afterwards—at length, believe me, hours on end, not by my choosing. They finally had to admit to themselves they'd get nothing interesting from me, nothing they could publish in a journal, no new data for medical science, not even a footnote. They would nod sagely at what I was telling them, but I'm sure they thought it was all bosh—that I was lying, or 'protecting the ego,' or maybe they just ruled me an old-fashioned Bedlam lunatic. Anyway, they turned me over to the chaplains."

"Why the chaplains?" Alec asked.

Maurice turned from watching the sea to face Alec full-on: "Because of what I told them . . ."

". . . ?"

"I told them again and again that I'd been dead."

Close as they were, Alec scrunched closer.

"I know it's crazy, but I'm *not* making it up."

"I believe you," Alec said.

"Truly?"

"Yes. What was it like?"

Maurice looked off over the water. "I was under the sea. The water was cold, and my limbs had no weight at all, and instead of fish, there were men, those I'd seen die and those I feared I'd killed. Horses too, those we'd shot and left on the shore. Sometimes the animals' carcasses were floating, like the bodies of some of the men, and sometimes, also like some of the men, they were alive in an otherworldly way, moving, galloping underwater, churning the floor of the sea like sand and spray on the beach." He turned to Alec and asked, "Still believe me?"

"Yes."

After a silence he continued, "When the volunteer was reading that poem to me, when I saw the water through the hospital window, I knew I wasn't under the waves anymore. I also knew you were out there somewhere."

32

He insisted on paying the hotel for taking care of Alec. He left generous tips for the staff and a check for the horse doctor. Sylvie, however, the child who lived upstairs, had grown attached to her gentle English soldier; she fussed and cried at his leaving and, to her mother's embarrassment, refused to say goodbye. Alec said that the only way to settle things fairly was to take her with him. When he picked her up and made to carry her off, she giggled and squealed and kicked till he put her down. She ran back to her mother, then back to him and hugged his legs. Finally, they parted as friends.

The lovers traveled to Thoronet. Alec saw that the home of the absentee baron was a timeworn hunting lodge, enlarged and improved since it was built, but still a modest place. Not so the décor. The baroness had recently hung the timbered walls with new paintings framed as lavishly as Old Masters, though the artists themselves were young and unknown. "The work merits the expense," she said.

Alec was drawn to a portrait of a woman wearing a Red Cross uniform and cape, who reminded him of the volunteer nurse at Slough. Behind her in the picture, he saw a sight he wished was not familiar: a scarred muddy field and a sky hardly lighter than the mud and, in the distance, flames. "Is it the sunset," Alec asked the baroness, "or a city on fire?"

"I can't tell—maybe both," she said. "The painter calls the woman *France*."

Maurice stood in silence before a picture of soldiers on the march, German prisoners together with American wounded, though it was hard to tell one side from the other. Four men were carrying a comrade on a stretcher on their shoulders. Most of them looked out at the viewer, except for one at the front of the line who was looking upward without seeing—blinded. Between the figures you could glimpse a rutted battlefield scored with barbed wire, and a flat sky the same dingy gray as the uniforms. When the baroness stepped closer to Maurice, she saw his lips moving, eyes glazed. She took his hand and led him away.

"You need more time by yourselves," she said on a terrace surrounded by woods. She suggested a digressive route home: "Instead of going right to Paris, why not take the train along the coast to Milan? From there perhaps a little side trip to Venice? It will be quiet now. Then back to Milan and across the Alps to Zurich. It's a beautiful ride. From Zurich you can get anywhere—back to France and north to England."

And so a week later, near midnight, walking across the piazza, they could still hear the musicians playing at Florian's, where they'd had a nightcap. Alec took Maurice's arm and drew him closer. The streetlamps, reflecting on the wet pavement in the drizzle, lit their way toward the Grand Canal. Alec sensed Maurice was lost in his thoughts again. "Hey . . . ," he said to him, "'twill get better."

"Are you sure?"

"Yes," he said with confidence, though he by no means felt it.

Even with the city's solid stones under his shoes, Venice seemed a stage trick to Alec. Otherwise how could these buildings float on the water? And like a show, the scene was always set to music, distant or near, played or sung, or sometimes just the lapping of the sea. The drizzle stopped. A woman appeared by the canal, wearing a filmy outfit with a scarf wafting behind, walking her Russian wolfhound on a leash. A motor skiff huffed across the lagoon. The lantern on the prow lit the profiles of two young men: the steersman gazed over the water, his companion gazed lovingly at him. Alec wondered, had he and Maurice ever been as young as those boatmen? What had the war done to them?

The sky cleared enough for the moon to illumine the larger dome of Santa Maria della Salute. Near the water's edge Maurice stopped Alec and looked him sternly in the eye: "Don't you ever die."

They were riding the Gotthard line to Zurich.

Maurice said, "After they ID-ed me, the army notified my mother. By that time she'd packed up and moved in with my youngest sister—she said she couldn't bear to stay in the house where she'd raised me. She kept the news of my safety in the family. She knew nothing about our friends, much less about you."

After the train crossed from the sunny southern face of the Alps into the gray northern slopes, the whistle shrieked on entering a tunnel. They kept quiet in the dark. When they emerged, Alec changed seats across the compartment to sit next to Maurice. It took him a moment to realize that the progress through the tunnel had been circular, not linear, that the descent into this valley was so steep that the tracks spiraled around it to ease the grade. They were viewing the scene they'd just passed from a new angle. "Look—it's that same church again," Alec said. "Like the train ride to heaven, i'n't it, this scenery? Llewellyn would know all about the church, who was the saint, when it was built; he'd have to tell you, you couldn't shut him up if you'd wanted . . ."

Maurice leaned forward with his elbows on his knees and held his head in his hands. Alec put his arm around him and felt him shudder: "Sorry, blatherin' on . . ."

"No, it's only . . ." Maurice rubbed his eyes with the heels of his hands. "That whistle shot right through my head . . . I saw things in the tunnel."

"You can tell me."

"Why pull us both down?"

Alec took Maurice's hand in his own.

"Sorry," Maurice said. Then he smiled a bit: "Train ride to heaven, eh?" He paused. "By the way, the baroness told me about my father."

"Ah . . ."

"She also told me she told you. I'd rather have told you myself."

"Are you vexed with her?"

"No. She said she thought it important for you to know and she wasn't sure of anything then, not that she'd see you again or that you'd see me again."

"Do you believe her?"

"About my father? Don't you?"

"Didn't know the man," Alec said. "Occurred to me maybe she conjectured what she said about him. The lady does keep some odd company."

"Like us?"

"Just so."

"No, I believe her, and I'll tell you why. I felt she was telling me something I already knew."

"Hmm."

"Funny, though—at first I was insulted," Maurice said.

"You mean, *How could you dare say such a thing that my da was one of those?*"

"Exactly."

"Tough habit to break, feelin' insulted."

"Poor Papa . . ."

"Why's that?"

"Oh come on, you know what I mean—marrying, getting kids. I wonder was he afraid not to?"

"Maybe he truly wanted to marry," Alec said, "maybe he truly wanted *you*." This idea, he saw, was new to Maurice. "I've never heard you say he was anything but good to you and the girls."

"Yes, but still . . ."

"Had it been only fear that moved him to marry, you'd have felt it. Fear and hatred, they're near the same, and you'd have felt the hatred from him. He must have wanted you, he must have loved you. Mrs. Hall too—you've never spoke of them quarreling. Always good to her, was he? Kind?"

"Oh yes, always."

"Then I'd say he loved her."

Maurice settled back, his face more peaceful than Alec had seen since their reunion. "Do you really think it's possible?" he said, almost to himself. "I guess people are complicated." The valley seemed to pivot for them in the train's descent. "You know, in one way I envy Papa . . ."

"How's that?"

"His fatherhood."

"What's that about, now? Provin' you're manly as your dad?"

"Who's talking? You bragged to me once that you could get a kid like snapping your fingers."

"Then I was a kid myself, to be makin' such a boast, puffin' out my chest at you."

"Hmmph."

"Or perhaps . . ."

". . . ?"

". . . or perhaps ya truly do wish for a Maurice III?"

The train quietly rolled on through the mountains whose tops merged with clouds. Maurice smiled a serene smile: "Or . . . why not a little Alexandra? Such a lovely name, don't you think?"

Alec summoned his Dorset brogue: "Would ya kindly wipe that smirk off yer otherwise pretty face, laddie?"

33

On landing in England, they traveled to Dorset, at Alec's request, to the village of Osmington. They paused in the lane before the Scudders' cottage, which Fred had listed with an agent for sale after Aderyn's death. The place, overgrown, was missing the care of the family who had once tended it as their own. The lovers had no key. They walked on to St. Osmund's to visit the churchyard.

"SCUDDER," Alec read on the marker of his father's grave. "Weird, i'n't it?" he said to Maurice. "Your own name on a headstone? Eerie. First time I'm seein' it; it wasn't in place for the funeral."

"Yes, stops you in your tracks," Maurice said. He didn't say that his own father's gravestone was eerier still, since it read MAURICE CHRISTOPHER HALL.

Alec spoke to the grave: "Da, I'm sorry Ma's so very far away." He edged closer to Maurice, feeling his warmth through his clothes. It reminded him of that uncanny sense of someone's presence on the day when he'd passed their old building on Bernard Street.

From the cemetery, they went on to visit the Blunt farm. Little Phyllis was nearly six years old. Mabel rang the triangle on the back porch to let her husband know their guests had arrived.

"Overseein' the second planting," Van said on coming in from the fields, "and doin' some of it myself." He shook hands with Maurice: "So you're the gentleman whose proposition kept our Alec from emigratin' to safety before the war."

Mabel said, "That's hardly a courteous welcome, Vanny Blunt."

Maurice took no offense. "Oh, Alec's his own man. I couldn't have kept him from doing what he truly wants. No one can, I'm sure you know. Of course I was glad when he chose to stay and work with me, but then none of us knew what was coming, did we?"

"Amen," said Mabel.

"And Van," Alec said, "who's to say I'd not have shipped back from the Argentine to sign on with all the other loonies?"

Mabel poured tea at her big kitchen table. Alec approved the lack of pretense. She knew who she was; she spoke respectfully to Maurice but was not cowed by his looks or manners. Alec decided Van had married a woman as confident as himself.

Maurice, meantime, was trying to puzzle out his host. Who was this prosperous farmer with the heroic figure and attractive face? Why so protective of Alec? He was sure the man gazed at Alec with fondness, but it seemed with longing as well. He could readily understand why he should be skeptical of a stranger from London, but, unless he was mistaken, Van was undressing him with his eyes. Also he thought he'd heard a certain tone in his greeting that suggested he knew their truth.

Van was puzzling likewise. Before the war, he'd scoffed at Alec (then hardly more than a youngster) when he told Van about his love for this gentleman. But Alec had since proven his mettle. He wondered who was this Maurice Hall, to inspire such devotion, even as far as leaving the safety Van had offered Alec in Paris and returning to harm's way for his sake?

His eyes passed from Maurice's face to that of the younger man. He remembered the beauty of Alec's naked form, remembered kissing his eyes closed in the passion of their embrace. He pictured Alec's surrender to the one who faced him across the table, their fierce pleasure together. He ached with yearning and envy. "I've written to Freddy," Van said to Alec. "I'm considerin' makin' an offer on the old Scudder cottage."

"Whatever for?"

"To rent to tenants, perhaps. We Blunts hold that property's the best investment. How would that sit with you if I were to do so?"

"Not sure. It's a sweet little place."

"Let me know, then, Alec. Should ya ever come back to these parts, perhaps you and Mr. Hall might lease it."

"Now tell me, was this the same Fanny Blunt—"

"Sshh," Alec said, with a glance aside to the other diners at the inn, "they're all ears, these villagers; they're already whisperin' about us. And, as you know quite well, it's Vanny, not Fanny. For Ivanhoe."

Maurice rolled his eyes, lowered his voice, and went on: "So was this the same fellow Mrs. Scudder once said 'smote his palm with his fist' when she told him you'd missed the *Normannia?*"

"Yes, one and the same."

"And why would he get so worked up about your staying?"

"Dunno." Alec shrugged. "He's an old friend of the family, mostly Fred's."

Maurice cocked an eyebrow. Alec offered a feeble smile. Upstairs in their room, he confessed. "Van was my first."

Maurice, reaching for his pipe, stopped short. "Oh?" He found the tobacco tin. "Well, that's understandable . . ." He turned around to Alec. "Striking fellow. Splendid physique."

"My first and my only, before you."

"Uh-huh."

"Truly."

Maurice tapped shreds of tobacco into the briar bowl. "Well set up, very handsome."

"No more so than you."

Maurice lit the pipe and drew on it.

"Come on, Maurice, you should be glad—"

"Mm . . . ?" He puffed. "Glad about Blunt?"

"But for him I'd have been an ignorant kid when we met."

"Taught you things, did he?"

Alec grabbed the pipe away from him.

"Hey!" Maurice said.

"As I'm sure Clive Durham taught you." Alec drew on the pipe. He frowned. "What's this damn stuff?"

"Louisiana perique."

"Pah—"

Maurice reached for the pipe. "Give it here."

Alec held it back.

"All right: since you've brought up old business, Clive Durham taught me nothing! He's cold as a dead fish. His idea of passion was a peck on the shirt cuff."

"Wha'—?" Alec giggled. "Shirt cuff?"

"You heard me." Maurice grabbed back his pipe. "All your jealousy wasted."

"You mean you and he never—?"

Maurice smoked and nodded.

"But they said . . ."

"Who, the servants?"

"*I* was a servant—"

"Lest we ever forget—"

"But you seemed—"

"What? What did I seem?"

"That you knew what you were doin' . . . somewhat."

"I was following you, at first. Then nature took over. I didn't need lessons, I only needed you." He sat down.

Alec caressed his hair. "My love, how very sweet you can be—at times."

"Well, it knocks me off my nut—to picture you having a joust with Sir Galahad." Maurice rapped his pipe against the side of the ashtray to settle it.

Alec started untying his necktie. "Listen, I was a kid with Van and lucky that he's an honest fellow, a kind fellow, and not somethin' else." He unbuttoned his shirt. "We had a little fun together, but it was nothin' like us, you and me." He stepped out of his shoes and trousers, standing before Maurice in singlet and drawers. "Nothin' like the way we are." He pulled the singlet off over his head. He touched his battle scar on his side. "Ugly, i'n't it?"

"What? No, Alec—it's not ugly. It's just . . . you."

"Now, *that's* why I love you! *You* understand. It's like a scar or a wound, I think, love is; hurts to acquire, but once you've got it, it's who you are. I wouldn't trade this scar for the perfect skin I owned when I was a boy, when I knew Van, before I knew you."

Maurice drew him closer to his chair; he slid Alec's drawers down to the floor, wrapped his arms around his waist, kissed his belly, closed his eyes, and rested his head there: "Alec . . ."

That night, as Van made his way to the big bed in the front bedroom of the farmhouse, Mabel Blunt could not help but notice her husband's prick—even concealed, as it was, by his nightshirt. She noticed for a couple of reasons. Since he had returned from the war she had seen him in no such state. And this particular erection was also noteworthy for its size and stamina, unprecedented, she believed, in all their marriage. When Van was under the covers beside her (with his back to her), she said, "You seem quite stirred up today."

"Hm?"

"Since our visit from Alec Scudder and Mr. Hall."

"What's that? Oh no, it's just the second plantin' got me worried. Gettin' the seed in on time and tryin' to get these lugs I've hired to shake a leg."

"Let's count ourselves fortunate we've found any help at all."

"Yeah, yer right, of course. Still, it's all a bit maddening. Goin' on these four years since the fields been properly tilled, and for what? The whims of our so-called Great Ones." He punched his pillow and resettled his head.

Mabel knew Van's secret—some of it. Her sister-in-law Rowena had gossiped to her about having spied Van once with the Scudder boy in the barn before the wedding. Rowena found it funny, as she found most things, and Mabel, though troubled, laughed it off with her. But then she started to notice how Van eyed comely lads and ignored striking girls. Practical as she was, she made peace with herself about the matter: better that Van should play with lads than squander their money on some other woman, or—God forbid!—a second family. Her husband was preposterously good-looking; she guessed people wondered how Mabel White, bony and sparrow-chested, could have fetched such a prize. Maybe it was her boyish figure that had appealed to Van. More likely her dowry, including that small but prizewinning herd.

She chose therefore to content herself with the comfort and warmth of his strength in her bed every night, with their house and the farm and the family they were creating, with his kindness. At last she answered him: "Oh, I don't know, I guessed that perhaps their visit reminded you of the war."

"Ah . . ."

Under the sheets, she embraced him best she could from behind; it was a stretch for her, so broad was his torso. "Van?"

"Hmm?" He caught her hand in his own and held it close against him.

"It's time, don't you think, Phyllis had a sister or brother?" He turned over to face her. She continued, "This farm is far too big to weigh its future on the shoulders of one little child."

He caressed her and took her in his arms; he raised the hem of her nightgown, feeling between her legs, squeezing, not tightly, then releasing, and again and again till she moaned, kissing her till she softened, dampened. Her breath deepened, her whole body relaxed and charged at once. Her mind pictured her husband's strong hands at last month's birthing of the lambs, helping to draw them from the ewes and then prodding the newborns, coaxing them to come alive, to open their eyes and bleat and stand on their legs to nurse from their mothers. Van and the shepherds as midwives—such tenderness . . .

Then she felt her husband fill her to her guts, it seemed, to her very heart. She pressed her face into his neck. What did she hear? Was he sobbing? Yes. Why?

She started counting the months in her mind. Come next winter, she was certain, there would be a baby.

34

Since returning from the war, Maurice had been careful to write or, if possible, to phone Mrs. Hall regularly whenever he was away from home. On the recent trip to France, he'd wired her about the success of his mission to locate the missing soldier; he then wrote that he would be making his way back to London at a tourist's pace and followed up with postcards from Venice and Zurich. In none of these communications did he name the soldier, much less mention that they were traveling together. When he'd reached England, he phoned her. "So you've been all right, Mother? And Auntie?"

"Yes, Morrie. Of course, it's rather lonely without you. The house seems a bit empty, two old women rattling around . . ."

Maurice sighed. How often had he heard that complaint? He tried changing the subject. "Oh, I'm sure that Ada and the baby must be keeping you busy."

"Ada was very patient with me during those horrible months you were missing, so very kind—I may have worn out my welcome."

"No, surely . . ."

"One senses these things. But then, I do have *two* daughters. What of my elder girl?"

Maurice recognized the bitter tone. "Ah, still no visit?"

"How could I have wronged Kitty, that she should treat me so coldly?"

"I'm sure it's her work keeping her busy, as she says . . ."

"And that place where she lives! If you could only have seen it . . ." Her voice was shaky.

"Mama?"

"I'm sorry . . ."

He did not like to get caught between his sisters and their mother, but now he felt an obligation as the only son to try to make things right for her: "Listen. I've a couple of friends who live near Sheffield. I was planning to visit them—to follow up on some business I'd started before the war. I was thinking I'd go later, but I could go sooner instead and . . ."

"And call on her? Would you, please?"

"Yes, I shall. Give me a few days. I'll wire you."

"Oh thank you. But Morrie—?"

"I'm here."

"On the Continent, you were careful where you dined?"

"What's that—?"

"I don't trust those foreign sauces. You never know what's in them—too many ingredients—"

Mrs. Hall's elder daughter had made good on her intention to volunteer as a nurse after the outbreak of the war. In public, the mother approved the noble gesture, of course. (Could she do otherwise?) But in private, she shook her head: she'd raised her girls delicately, not to confront God-knows-what horrors in hospital wards. Besides, Kitty did not have the constitution for such work. She'd nearly died of scarlet fever as a child; she must therefore be exceptionally prone to infection. Mrs. Hall blamed herself for her daughter's rashness. When was it—in 1912, 1913?—she'd allowed the girls to take that course offered by the Red Cross on how to apply bandages in an emergency. If she'd only stood more firmly against it. But they wheedled and pleaded about "all the other mothers" till she gave in—on the condition that she accompany them. To be sure, it seemed harmless then. They even cajoled dear Clive Durham into letting them practice on him and wrapped him like a mummy. Those were happier times, when Maurice and the young squire were friends. Who could have known what was coming? But even now, with the peace, Kitty continued her medical work, despite her mother's reminders that her twenty-fifth birthday was approaching, and she might give some thought to her personal life, particularly marriage. "At your age, I was expecting my second baby. Who, by the way, dear, was *you*."

"It's selfish of you, Mama, demanding that I visit when there's so much need all around us. Remember, your own son once relied on the care of his nurses."

With Maurice, Kitty tugged the right maternal heartstring. Mrs. Hall considered perhaps it *was* selfish of her to expect her daughter to come to London. Therefore she went to Sheffield, where Nurse Hall was living and rotating her service among three military hospitals.

She went uninvited, unannounced, and prompted by an intuition that something was amiss. She made her way through the town's dirt, the miasma of soot, the squalling children, the want and envy of those who hated the sight of such a well-dressed lady as herself. She was particularly pained by the eyes of those young veterans (often maimed) who stood about idle or begging. Of what did they wish to accuse her?

At last she reached a building on an unpaved street and asked a neighbor for Miss Hall.

"The nurse?"

"Yes, Nurse Hall."

The neighbor climbed the stairs and returned: "No answer at the door."

"I'd like to wait in her room, then. I'm her mother. I've traveled from London to visit."

"I haven't a key."

"Oh." She looked up at the frayed curtains in the window that she imagined was Kitty's. She offered the neighbor a coin. "Would you please say I called?"

On the train back, Mrs. Hall was upset: she could not dismiss the feeling that Kitty had in fact been there in her room when she called. She was unsure if she was more concerned for her daughter's well-being or infuriated by this slap in the face.

35

On Empire Day in the spring of 1919, children all over the kingdom had been singing:

> *And did those feet in ancient time*
> *Walk upon England's mountains green?*

Alec couldn't get the tune out his head, nor the words, nor the music of their treble voices all mixed up with the military bands, parades of open motorcars, carriages, and officers on horseback. Men in uniform—Canadians, Anzacs, Indians—still marching, why? What next? "Bolshevik Terror!" The dailies were screeching that the BEF would go off to fight the Reds next. "Oh for Christ's sake," he thought, "just send the weary lads home."

> *And was the holy Lamb of God,*
> *On England's pleasant pastures seen!*

> *And did the Countenance Divine,*
> *Shine forth upon our clouded hills?*
> *And was Jerusalem builded here,*
> *Among these dark Satanic Mills?*

Before the war, at the Working Men's College, Harrison Grant had decoded Blake's mystical verses for his students.

Once upon a time, he told them, according to legend, during the Hidden Years of his unrecorded life, the young Jesus had sailed to England with Joseph of Arimathea. Yes, the holy Lamb of God in the company of the man whom the legend called a tin merchant and who, in due time, according to the St. John gospel, would receive his young charge's divine body from the cross. He would bury Jesus in the tomb he'd had carved for himself.

Alec wondered if Professor Grant had volunteered for battle. He seemed the sort that would have made the valiant gesture, even in his fifties, so devoted to his students that he would wish to fight with them and for them. Had he survived the war? Or had he died, along with all his knowledge and passion . . . ?

George's prediction, made back when they enlisted, turned out right: the parcel of forestland they'd found before the war was bought up while they were in battle, its great trees felled for Satanic Mills. They were now standing in front of the weapons factory built there, put up as fast and cheaply as possible and meant to be temporary, but proving to be permanent, along with its warehouses and service roads. Scores of additional acres had been cleared for a much different purpose: for summer cottages, each featuring a picturesque little turret.

The children had sung:

> *Bring me my Bow of burning gold:*
> *Bring me my Arrows of desire:*
> *Bring me my Spear—O clouds unfold!*
> *Bring me my Chariot of fire!*

Now there was no other forestland for sale—neither nearby nor anywhere, it seemed, in all of England. Where to go now?

Maurice sighed and said, "Seen enough?"

36

Ted and George had welcomed their young friends back to stay at Millthorpe. There, they decided that Maurice should seek out his sister in Sheffield on his own. Alec would meanwhile return to Osmington. He'd given Van the go-ahead on buying the Scudder cottage, and Van invited him to visit to see if there were things he wanted.

The cloudless sky brightened the sight of Alec's empty home. The agent had offered him the key, but he'd found his own in a pocket of his old army pack. He'd had it with him, forgotten it, all through the war.

He hesitated before opening the door. Why the dread? He was tempted to walk away and tell Van to sell what he could and toss the rest. His parents owned nothing valuable: unloading their things would likely cost more than the lot was worth. But what of the pictures, mementos? He conceded a family obligation and turned the key in the lock.

Inside it was hazy with dust, motes scattering in the air when he closed the door. All else was stillness. In the kitchen, he saw breakfast dishes by the sink. Had Aderyn left them to wash on that morning more than two years ago when she'd planned to come home after seeing Fred off from Southampton?

He heard the faintest of sounds, something rusty yet musical. What was it? His grandmother's spinet. He must have stirred the air enough to make its wires vibrate. He stood at the yellowed keyboard and pressed a key. Instead of a note, it yielded a little thud, the hammer within likely broken. He ran his finger along an octave.

He took down some pictures from a wall in the parlor, tintypes of forebears, bridal couples. These he would send to his brother, along with Fred and Jane's own wedding photo, colored by hand. There was also a wedding picture of Ma and Da, posed in a studio against a background of a painted garden scene with a real balustrade. That he would keep for himself.

He braced himself to go into his parents' bedroom. (Maurice had warned him the visit would be hard, and so it was proving.) In that bed between the windows, his mother told him, he'd been born. He'd been an easy birth, as births go, she said, easier than Fred, and . . . She did not complete the thought and her eyes turned sad. Was she remembering the twins, stillborn? Or maybe Susan's fevered cradle beside the bed? How it must have pained her when her granddaughter took ill, remembering her own baby's ordeal. His knees suddenly went weak with sorrow and he sank down on the floor at the foot of the bed. He cried out loud, "Oh, Ma . . ."

He took hold of the footboard to pull himself up. In the patchwork quilt, he thought he recognized some squares from old curtains and such. Then it struck him that he'd been conceived in that bed as well as born in it, and Fred and the others too. The room seemed a shrine to his parents' life together, their most ordinary life.

His mother's clothes were already gone—sent on to Buenos Aires by a neighbor at her request. He was glad of that. Only his father's things remained to be looked through. He turned away from the bed to cross to the dresser. He was surprised to see his own face on the wall, a photo of him in uniform taken shortly after enlisting, hung where his parents could see it when they were lying in bed. The picture was not yet five years old, but how much younger the face appeared than the one he could see in the film-streaked mirror.

He opened a drawer—Da's shirts and long johns and a thick-knitted cardigan. He knew his father's clothes: in the closet would be two coats and four pairs of trousers, overalls, a mackintosh, a topcoat, but not his Sunday black suit—he'd been buried in it. None of the clothes would fit Alec; and Fred, whom they might fit, wouldn't want them. He opened a small top drawer. There, with his father's collars, was his watch, also his cuff links, a wedding gift from his bride. Aderyn must have held them back from the coffin to pass on to their sons. Beneath these valuables, he found an envelope, unsealed and unaddressed, holding a letter. He opened it and read:

My own dearest son,

We just returned from the train to see you off. I sat with your mother for a time with no word spoke betwixt us but at last she sed she woud lay down & has done so upon our bed where I hear her talking to your picture.

Thryce the Lord has taken you from us. First three yeers ago when you were to cross the sea with Fred. But then you upeered befor us the very next day! You will never know how my heart did leep when I saw you. Then to leeve us again for this curst war. That was twyce. But again you came back to us hurt but alyve. Now to set off again back to that place of death. I have no words for such back & forth joy and sorrow. Pray God bring you home to us onct for all.

I shall not post this to you now, lest the sensers

tare it up or you shoud be sad for our sake, but when
the war ends & you are returned to us forever then I
shall read it to you with lafter & care nothing for how
foolish I upeere to hold you & kiss you, man that you
are, as my own sweete boy.

—Da
30 Aug 1916

Walking toward the address in Sheffield, Maurice encountered veterans (as his mother had done), but instead of has-
tening to pass them by (as she had), he stopped to greet them,
a pair of men, one lame, the other missing his left hand. He
asked where they'd served and with what outfit. When they
ascertained that Maurice too had seen battle (at first they'd
taken him for a lily-white staffer), their attitude changed from
resentment to a gruff kind of brotherhood, and then to respect
when they learned he'd fought at Gallipoli. He urged them
please to accept some money and enjoy a couple of rounds on
him, assuring them that he'd join them for a pint himself but
for urgent family business. As he reached for his wallet, he
heard a woman behind him also greet the men. He turned to
face his sister, who was even more surprised than he.

Alec sat on the bed and read the letter again. He closed his
eyes and pictured his father writing . . . Where would he have
sat? At that little table in Alec's old room? Yes! Where his

schoolboy son had worked equations and drawn triangles and identified parts of speech. He pictured his father, hunched, his rough large hand guiding a pen in the delicate task of forming words on paper, giving shape to a passion beyond words, that of his fatherhood. Alec kissed the letter. He said aloud, to no one, "I want to be buried with this."

And for the second time in his life, the knowledge of being loved overwhelmed him. The first time, when the kingfisher danced near the boathouse at Penge, the knowledge had washed over him like water, like the rain on the pond, cleansing him of his doubts and freeing him to trust Maurice and to stay in England to make their love real. This second time, in spite of the cottage's dust and shadow, the knowledge came as light. The light revealed that he was loved to his core, also that he had done nothing to earn or merit such love, but that it was love's nature to love.

37

"She's with child," Maurice told him in their room at Mill-thorpe.

Alec made no reply. He watched the rain on the greening hills through the window. Then he asked, "Is she well?"

"Healthy, you mean?"

"Yeah, comfortable?"

"Far as I can tell. She didn't complain of any illness. Her face is quite serene, even radiant."

"Ah . . ."

"But she's troubled, very . . ."

"Of course."

"There's the marriage thing."

"The father's dead?"

"No, alive."

"Oh? Then he's got to—"

"He's married."

"Oh . . ." Alec shifted in the old overstuffed armchair. "Even so, there's a duty on his part—"

"Alec, the man's . . . not English."

"Catholic, you mean, so he can't divorce?"

"No. Oh Lord . . ."

". . . ?"

"He's Indian."

Alec's eyes widened: "From India?"

"Yes, an Indian officer, with a wife and two kids in Madras—wounded in France. She was caring for him shortly before the armistice. He's returned home and knows nothing about the child. She does not intend to tell him."

Alec let out a long breath: "Indian . . ."

"That's right."

"So he's—"

"Yes, colored. As the child will be—"

In his mind (in a flash), an imp drove Alec through a gauntlet, where other imps (with ugly little faces, some wearing monocles, others tiaras) cudgeled him not with clubs but with the English language's array of hateful words about the pregnant woman and her paramour. He held his tongue till his mind escaped into his father's arms, so to speak, into the embrace of the letter he was carrying in his jacket pocket near his heart. Finally he said, "We need to help her."

"Yes. I've thought about going to Madras."

"Whatever for?"

"To find him."

"But why?"

"That man has insulted my sister—"

"Wait—no!—are you sayin' he *forced* himself on her?"

"Oh no, nothing like that. She said she loved him."

"Then what insult are you talking about?"

"I'm talking about my family's honor."

"And you're going to fix that—how? A duel? Like *The Three Musketeers*? How the fuck would that help her?"

"Alec—"

"What, you kill the man? Brilliant! Then you've got a couple of Indian kids with no dad in addition to your sister's. And you're locked up in Madras till an Indian jury finds you guilty of murder and they hang you—" Maurice wanted to interrupt, but Alec barreled on: "Or, *or*, what if you lose this honor match of yours, eh? Could happen, ya know. What if *he* does away with *you*? Then your sister's got no husband *and* no brother, plus your corpse to fetch home from thousands of miles away. Plus they hang *him* for killin' *you*, so we're back to three fatherless kids—"

"Alec—"

"And what about *me*?"

"You clearly do not understand."

"Yeah, I understand, rude and menial that I am—"

"Aw jeezus, here we go—"

"I understand it's the stupidest thing I hope to ever hear you say."

Maurice stood to leave. "I don't have to listen to this."

Alec stopped him: "Tell her about us."

Maurice opened his mouth to speak and shut up without a word. Then he said, "That's—ridiculous! The absolute limit! And you call *me* stupid?"

In truth, the suggestion (blurted out with no forethought) had stunned Alec no less than Maurice. But now he stuck by his idea: "You let her know she's not the only outcast, she's not alone. That's how we help her, to start."

"You want me to tell my *sister* I'm a criminal?"

"Tell her that you love me, and that I love you."

Nurse Hall, now that she had nothing to hide from her brother, readily agreed to meet again. She suggested a tea parlor in the Abbeydale section of Sheffield, near St. John's Red Cross Hospital. Alec waited in a park around the corner, where raw drizzle was yielding to sunshine so warm that the hyacinths seemed to open while he looked at them.

Alec had prevailed in their dispute by reminding Maurice of his own courage, of the night when he'd taken leave of Clive Durham and told the squire frankly that he loved the gamekeeper. That was that. No second thoughts, no hesitating for fear of possible consequences. He'd simply spoken the truth.

"But family . . . ," Maurice protested, "complicates everything. Besides, much as you dislike him, Clive's a gentleman and so I could trust him to be straight up in our quarrel and not try to knife me in the back later."

"All right, then, let's be gentlemanly ourselves."

"How so?"

"Judgin' from what you tell me, Miss Hall is likewise someone to be trusted—I mean that a lady like her should choose, *choose*, out of a sense of duty or kindliness or greatheartedness, to slop around in hospitals and tend the sick and wounded and dyin'. That's fuckin' noble, if you ask me, even heroic. And now she's been truthful with her brother, though she might rather have done otherwise."

"But—"

"Granted, she had little choice in the circumstances. But that accords you the chance to speak the truth in return, freely, by no force of necessity."

So they were here today in Sheffield, Alec in the park while the two Halls drank tea. The brother, it was planned, would break the news to the sister and then bring her to meet his beloved. But as the afternoon lengthened, anxiety started to prey on Alec, dragging his thoughts from calamity (i.e., what if she becomes enraged and threatens to expose them?) to catastrophe (i.e., what if they should consequently be ripped apart and imprisoned?), thence to bleak rumination about the war: though it had not killed him outright, it had so crushed him that he would have died in France but for the charity of others . . .

"Alec," Maurice called from some yards away.

As they approached, Alec thought the sister looked familiar. Her hair was as dark as her brother's, and she had lovely eyes, greenish, magnified by her glasses.

"Kitty," Maurice said to her, "I'd like you to meet my friend, Alec Scudder."

Then Alec said, "You're the VAD nurse."

"Beg pardon?" she said.

"At Slough. Sorry. Did you volunteer at Slough?"

"Yes, I worked there . . ."

"I was your patient."

"No."

"Truly."

She laughed out loud. "No! When?"

"Summer of 1916. First battle of the Somme. Collapsed right lung."

At a loss for words, she said, "I'm sorry, but so many . . . Collapsed lung, you say?"

"That's correct. Welsh Fusiliers, Private Scudder."

She looked from Alec to her brother and then back at Alec and said, "And you—? And Maurice—?"

In her rooms, Alec listened quietly to the sister and brother talk. Her place was as shabby as the building was run-down, but she did not apologize for it. Alec liked her for that.

"I've put off thinking about what to do next," she said, "keeping busy with work. But that's changing. St. John's is closing. Earlier today, before I joined you, I was saying good-bye to friends and patients. Next they'll close the military wing of the Ecclesall Infirmary . . . Of course, there's still Wharncliffe—they've treated forty-seven thousand over the last three years."

"But surely, Kitty," Maurice said, "you can't keep working."

"You're right, I can't. I'm 'showing,' as we say, and I've long since felt life . . . Oh, Maurice, I was so very angry with you when you came up on me with no warning. But now I'm relieved. The family must know sometime. And it's best you're the first. We're more alike now than we ever were growing up."

"How's that?"

"Because you were there, and saw it, and lived through it, as I have, and your friend. And that makes us different from all those people who were not. It's like I'm watching them from another world. What do you say? We can't describe it, and they can't fathom. I couldn't face Mother that day she came to the door, I still don't want to."

"I understand."

"Please don't think I'm brave. Don't think for a minute I haven't wished I might lie, invent a secret wartime marriage to an officer who died in combat and then play the respectable young widow. But that lie won't work for me. My child's color, they'll call that a worse crime than illegitimacy. Listen to me! *Illegitimate*, as if a child's birth needs the approval of a magistrate! My child's color, that will be my mortal sin, unforgivable in the eyes of the Hall family and jolly old England. Thou Shalt Not. Ever.

"I've thought, should I go to India, where the baby might fit in? Would we, though, among our colonial sahibs? 'Touched by the tar-brush,' don't they say? As for me, I'm sure they'd fling their arms wide open to the fallen Englishwoman gone native before she even arrived. Besides, I know nothing of India. Why should I pass my years like a criminal in exile in a place where my fellow countrymen will despise me? Does *my* life count for nothing? Truly, I cannot see a way forward."

As they walked to the train from Kitty's rooms, Maurice told Alec about their talk in the tea parlor. "She said she's amazed to learn of you and me, but by no means upset, much less scandalized. 'Why are you amazed?' I asked her. 'Because you always seemed such a conformist,' she said."

Alec chuckled: "Not since I climbed in your window."

"She makes a good case that tending the wounded is like being wounded yourself, maybe worse, time and again, with no chance for healing, always another casualty. Good God, she's witnessed so much misery! And suffered plenty of her own. Anyway, she says she welcomes love any way it manifests. 'It's the enemy of war,' she says. So she's glad for us."

"Now, that is amazing."

"Yes. When I hear her talk like that, I can understand how the baby came about."

On the train, Maurice and Alec each kept to his own thoughts. Alec reluctantly acknowledged to himself that he'd been afraid to meet Maurice's sister, of how she might look down on him. But in the face of her hardship, he now renounced such emotion as unmanly, selfish, silly. Maurice stared out the window, elbow on the armrest, chin on fist.

Alec spoke up when they were approaching Millthorpe: "Can *you* see a way forward?"

Maurice shook his head. "I was just thinking about breaking this news to Mother and Ada and my aunt . . ." He shuddered.

38

Teddy opened the door and said quietly, "Morgan's reading to us." They paused in the parlor archway to listen:

When one of them used to pass by the market-place
of Seleucia, about the time of nightfall,
a tall young man of perfect beauty,
with the joy of immortality in his eyes
and perfumed black hair,
the people used to watch him
and ask one another whether they knew him,
whether he was a Syrian Greek or a stranger. But some
who looked with greater attention
understood and made way;
and while he disappeared under the archways
among the evening lights and the shadows
on his way to the place that lives only at night
with orgies and drunkenness
and every kind of lust and debauchery,
they wondered which of Them it was
and for what unavowed pleasure
he had come down to the streets of Seleucia
from the Sacred and Hallowed Dwellings.

The listeners murmured. When Morgan looked up from the page and saw Alec framed by the arch, he beamed. "Here he is! My dear, old, young friend—"

They crossed to each other to shake hands; Alec drew him closer and kissed him on both cheeks. Morgan reddened. "I have *agonized* over your safety these last months," he said. He turned to the others. "But doesn't he look well, Risley? Fully a man now—"

"Well indeed," Risley answered.

At supper the talk got around to the verses Morgan had been reading, the work of a Greek man he met in Alexandria when serving with the Red Cross at the military hospital there. "I do love that city," he said. "Sights, smells, attitudes—thoroughly cosmopolitan, with expatriates from all over the world. Greeks have been living there since Ptolemy."

"That last poem you read us," George said, "about the stunner on his way to orgies—what's it called?"

"'One of Their Gods.'"

"Aha!" Risley said. "The pronominal key in the title! *Their* gods—that is, the Hellenists, the 'pagans' in Alexandria. Unlike the speaker of the verses, no doubt a timid Byzantine Christian, terrified of his own urges."

"Oh, I think otherwise," Morgan said. "It seemed to me the only 'timid' people in Alexandria, scared of their 'own urges,' were we English. For instance, when we took charge, we right away shut down the brothels, though they'd been flourishing for centuries. And it goes without saying they tried to close the men's bathhouses," Morgan said.

George thwacked the table and protested, "*No!*" They all turned to him. "I mean, where else could a man bathe?"

"Don't fret, Georgie, with the bathhouses they had no

luck," Morgan said. "And on the streets, boys and men were flirting openly with one another."

"Good for them!" George said.

"Tsk, tsk, it's the climate, no doubt," Teddy said. "Excessive sunshine causes hypersexuality."

"One must visit," Risley said.

"But about the poem," Morgan said. "I take the speaker for a Hellenist, one who recognizes that the dark young man is divine, maybe even the god Eros, a visitor from Olympus. On the other hand, in the *title* the poet himself is speaking, giving the verses a curatorial touch, don't you see, as if we're admiring an antique text. *Voilà!* Timeless artifact! Spanking-new museum piece! At once ancient and au courant, and therefore perfectly Alexandrian and equally at home in Bloomsbury."

After the others had gone to bed, student and mentor sat together in the parlor with a little brandy.

"I didn't know how much I'd missed you till I saw you," Alec said to Morgan.

"Thank you. You've been my consolation in all this—and my hope."

"In the war, you mean?"

"Yes, and after. You and Maurice together. Hope for all of us." Morgan sipped his brandy. "You were quiet at dinner."

"I was happy to listen. Lots of wisdom at that table tonight, from books and from life."

"Maurice was quiet too. Are you all right?"

Alec stared at his glass. "Well enough, I guess." He sipped, looked up at his friend: "Truth be told, Morgan, I'm a fuckin' wreck. Maurice too. He wakes up wailin' in the night, like a child, enough to break your heart." His voice began to quaver. "It's all changed now, everything, i'n't it? We were goin' to live in the greenwoods—remember? But there's no woods left. And even if there was such a place anymore, or had been ever, how could we go there, the two of us, changed like we are?"

They were quiet together. Morgan wanted to comfort his friend. He said, "You've changed, eh?"

Alec nodded.

"Would you rather you hadn't?

"How's that—?"

"Would you rather be as you were?"

"Before the war?" Alec asked.

"Before the war."

"Not much use sayin' yes, is there? Or no . . ."

"Perfect answer. There's no *un*-changing, is there?" Morgan paused, then went on: "The war has forced memories on me, as it has on you and Maurice, of things I wish I'd never seen, things I wish I'd never even heard about. Shattered my beliefs. What I'd been taught to call civilization and barbarism, the war turned those ideas upside down—along with my notions of being English, or being a man." He finished his brandy. "It hurt like hell and still does." He poured a bit more. "'Respectability.' That's what I once called my way of life. In truth it was cowardice."

"I've always thought of you as brave," Alec said. "In the trenches, when I'd think of you, I'd say to myself, 'I'm lucky to know such a man.'"

"How kind you are. Before the war, I'd no experience—with sex, or intimacy. That's changed now."

"I'm glad for you."

"Sex was easy, once I'd made up my mind. So many of

us lonely men, patients and medics, at the hospital where I worked. Right on the beach at Alexandria. What a scene: scores of convalescing soldiers playing in the sea all day long, as naked as if they'd never worn clothes, and lying on the sand side by side well into the evenings. To no one's surprise, there was a trysting place . . ."

Alec grinned: "And so . . . ?"

"And so."

"Wonderful!"

"Yes, entirely delightful. But why had it taken a war to set me free? I'd pinioned myself, trapped myself—or aided those who'd sought to do so. I look back and shake my head at my own cowardice.

"But love, I soon learned, and as you know well, takes far more effort than sex. We've so few models, men like us, for intimacy, for devotion that endures. By no fault of our own. How many of our stories have been expunged—from history, from memory? With no stories, we're made to feel alone, unnatural, ashamed. But I'm lucky: I know Ted and George, and you and Maurice, so at least I understood what I was seeking."

"Tell me his name."

"Mohammed." Morgan chuckled.

"Why is that funny?"

"Because his family's Christian! Not that he cared much for Christianity: he complained it caused too many problems and that the English called themselves Christians, and they were often nasty."

"But not you."

"Not me. Very English, but not nasty. What a hopeless life I'd lived before him! He was Egyptian, beautiful to my eyes—with such a very bright mind and wit! When the war broke out, he had come to Alexandria from his village for work. He got a job driving one of the new electric trolleys. That's how we met. I'd taken to riding the trolleys all over, into the old parts of Alexandria, where the English never go. How could I have stayed in my room on those endless balmy twilights by the sea?

"I'm so grateful we had those many hours to talk in a public space, because that's how we got to know each other as friends. He insisted we speak English—now *that* caused lots of laughter. And when we met for our real first date, I didn't recognize him. I'd only seen him in his tram-driver's gear, and he showed up in these dazzling tennis whites! The joke was on me.

"That night he invited me to his room near the bazaar. He asked if he could try on my uniform."

"The clever rascal . . ."

"Absolutely. It was marvelous to love him—at thirty-eight, I thought I was too old to know such love. How ridiculously I was mistaken!

"But as the war was winding down, so was our time together. He was obliged to return to his village, to the marriage his parents had arranged for him there. We wrote each other, and even managed a couple of visits.

"But not long after the armistice, the Influenza killed half his people, among them Mohammed and his infant son, whom they'd named Morgan."

Alec took Morgan's hand as they sat together and leaned his head on his friend's shoulder, enjoying the shared silence and the warmth.

At last Morgan said, "I won't be stopping long in England."

"No?"

"I'm setting things in order for my mother—property, finances, getting the right help for her—but I don't plan to stay.

This country wants to destroy us. It's dangerous, worse than you know. I finally learned why no one had heard from me for so long. Early on, I'd written Teddy some cautious words about Mohammed, but not cautious enough. The army decided I was a pervert, so they started withholding my letters, even to my mother.

"Before the war, before Mohammed, I might have endured England's slow suffocation. No longer. I've changed. I'm leaving. For India. I've been recommended for a job with one of the minor rajas. He's a delightful fellow, wants an Englishman to work for him, to bring his family up-to-date, and his realm. Maybe you'd consider a visit." A candle guttered out. "Am I keeping you up too late?"

"No, not a bit. But please, while we're here, just us two, could you help me sort through some things in my head?"

Morgan listened. He gave no advice. Rather, he asked questions of his young friend. The most perplexing to Alec was also the simplest: "What do you truly want, what's your deepest desire?"

Alec hesitated: "I can't say . . ."

"That doesn't surprise me at all. Many people can't. Most, I believe. Oh, they might say something vague like, *I want to help others*. But in truth they're afraid to ask themselves the question. Or maybe they don't know they're allowed to. Not you, though. And, Alec, when you can name that desire, I'm confident you'll pursue it."

Upstairs, Alec couldn't sleep. First it was too warm next to Maurice under the covers, so he kicked them off. Then it was chilly without them. He got out of bed, went to the old wing chair, wrapped himself in a quilt, and nested there, swami-style, in the dark. He wanted to smoke, but he might wake Maurice; then he'd have to explain his state of mind, which would change his state of mind, and he needed to stay with it.

What *did* he want? He wanted Maurice, always and forever. No doubts or hesitation there. But love was only half the answer. What did he want to *do*? What would he do with life itself, snatched away from Llewellyn and Billy Wrenn and Swavely, but lavished on him? He was certain of what he did *not* want to do: he did not want to be always sponging off Maurice's money, nor did he want to squander his mind and his strength on work he deemed meaningless.

Through the window he saw that tonight's sky was perfectly clear. Here in the country, unlike in town, no man-made lights distracted his eye from the stars. He found the North Star. Though he could not name the constellations, they seemed to gyre, to pivot about it, their music silent to his ears, their order unknowable and sublime. How rich the endless canopy appeared tonight!

He wanted to keep learning, to study. That was the answer to Morgan's question! It was by no means the final answer, but it was the right place for him to start.

39

Maurice was restless with his own question: how to acquaint
his family with Kitty's circumstances? He stalled for time.
On the phone with Mrs. Hall he said, "She's in perfectly
good health, I promise. No need to worry. But, you see, several military hospitals in the area are shutting down, and it's
absurdly hectic for her right now, trying to get her patients
discharged or properly transferred. You do understand, don't
you, Mother?"

No answer.

"I told her I knew you would."

Much as he valued their Millthorpe friends, he did not
wish to discuss this particular matter with any of them. He
believed he needed a woman's advice, someone wise and
trustworthy, so he called on the baroness.

In the foyer of her house on Bedford Square, Maurice and
Alec encountered another guest, about to depart, whom Alec
recognized and greeted.

"Oh yes!" said Madame Mardash. "I remember you. Who
could forget such a kindly face? Thank God you've survived,
dear boy. My heart breaks these days, dozens of families coming to me, hoping they might speak to sons who've died. But
for you I recall feeling a certain confidence that night, because
the Hanged Man had just turned up when you did—" Then
she seemed to recognize Maurice. "You were also there, sir."

"No, ma'am."

"But surely—you must recall—such a vibrant soiree—I had an awful cold—and you were with your friend, standing by him, as close as you are now."

"That's impossible. I was serving in the Dardanelles."

She closed her eyes. "I see." She opened them. "Someone very much like you, then, but older, considerably, in civilian clothes. An uncle, your father?"

The baroness entered from the hall and interrupted: "Roxana, I assure you, Mr. Scudder was alone that night. It must have been another guest you saw with him." She greeted her young friends.

But Maurice was intrigued by the clairvoyante and wished to answer her question. He said to her, "I've no uncles, ma'am, and my father died more than twenty years ago."

"Ah . . ." Madame Mardash closed her eyes once more. She smiled and opened them: "Then perhaps it was he." She bade them goodbye.

The baroness brought them into a small parlor and closed the door. When Maurice finished telling Kitty's story, she stood up and paced, her arms wrapped tightly across her chest. "What a painful situation," she said quietly; then, "I'm so very touched that you would come to me."

"Do you think we should tell my family?"

"How can you not? Since you've asked me, I'll tell you I believe you'd make a great mistake by trying to hide the truth." Her eyes were distressed in a way Alec had not seen before: "I suppose one might try to weave a fiction of adopting an orphan, but such deceit has a way of playing out its consequences over decades, even lifetimes, and how unkind to the child . . ." Then her expression turned calmer: "But your sister is so very fortunate in your care for her, Maurice. You know, I'm thinking of your father—and my recollection has nothing to do with the visions of Roxana Mardash. He would have protected his daughter and her child. I'm certain of it.

"Please let her know she's very welcome here. Or, better, ask her if I may write to her and I'll invite her myself. It's a big house; she'd have her privacy, and we'll get proper attention for her. She has a friend in me, and, believe me, I've learned to keep my mouth shut."

Kitty accepted the baroness's heartfelt invitation. In June 1919, she gave birth to a fine baby girl.

40

In due time, Maurice called to let his mother know that he and Kitty wished to visit together; they hoped Aunt Ida might also be at home and that Ada would be there too.

Brother and sister had discussed the visit in advance. They'd considered saying more to Mrs. Hall ahead of time, or even writing her, but finally agreed the news was best delivered in person. They asked the baroness to listen to their plans. The lady promised to speak up if she believed at any time they were making a mistake, but requested otherwise to be excused from suggesting strategies in this family matter.

So Maurice and Kitty brought the baby to their family. When the maid, answering the door, saw the infant, her eyes widened. "Good afternoon," she said, "Miss Hall, Mr. Hall." She parted the double pocket doors of the large parlor, where Mrs. Hall, Aunt Ida, and Ada were waiting for them.

The women's eyes, like the servant's, also widened on seeing the baby, and their lips opened in surprise. Aunt Ida gasped audibly.

"What's this?" Mrs. Hall said. She looked at her son with a painful, reproachful question in her eyes: "Maurice?"

He and Kitty had failed to anticipate that Mrs. Hall would first take the baby for her son's. She made her assumption clear: a child born from some illicit wartime union, perhaps a foreign one—in Malta, or on the Continent. Yes, men did that sort of thing and women were left to make the best of

it. Deplorable, unutterably common behavior—so shocking
from Maurice! But by no means unheard-of. Against her
advice, he had waited too long to marry. Now this disgrace.
What respectable family would permit their daughter to have
him now?

Kitty did not wait for Maurice to address their mother's
unspoken accusation. "The child is mine," she said. "Her
name is Anjali."

Aunt Ida sat down immediately and held her forehead in
her hand. Ada began quietly to weep.

Mrs. Hall said softly, "Oh no, no, no . . ." Her denial was
suffused with a certain tenderness, imagining her daughter, like so many others, married secretly in desperate circumstances and widowed by the war. "Oh, Kitty, had I but
known . . . Have you no mourning dress?"

As decided in advance, Maurice told their family why it
was impossible for Kitty to marry the baby's father. When he
had done so, Aunt Ida rushed from the room, Ada sobbed out
loud, and Mrs. Hall was stunned to silence.

At last she said to her son, "How could you do this to me?"

"What has he done?" Kitty asked.

She ignored her daughter and addressed Maurice again.
"Have you ever seen me weep?" And then came the downpour
of tears.

"Now, Mama . . ." He tried to comfort her. But she would
have none of it. She waved him away and wept louder. He
said, "All right, then, maybe you need to cry."

The tears stopped immediately. "What do you mean, 'need
to cry'?"

"Maybe the tears will open your heart. It seems to me that
the choice is yours, you can have your pride or your grandchild."

"I have a grandchild, thank you—Ada's little William. This nigger bastard is not mine."

"I'll be outside," Kitty said to Maurice and left the house.

Ada, without a word, ran upstairs. Alone with his mother, Maurice said to her quietly, "I've never heard you use such language."

"Oh, now my *language* offends you? Yet you accept . . . *that*? You expose your mother and your aunt and your sister to *that*? I raised my son to be a gentleman, an English gentleman who defends women. If your father were alive, would you dare to so insult us? Where is my son? Do I even know you?"

He felt an agitation raging in his gut, a surge of nervous energy like what he'd often felt during the war, his body's groundwork to fight or to run. She had the advantage of surprise: he'd no experience of such behavior from her—the vulgarity, the phony tears. In this gracious home where he'd been assured of her love throughout his life . . .

He turned away from her. He was shaking and knew that, if he tried to speak, his voice would quaver, or, worse, he would raise it, shout, yell, in an effort to dominate. So he did not answer.

At the window, he saw Kitty with the baby in her arms. She was walking down the curved brick path through the front garden, where Mrs. Hall's prized dahlias, some nearly as tall as his sister, were starting to bloom, their tropical colors at odds with the tamer native hues. He saw Alec, who'd been waiting in the lane, meet her at the gate and open it for her. He understood at that moment that Alec, Kitty, and the baby were where they belonged: outside this house. He also understood that he belonged with them. They were his family now.

At some time in the past, before the war, he might have craved the safety of this home, of all it represented, and sought a way to remain inside, as his father had done. But now there was Alec.

If your father were alive . . . Maurice had told no one, not even Alec, that he had seen his father's shade among the dead in the depths of the Aegean. And so he was less skeptical than the others that the clairvoyante might have seen his father's apparition, or that Alec might have felt his presence that day on Bernard Street while his son was buried in madness.

He turned to face his mother, seated in a fauteuil, her smooth wrist resting across the chair's satin-covered arm, her hand relaxed and graceful. She fixed her gaze on the carpet. Sensing his attention, without raising her eyes, she repeated her question. "Do I even know you?"

"It seems not."

Now she looked up.

He continued calmly, "If Anjali is not your grandchild, as you say, then Kitty must not be your daughter. But she is my sister, so tell me, who am I to you?"

"You side with her?"

There was no point in answering her question. He might have pitied her, except for her power to hurt and her willingness to do so.

"Why do you stare at me?" she said at last. "Is it a crime to be decent?"

"I wish to tell you something."

"Yes?"

He looked back out the window. If he wanted to hurt her in return, he might tell her about his father's secret life. But no, what was past was between husband and wife; it would be dishonorable for him to intrude on the privacy of their marriage. He could speak gently now. He knew that his own particular truth would be painful for his mother to hear, but he could say it with no wish to hurt her.

He said, "Look out the window, Mother. Do you see the nice-looking fellow waiting with Kitty by the gate? His name is Alec Scudder. He fought in the war, like me, and like Kitty, too. Well, much to her credit, she was fighting *against* the war. He's the one I went to the Continent to find, when he'd gone missing after the armistice. I love him, and he loves me. We plan to live our lives together. We'll stand by Kitty and the baby."

He left the house, along the path through the garden. His step was light; he felt unburdened, happy. The feeling reminded him of the night he said goodbye to Clive at Penge, with Alec and a new life waiting for him in the boathouse.

Maurice caught the baby's eye as he approached. He made a very silly face at her, threw his arms wide open, and flapped his hands, and that made her smile.

EPILOGUE

41

"Kitty?" Maurice poked his head in at the stateroom door. "Up on the main deck, please? There's one last document to sign for Anjali."

"Yes—coming," she said.

Alec opened his arms to receive the baby. "Here. Those stairs are steep."

"Thanks. We won't be fifteen minutes." She followed her brother.

Uncle Alec was practiced in the drill: head elevated and supported in the crook of his elbow; if she fusses, pace and talk and pat her bottom. But she was being quiet, except for that baby thing where she flexed her feet and kicked her legs and clenched and opened her fingers and moved her lips and slobbered all at once, barely opening her eyes. Alec blotted the edge of her exquisite little mouth.

Even before the confrontation with Mrs. Hall, Alec and Maurice had talked of leaving England. But where to? France or Italy, where they might be despised but at least not imprisoned for their love?

Kitty and the baby brought new considerations to the table. Europe had done its best to "commit suicide," as she put it, in the war—annihilating an entire generation of young citizens; maiming, both physically and psychologically, those who had managed to survive. Did she wish to raise her child in the midst of such depravity?

They talked about Canada; they talked about South America; finally, they settled on the States. The country was vast, its language their own, its culture familiar. They would all find work. Three healthy young adults would surely be able to create new lives for themselves in that nation's promise of opportunity. And the child would thrive in its openness. Or so they hoped . . .

Alec looked up from Anjali's face and out through the porthole. The sky was clouding over. But a little rain could hardly deter the departure of this enormous ship.

At first sight of the RMS *Elysia* he'd gasped: the low-slung design of the hull made its vast length seem impossible; the massive smokestacks, slanting backward at a vertiginous angle, suggested speed as well as might: one, two, three, four black colossi in a row. Arriving at the dock felt like stepping into a newsreel: gangplanks draped with bunting, a brass band playing, crowds boarding, larger crowds seeing them off. August 1919. Six years, nearly to the day, since he had not sailed on the *Normannia*, Alec was beginning his great transatlantic voyage, bound not for Buenos Aires but New York, New York.

The baroness had booked the travelers two cabins side by side, one for Kitty and the baby, one for Maurice and Alec. She was there today to say goodbye, with Risley and with Morgan, who would soon be departing from Southampton as well—for India.

Then Van joined the farewell party onshore. Risley was thunderstruck by the stalwart yeoman's beauty and did little to conceal his admiration. To his delight, Van accepted his invitation to join him for a drink in town before going back to the farm.

Now the whistle blew to signal imminent departure. The

baby squirmed at the shriek. Alec sang to her softly, the first tune he thought of:

> *Da dada dum, da dada dum,*
> *Alexander's Ragtime Band.*
> *Da dada dum, da dada dum . . .*

He felt the *Elysia* move. Singing, he rocked the baby in his arms, gazed through the porthole, and, as he often did, pondered Morgan's question.

Acknowledgments

In Part II of *Alec* ("Kingfisher"), the story coincides with that of *Maurice*. By permission of the Provost and Scholars of King's College, Cambridge, and the E. M. Forster Estate, I quote from Forster's work there, mostly in scenes where the lovers appear together or write to each other. The passages, by permission, are not identified in the text, for the sake of continuity. To adjust the point of view, I sometimes, also by permission, weave my own words into the quotations.

The relevant passages occur on the following pages:

- 52–53
- 57
- 59
- 62–68
- 70–72
- 74
- 76
- 82–85
- 89–105
- 115

I wish to thank the Forster Estate and King's College, Cambridge, for granting the necessary permissions, as well as those who guided me in the process:

Sarah Baxter, Contracts Advisor & Literary Estates, the Society of Authors; Kevin R. Casey, Chair, Intellectual Property, Stradley Ronon Stevens & Young, LLP; Lisa Dowdeswell, Head of Literary Estates, the Society of Authors; Patricia McGuire, Librarian and Archivist, King's College, Cambridge; Wendy Moffat, Professor of English, Dickinson College; Philadelphia Volunteer Lawyers for the Arts.

With thanks to my friends, who were first readers and consistently encouraged me:

Barry Ahearn, Peter A. Battisto, Neal Bell, Cordelia Frances Biddle, Joe Byers, Paul DuSold, Robert Hansen, Emma Lapsansky-Werner, Damian McNicholl, and Gary Westerfer.

With thanks to my professional colleagues, who are now also friends:

Matthew Carnicelli, and my skillful, patient editor, Jonathan Galassi.

With deepest gratitude to my beloved spouse, James Harrison Anderson.